The Stones of Destiny

First Published by Vivien Smith on 22nd November 2024

Edition 1

A catalogue record for this work is available from the British Library.

ISBN 978-1-0369-0281-0

For my boy, Liam.
Love Always,
Mum xx

PLAYLIST

As part of the creative process for my story, I spent a fair bit of time enjoying listening to tracks that I think best reflect each chapter in the story. I had a lot of fun preparing the music and had hoped to share my own personal playlist with you. However, I have been unable to secure the necessary permissions to use the artists name and song title at this time. I intend to keep trying to get permission and if I'm successful, I will of course update my book to reflect that.

In the meantime, I am hoping that you will forgive my blank playlist against each chapter, as I have decided to go old-school and intend to write my playlist in my own copy of the book.

You may wish to do the same if, like me, you are a music lover and have an interest in blending a story with music that is important to you? Music that best reflects what you think the chapter is trying to say through song. I find the tracks I have picked evoke an emotional connection with the characters in my book and the actions they are taking.

Of course, the story stands on its own merits and the playlist is not an essential factor to the enjoyment of the book. Think on it as an added bonus if you like, as I too picked tracks for my playlist to match the story, and not the other way around.

I do hope you enjoy my story.

Vivien

PART ONE

OBSIDIAN

FIRE

EARTH

AIR

WATER

CHOICES

PROLOGUE
PART ONE
SON

The behavior was unprecedented he knew, but he would take the risk regardless. Feeling sure that there was nothing to mitigate against the greater risk of doing nothing. He burned inside, hoping against hope that what he planned to do now would be worth the sacrifice to his own people. Only time would tell…

He stood in her bedroom, cloaked in his wings, watching the rise and fall of her breathing and finally decided that his observations had now reached their climax. He would reveal himself to her this very day. There was no other reasonable alternative open to their people in his mind. It had to be this way and, in fact, he had already decided that compulsion would be his tool.

***

Birds were singing purposefully outside the window calling Iris towards wakefulness. She awoke gradually, not wishing to be hurried from the softness of the in-between state. The sun streamed into the room through chinks in the shutters. One stripe softly caressing her face with its warmth like a summer kiss. Lingering longer than the brush of lips and reaching deeper than skin.

Snuggling down into her covers for a few more stolen minutes, she stretched her lean body, climbed out of bed, gave her duvet a shake and crossed the sun striped floor to the window. Issuing her command nonchalantly, 'Open', the shutters glided into their recess in one smooth motion.

Surveying the view from her window, she decided that she could never tire of it, most especially the majesty of the hills in the distance, now crowned in morning glory. Reveling in the beautiful vista for a few moments as she watched the morning light dancing across the hills, noting where the shadows that were created by crag and cloud sought to steal the light away.

Chuckling to herself, she opened a window manually thinking that old habits die hard. The house could have done this for her, but she liked the feel of the cool brass handle and the soft pop as the window disembodied from its frame. She was rewarded by a light, fresh breeze on her skin. Not enough to pucker her arms to goosebumps, more like a cool breath from the universe sliding over her skin.

Knowing she wasn't meant to open the window unless there was an emergency, as the house was regulated for maximum efficiency and low impact, she still liked this feeling more than she cared to admit to her city friends, so the house would just have to put up with her little bad habits. Her boss would no doubt be on her case on her return to the city though. He would have received all of the house data and this little pleasure would give her a big red mark in his book. Too bad. It was worth it to her in this moment, knowing she was good for the job and the company, and feeling sure that it was likely he would overlook the issue. Again!

Aware that her love of this part of the world was constant, Iris was more than pleased that her work meant she could undertake her field studies here. The bio diversity of the area was second to none, with plants and animals surviving in this climate better than any other place on earth.

Shrugging off the tee shirt that she favored for sleepwear, she was at once naked. No one to see me here, she thought to herself, relishing the faint breeze on her skin as she passed the open window on her way to the shower room.

Following her shower, she continued her morning routine calling out for breakfast. 'Two slices of toast and coffee please.'

By the time she had dressed in her favorite comfy jeans and donned a fresh Tee Shirt sporting the slogan, 'It's Your World Too', her breakfast had appeared in the house hatch. The toast was buttered the way she preferred and her coffee had the designated half sugar that she allowed herself. At just under six feet tall and 54 kilos, she was suitably slim and knew she could easily afford the half sugar in her coffee. Another one of her very own self-treats.

Iris had programmed the house hatch when she had arrived to her own personal requirements and it had been reliable with the results. Technology had a way of ensuring that sameness. But, she gave it no real thought, instead expecting the result to be the same each time. She breathed deeply of the roast coffee aroma she so loved, while also drinking in the peaceful morning.

Listening to the quiet as she finished off her breakfast, broken only by birdsong, Iris again reveled in the advantage of pursuing her line of work. The city would be teaming already at this hour she knew. In fact, it never stopped. One of the main reasons she had decided to 'get away from it all' at every opportunity.

Back to nature, quiet and a whole lot of species just waiting for her to investigate. Species of insect, flower and fauna that could hold the key to new innovations and cures. Feeling the pull of her research, she collected her bag from the hallway, grabbed her camera and set off.

The door closed and locked automatically behind her.

Ambling down the path that would take her to where she had finished her work the day before, well, she surmised that it couldn't be called a path really, more like a track in the grass made by the animals who roamed around these parts, but she followed it nevertheless.

She hadn't gone far when she experienced a blurring in her vision. 'That's the third time that's happened,' she said aloud, somewhat warily. Twice before she had experienced the same blurring and it was gone almost before she could take two steps. Thinking grimly that she would have to visit the hospital on her return. It was possibly a brain tumor? She had known several people who had had these and they had all associated blurring of vision of an early sign.

At least it wasn't serious; she could be treated in a day. After all she was only thirty-five years of age and had experienced nothing other than a few minor skin cancer eruptions. Nonplused, she continued on her way, all the while considering when she could fit in the day needed to take up the treatment she would likely require.

A small whisper, like something she had never heard before, entered her thoughts. It was a man's voice. 'You are a beautiful woman Iris.'

That stopped her in her tracks. No brain tumor stories ever sounded remotely like that. She wondered briefly if she was going crazy?

'You are not going crazy Iris; may I touch you?'

Her lips parted as she gasped. Eyes darting all around. 'Ok, I know someone is there. You have learned a new trick that I don't know about and I don't like it! Get out of my head now and show yourself,' she shouted as authoritatively as she could muster in the moment.

Feeling somewhat foolish shouting this out loud to the air itself, she swore, 'one of me.' The house hatch must have put a dose of narcotics in her food or something, thinking perhaps it wasn't operating effectively after all. She wouldn't touch any of those manufactured high givers, preferring to keep her feet most firmly on the ground, thank you very much!

Picking up her pack, which she had dropped when she first heard the voice, she took out her water bottle and had a quick drink. A feeling of uneasiness was beginning to creep in like a slithering scent. She really was beginning to feel a bit afraid. Remembering there were some new fungi that she had been studying, she briefly wondered if her imagining a voice could be related to them?

'May I touch you?'

The voice was outside of her head, by her ear now; she jumped and turned… nothing!

She swore again, 'One of me!'

A sigh, had she heard a sigh?

Becoming more anxious by the minute, she said self-consciously, 'If you're really there show yourself,' her eyes still darting here and there. Assuming a crouched position she held her arms out in front of her, in what she hoped was a good mimic of someone who was able to take care of herself.

This really is ridiculous she thought eventually. Her heart was hammering in her chest, but, she also realised that she didn't really feel frightened or threatened. More… excited. The voice had been unfamiliar, almost musical, but she felt she knew it somehow?

Coming out of her crouch uncertainly, she dropped her arms and spoke out loud, 'Yes you can touch me.' Feeling a shiver of anticipation running down the length of her spine, she drew in her breath and held onto it.

All at once he was there, standing right in front of her, filling her eyes with his beauty. She gasped even more air into her already full lungs, and her eyes widened in an attempt to take in all of him simultaneously.

He was taller than her by far; perhaps by around 6 inches and his golden hair framed and softened his sharp facial features. His eyes were of the lightest blue and were rimmed with the deepest blue, almost indigo. They were almond shaped and framed exquisitely with brows that rose and tapered to his temple. His nose was, well perfect, as were his high prominent cheekbones that were so pale to be almost blue. Gashed against the pallor were his full ruby lips.

He was by far the most beautiful creature she had ever encountered. His arms were long and strong. She had noticed this as he had raised one. His hand with its long fingers had reached out and tucked a strand of her hair behind her ear which popped back out almost immediately, but he didn't seem to notice or care.

His fingers moved from her temple, traced the outline of her eye, slid caressingly down her cheek, then his smallest finger brushed her bottom lip.

Groaning aloud as he pulled her towards him in a tight embrace, she released her pent-up breath.

'You are mine Iris,' he commanded.

Iris felt compelled to agree. 'Yes,' she breathed, but pulling herself together, least she was taken over completely she continued, 'You, you have.... wings?'

'All Fairies have wings Iris, they are a part of us, I thought you would know that and remember. I have visited you often in your dreams here.'

Colouring slightly at the thought of her dreams, half remembered, when she had awoken filled with the desire of an unknown source. She felt her real, wide awake desire for this man start to form. Reaching up, she touched his wing gently.

'Is it sensitive, can you feel it when I do this?' It felt almost muscular and yet soft at the same time to her inquisitive fingers.

'Yes, I feel it, and yes, I feel you, and yes, I want you as much, if not more, than you want me. You do want me?'

It was only half of a question, more a statement of fact she realised. But, she didn't mind. Moving closer to him, she breathed in his ear, 'Yes, of course.'

His sigh was like the first breath of wind in springtime.

They abandoned their cares. All rational thought was suspended.

Afterwards, in the quiet time she somehow knew what they had grown together that day. A new seed had been planted.

In the morning she awoke to the scent of crushed petals

and cinnamon, the only sign of her wild lover's presence. She snuggled down once again into her covers.

There was a whisper in the air, 'Our son can save our worlds.'

CHAPTER ONE

FIRE

Fire frolicked across the sky. Its orange glow bathed the evening in the promise of a calm night. Viktor watched on as the sun dipped and withdrew its tentacles before turning to enter his tent.

Inside, he was greeted by a smile from the woman he cherished more than life. He noticed her glossy auburn hair which shone with bright lights, highlighted by the glow from the hearth fire where she and four of his daughters were preparing the evening meal.

'Where is Ayesha?' he enquired.

'Out watching the firedance, I expect. That girl is nine going on twenty,' Melody laughed. 'She said it is her duty to ensure that the people see that we are still leading the Clan, and that I will have a son soon enough to prove it,' she continued, watching closely for her husband's reaction. She was satisfied when as usual when there was none.

Melody knew that her husband Viktor was a strong man and a strong leader. He had led their Fire Clan to reasonably peaceful and prosperous times. Their life was not an easy one, living as they did in the valley below Mount Sepit Mhor, a great, but now dormant volcano. However, the Clan's tents had remained in place for ten years, strengthening the sense of community and stability. In fact, their own tent was a grand affair with many features of comfort that could only be possible with long years in one place. She was very happy, contented even living here, and had no desire to give up her place as the Clan Leader's wife. It suited her very nicely.

Viktor knew he had been lax in performing the sun's last dance ceremony all too often of late. Trying to avoid the questioning eyes of his Flames, the men he trusted to rule his Clan's sects. It was always the same question he saw in their eyes, 'Where is your heir?' He struggled to answer that challenge. Although, it wasn't for the want of trying, he reminded himself ruefully.

Melody put down their youngest daughter, Bella, who had been 'helping' to knead the dough for their flatbread, even although she was just shy of three years old. 'Seraphina called in while you were out, walking,' she began. 'She wants to talk with you this evening and asked that you go to her tonight.'

His response, if there was one, filled the space between them with silence.

Turning directly towards him she pleaded with her husband, 'You must my love. It's the cusp tonight and tomorrow will be too late.' Her eyes met his with a challenge of her own. There, she had said it! She had given her approval to the man she loved to go to another. With five girls at her knees, she could do no more.

Melody knew that she really had to convince him to go tonight. It was the last window of opportunity to ensure their son was born at the right time as a Fire boy. Another couple of days and the timeline would move into Earthlander territory. All of their efforts and sacrifice would have been in vain otherwise.

She watched as the lines around the eyes of her strong, wonderful husband tightened. He had never shown weakness of any kind in public, but he had cried the previous evening. She had felt the strange dampness on his cheek, as they went over again the choices open to them. But there was never any real choice; outcasts do not survive, especially not with five small mouths to feed.

The Fire Clan was survival for all. She was acutely aware that it was also not possible to pass Leadership of the Clan onto another and remain within. Everyone knew that, but you don't think about that when you are starting a family, secure in the knowledge that everything will turn out well for you in your life. But, life has a funny way of testing you she thought, and they needed a son if they were to stay. It was a conundrum neither could unravel alone she now knew.

The Leadership covenant was harsh in its rules. Designed to bind all of their Clan to one Leader. There could be no divisions in the Sects for the safety and protection of all. Already she had heard there were murmurings. Had been murmurings for some time in all honesty, and it had been three long years since she had carried their last child. Their people needed to see an heir. Everyone's future and their own children's future depended upon it. It was never an easy life in the Firelands she acknowledged again to herself, unwittingly shaking her head and causing her auburn locks to sway. She supposed that life was never meant to be easy. But, this hard, was bordering on too hard and, she knew, was creating a vast chasm between the two of them.

Viktor almost sighed, but he held it back. 'As you agree Melody, I will visit with Seraphina this evening.' His eyes slid away from his wife's challenge, defeated.

Just at that point, Ayesha came running into the tent at full pelt and threw herself at her father. 'You're home. Did the hunt go well? Did you see the firedance tonight father? I was there at the stone. Derrik put me in your seat. It was great,' she gushed.

'One question at a time little flame.' Viktor's face had warmed as he bent down to scoop up his boisterous daughter in his strong arms. He birrled her around, her legs flying outwards with the motion.

Ayesha responded by whooping and nuzzling her head into her father's chest to manage the dizzy feeling in her head.

'You were sitting in my seat,' he bellowed as he birrled her. 'And your mother is here cooking dinner for us all. Shame on you little flame,' he said with laughter in his tone.

He knew that Melody liked to let Ayesha roam free when she could and he loved his beautiful wife all the more for this. She had often told him that there would be plenty time for their children to be fully responsible for chores when they came of age. As a consequence, his children were usually always willing and ready to help whenever needed or asked.

He caught up Ayesha's legs in one arm and carried her like a babe to the table, with her giggling all the while. She was such a bundle of joy and energy. Already at nine, she had captured the hearts of many in this Clan. It was another strong reason for him to go tonight. Another reason amongst many he thought ruefully. He felt he had only one choice open to him now, and it was a poor one at that.

As a family they always shared dinner together. The flatbread, warm and aromatic, was used by all to scoop up the staple rabbit stew Melody had prepared for them that evening. The mood was as normal as they could manage for their children, but their eyes met from time to time in shared understanding and sorrow.

Later, Viktor emerged from his home with a destination in mind. However, he knew that he had to be noticed going there. So, he put on his biggest smile and moved through the camp with ease. Not stopping to speak, but passing comment to those out tidying the camp for the night to come as he passed. Some were busy about their tool's, cleaning and sharpening their long knives and spears for the morrows hunt.

He generally liked this time of day, with noises somehow dulled by the dark and voices held to low decibel murmurings. In truth, it was a perfect evening, but mostly lost on him due to the darkness of his thoughts and fears.

He strode on through to the center of the camp, where he knew he would find some of his Flames awaiting his promise. Good news travels fast in a tented village he knew. Faster still, bad news.

Walking through the clearing ringed by their tented village, he stopped just short of his destination. It was a large clearing that had hosted many Clan celebrations, including the Clan's branding ceremonies, marriages, feast days and more.

Viktor's eyes travelled over the clearing which began at the base of the mountain, where a great stone protruded and shelved for roughly 20 meters by 10 meters. The great stone shelf then met the mountain, rising steadfast and strong in solidarity, protecting their Clan gatherings like an immovable fortress. The stone shelf at the base made a wonderful stage setting, rising as it did to around 3 meters above ground level. The main rock plateau was granite and part of Mount Sepit Mhor, the great mountain that shielded their village. He was forever grateful to have found this place.

Set upon the great plateau were rocks, fashioned into wonderful, fanciful seats, and he smiled at the various shapes they made, like a collection of life relived. Brian had carved the seats on the plateau from the pumice, so readily available in the region. His ability to craft the pumice into fanciful shapes was legendary and often other Fire Clans would come to trade for some of his smaller offerings which suited their Clan down to the ground as it meant they were known to be a strong Clan each time others ventured in.

Viktor knew how valuable this seemingly fanciful offering was to their safety. It helped to protect them from possible ambush or Clan infighting. The women of their Clan had sewn the hide around the structures Brian had created, and the resulting 'animal dance' had been written into their Clan histories.

His eyes were adjusting to the evening light and he could now see in the light from the torches on the plateau that more than half of his Chief Flames from each of the Sects were now present at the stone. Some waiting patiently alone on his arrival, others banded into small groups chatting amongst themselves. He noted the makeup of the groups and knew instinctively that they talked of more than the weather or the next day's hunt.

Clearing his throat as he volleyed, cat like, onto the plateau, intending to alert those in deep conversation to his arrival, having no wish to overhear any slights or threats to his Leadership that evening. There were more important matters to deal with and a battle now would not improve his mood.

'Well met Flames of Sepit,' he said as he threw himself into his position in the most frightening looking animal seat. 'Derrik,' he nodded, 'My thanks to you for looking out for little Ayesha this evening at the Sundance.'

'No problem,' Derrik replied, as he took up his position to the immediate right of Viktor as was proper for his deputy.

Others followed suit, and moved to their own seats.

Judging that he had everyone's attention Viktor began. 'As you are all aware, I need an heir,' he said unusually getting to the point immediately. 'I am painfully aware of this myself, as is my beautiful Melody. I have five lovely daughters, who I love and adore. I am blessed.'

A few people moved and harrumphed at this, where before there had been breath held as a result of his directness.

He held up his hand and smiled, breaking some of the tension. 'But, not blessed enough. That is why I have been seeking the ministrations of Seraphina. That is why I go to her tonight for her final blessing, for my healthy baby son to be born in 9 months to this day. Melody will be happy tonight,' he said smiling suggestively outwardly, while inwardly cringing.

'That's as maybe,' Miele spoke up, 'But, tomorrow is the cusp. Who's to say we won't end up with some down to earth boy as your son and heir?' he finished with both scorn and distrust dripping from his tongue.

'A good question, I grant you Miele. Both Seraphina and

Melody have an ACCORD to ensure that this doesn't happen. Melody will go to Seraphina for the last month of her womanly term,' he responded easily.

None of them would know that his responses had all been thought through in advance. Nothing had been left to chance!

There was a sharp intake of breath around the gathering of men however, and Derrik leapt to his feet. 'It cannot be Viktor; you cannot do this to Melody. No one lives through an ACCORD!' Derrik emphasised the last word, and by doing so had again come close to reveling the love he felt for another man's wife.

Viktor's mouth tightened. 'Enough! It is agreed. This is what I and we must do. A son and heir this time, or, or I step down willingly and take my chances on the lonesome path with my family.'

Sensing the finality of his statement, the Chief Flames rose and each shook his hand muttering 'Luck to you.' Some were sincere, others less so. Neither Derrik nor Miele were amongst the well-wishers, which he dually noted.

Leaving the plateau, he made his way across the clearing, through the tents and on into the wilderness, with only his long knife at his side. Purposeful and calm on the outside, but inside he wept.

Outwith the security of the tented village he broke into an easy jog. He knew that his destination would be reached all too soon for his liking, but reach it he must. He ran on oblivious to the sounds of the night gathering around him.

Seraphina, the Clan's crone kept herself apart. Choosing to make her home in one of the abandoned caves on the back of their mountain. In this way, she was able to pursue her crafts of potion making, childbirth, death rituals and whatever else was needed by the Clan, without the fear of being cast aside. By making herself available for very private matters, she was more than useful to them. This was one such private matter. A son and heir!

Viktor's thoughts whirred around as he ran, like the stone he used to sharpen his blades, going over and over old ground in his mind.

Seraphina had come to him three years earlier and told him that she had read the flames in her fire. They had told her to help him as he would never have a son with Melody. The solution she had suggested was a sour one indeed. She had said then that Melody could not and would not bear him a son and that he must mate with another. How right she had proved to be.

Their conversation had burned in his brain for too long and he had chosen not to seek her help for far longer than he should have he now knew. His Flames were growing restless. The whole Clan was in truth. Before long they would be exposed to a takeover from a rival Clan, and no one wanted that to happen. That would bring significant change and his Clan were getting just too comfortable for that to be a palatable outcome for any of them.

His daughters were also too young to be matched and their husband, yet to be discovered, let alone be assessed for his Leadership qualities.

Seraphina was right of course. For whatever reason the Sun god refused to bless him and his beloved Melody with a son. He knew his love for Melody was too strong to put her aside for the sake of the Clan, as other Leaders in their histories had done when faced with the same problem. He also knew that Derrik would have taken Melody and his girls willingly. Some inner part of his soul could not for one minute comprehend this though, and his stomach soured again at the very thought of it.

Perhaps he was weak? Perhaps he was selfish? Viktor gritted his teeth and spoke aloud, 'No, you have been over this soul-searching ground a million times. The decision is made!'

Picking up his pace he ran on with grim determination. Seraphina had told him not to worry, that she would take care of the details. The woman would be young and comely. He would have no trouble bedding her. The woman would be cared for while the baby grew, and it would be a boy. A boy he could be proud of, a boy who would secure all of their future happiness within the Clan.

He had arrived.

Seraphina stepped out of the darkness to his left. 'What would you say if I told you that right at this moment Derrik is at your tent begging Melody to come away with him? I wonder if she will go?' Seraphina spoke almost wistfully. 'Ayesha is awake still and listening. She loves Derrik too; do you think she wants Melody to say yes?' She paused and then asked, 'What does she think I wonder?' This latter was more of a statement to the air than a question to him.

'What does who think woman, are you trying to drive me crazy? I can't be in two places at one time. You brought me here to solve a problem, not give me three more I hope,' he blurted out. He was nervous enough and just couldn't take very much more from anyone and most especially not from this little woman. His stomach was already clenched and he felt like he wanted to be anywhere but in this spot at this time preparing to betray the woman he loved to the very core of his being.

'You brought yourself here Clan Leader and I would have some proper respect from you,' Seraphina barked back at him.

Quickly appraising the situation, as he knew that not to show respect at the outset risked the Sun god's wrath on his needs and the needs of his family. The woman who stood before him was small in stature, but huge in presence. She had a pretty face, he knew, when she smiled, but right now it was contorted.

Her scathing look brought him swiftly to his knees and he bowed. 'Sun Mother I come to you willingly. I come to seek your guidance and good council. May the sun always shine brightly on your hair,' he submitted.

She touched his bent head with her right hand. Taking a lock of his hair between her fingers, she snipped it off at the crown. 'Clan Leader you are welcome at my home. I will help you find an answer to your need. You will be blessed with a boy and I ask only that you call him Orrison, after the great Orrion of our forefathers. Like him, he will secure a bright future for us all,' she prophesied.

Well in truth it wasn't her prophesy, the woman she held for him had asked for this favour from her. But Viktor would never know that. 'You are nearly ready, come,' she motioned turning towards her abode.

Seraphina helped to raise him to his feet. Not that he needed her help at all. It all felt a bit surreal, slightly ceremonial even, but he followed her without question into her home.

Viktor couldn't feel less ready though and had no idea how he was going to manage an arousal, never mind impregnating anyone with the longed-for son. It was a tricky dilemma for sure. One that had been keeping him awake in recent nights. What did it say if he couldn't manage to do this, and worse still, what did it say about him if he did manage? He truly felt like the twine on the master huntsman's bow, pulled to maximum stretch and longing for a smooth release.

Inside Seraphina's cave dwelling was bright, as she had many firesticks lit in their holders on the wall, and a waxy substance that glowed in bowls around the room. It was warm and the fire was alight. Drawing him towards the fire, she gestured to him to sit in the closest seat to the flames.

A million questions surfaced and subsided in his head unanswered. It was too late for questions now he knew. He had already conceded defeat when he had agreed to this course of action, and was truly unable to walk away now. That would just let everyone down he acknowledged. The weight of his responsibilities bore down ever heavier on his strong shoulders, until he thought he might break.

Was he even considering walking away? No! Again, he reminded himself there was no other option for their family. It was this charade or nothing. Well not nothing, certain death more likely for his lovely girls. He would go through with this for them and for his Melody. He really felt like he was cheating all of them though. And cheating himself most of all.

Seraphina placed a warm drink into his hands. 'This will help you to relax Clan Leader.'

He drank it rapidly, and as he did he savored the smell of spices, never before known to him. Almost immediately he felt the warmth turn to fire in his belly. He sat on waiting, trying very hard to calm his spiraling thoughts.

After a short time, she beckoned for him to follow her. And follow he did.

The walls of her cave home were adorned with animal skins and she pulled one back to reveal an inner alcove. This was darker than the room he had just left, but still boasted a warm fire. In front of the fire was a mound of skins upon which lay a vision of such loveliness. Never before had he seen a woman so pale. Her long silken, silver hair tumbled over one shoulder, covering only one breast, and finishing just above her mound of womanhood.

He gasped and drank in the sight of the woman who almost floated before him. Barely noticing that Seraphina had removed his shoulder clasp and unknotted his belt, allowing his own skins to fall noiselessly to the floor.

Viktor couldn't take his eyes from the woman before the fire as Seraphina washed him down with a cloth, chanting all the while in a low hum. 'You do it now Clan Leader. I give her to you.' And with her gift given, Seraphina left the room.

He could almost feel the fire in his blood, pulsing to the beat of his heart and coursing through his veins. He knew beyond any doubt, that for this night he would live in the moment. Crossing to the fireplace he took the woman who would give him a son. A son was not in his mind however, as he made wild and passionate love to her. Never before had he felt so virile and strong in his lovemaking.

Finally, he heard her sigh. Her sigh broke the spell and he gagged as he noticed the clamp on her wrist. And the chain that held her fast to the wall. How could he have missed those?

'Oh, one of me, what have I done…' he exclaimed! His lust for the woman had died in the instant she had sighed. He pushed back horrified, stood, gathered his skins, and left the room as quickly as his legs would carry him. His shame followed him as he thrust aside the animal skins covering the room, and let them drop closed behind him, shielding his sin.

Seraphina was right there to greet him though. So close

that he nearly fell over her in his haste to get out.

'You have done well this night Clan Leader. Tell Melody to come to me when it is her time. I will have the babe for her.' Seraphina simpered. 'Melody is with child now. I checked today when I visited with her. It is all working out to plan. Couldn't be better eh?'

Viktor was too caught up in disgust in himself and guilt for his total betrayal of Melody to choke out any words other than 'It will be done Sun Mother.'

He didn't even take the time to consider the news that his Melody was with child again. Their child!

Leaving the place feeling half the man he had been a few hours before, he walked back home slowly through the darkness to his beautiful wife and family.

PROLOGUE
PART TWO
BEGINNINGS

It was almost time, Orrion thought. They would be here soon. He had perhaps a day at most for the last of his preparations. He had resigned himself to meeting this day calmly and confidently. As well as anyone who could face his or her own end knowingly, he was sure. But, so little time and yet still so much to do. He knew that he would never see the results of his lifetime's greatest work. He could only hope for a new tomorrow, albeit he planned to sacrifice himself in the making of it.

Considering the situation to be of his own making, and in every respect, it was. He knew he had forsaken his heritage and many millions of people had died as a result. However, this had been planned all along by another. His surrogate father in fact, the man he had called Uncle.

In any event, he was still unsure whether the mechanism he had built to save the world, he thought of it fondly as 'Anew', would prove to be his most powerful legacy. Or if the Liferods, the tools his real father had brought over into this world, would prove to be his undoing amongst the people from both worlds?

Still unable to grasp the significance of the Liferods even now, he recalled the time his real father had presented them to him. There were twelve Liferods in total, each one representing the twelve phases of the sun as it traveled through the year, transecting the fire, earth, air and water elements in sequence three times each. His father had told him that the Liferods were each designed to represent the basic sun qualities of the twelve phases of suntime, a calendar year. They were about a meter long and fashioned from finest walnut. Each was carved along its length, in minute detail, with the most exquisite creatures. The sun, moons and stars joined with the creatures on the Liferods and made a perfect whole in line with the grain of the wood. The effect was that the Liferods were both sturdy and somehow delicate at the same time.

No crafter on earth could have created objects such as these, even with the greatest imagination. The creatures depicted on the Liferods could not have been thought of, let alone carved to the detail of hair and wing. His father had told him they were his people.

The top of each Liferod was smooth with a groove so that the holder's fingers were supported. Each also contained a thought release, whereupon an inner section emerged, around an inch beyond the main Liferod. On this inner section were four designs representing the elements: fire, a flame; earth, a mountain; air, a wing; water, the crest of a mighty wave! It was these four, in each of the twelve Liferods, he had been told, that contained the power of life and death.

Having been shown that the Liferods would tune to the wielder by his father, when he brought them home he had considered who would be the best, most trustworthy and able person to give them to. He looked back on his boyish decision with deep regret, however, it no longer burned in his stomach and in his heart the way it once had. His mother, Iris, having worked on environmental projects had many friends in the government of the day. It was his own decision to make the connection with the man he thought of fondly as Uncle Tarramore, her mentor.

Although not his real Uncle, he had been the closest thing to family, besides his mother, that he had ever known. Tarramore was a large man at 6 foot 4 inches tall and most people looked up to him as a result, but Orrion had truly valued his relationship with him, especially confiding in him as a boy. Tarramore was a natural leader and inspired confidence in most people. A factor he now knew that Tarramore used to his full benefit, always.

Tarramore alone knew that he wasn't fully of this world. Accepted and nurtured his relationship with him and his mother as a result. Often finding the time to play with him and most especially finding time to listen to his deepest feelings. Orrion still cringed at the blind trust and love he had felt as a child towards the man who was now his greatest enemy.

Tarramore had been like a father to him, trusted and revered, so it was a bitter reminder that some people could never be trusted to do the right thing when faced with such power that the Liferods contained.

Coaching Orrion over the years to trust and respect him, Tarramore had also not shared Orrion's secret of having a Fairie for a father with another living soul and had no intentions of doing so. It was powerful information and Tarramore had kept it to himself, sensing naturally that it would be useful to him at some future point.

Everyone liked Tarramore. How could they not Orrion thought? The twinkle in his eye, his jovial disposition and of course his presence. He was the natural choice to share his new treasure with.

Orrion's thoughts revisited the day…

'Uncle Tarramore, may I speak with you privately, it's really important,' he had blurted out while hurrying into the room.

Tarramore had looked towards him and sensing the urgency of the moment instinctively, did not chastise him for interrupting his meeting with the Leaders of the Twelve states remaining on the earth.

Having previously advised his secretary that he was not to be interrupted, Tarramore had realised immediately that Orrion couldn't be kept waiting. He must have run right past the woman, Tarramore thought, as he could see Orrion was panting and had obviously been hurrying hard to come to see him.

However, the Leaders were at an important point in their discussions and it was not a timely interruption. His best defense, as always, was a smile; he spread his arms wide, shrugged his shoulders and laughed, breaking the tension that was developing in the room. 'Children, eh, what is the world coming to when a man can't have a meeting in peace?' he asked, at the same time as rising and continued, 'Refreshments everyone, we will take a break and resume our important discussions in,' he checked his watch, 'Say fifteen minutes?'

There was a general murmur of agreement around the room and each of the eleven men called for the refreshment of their choice which momentarily appeared on the tray in front of them. Tarramore noted that most had called for water or soft drinks, with the exception of Peter who had called for his usual spirit. The general abstinence from spirit more widely in itself depicted the seriousness of the discussions he was engaged in.

Moving quickly and gracefully to Orrion's side, Tarramore pressed his large hand on his shoulder, personally directing him towards his inner sanctum. With the door closed, he turned in a seemingly relaxed fashion towards Orrion and said 'What is so important that you interrupt a meeting of the Twelve Orrion?'

Orrion's mouth went dry, he hadn't realised in his excitement that the meeting had been such an important one. He hesitated and then burst out in a rush, 'I'm sorry Uncle Tarramore, for interrupting your meeting I mean, but you told me to let you know immediately if I ever had any contact with my real dad, and I have, and shit, he really is a Fairie and everything, and I have these, and they will save us, I know they will.' He had then emptied his rucksack onto the big desk in a 'ta da' fashion.

'Will they indeed,' Tarramore chuckled at his protégé's enthusiasm. 'Let me see, what are they exactly?' He picked one up from the pile that Orrion had dropped unceremoniously from his bag onto the desktop. 'Ah, but they are beautiful and feel somehow alive, I can't describe it, I just know that this stick is aware!'

'They are called Liferods Uncle Tarramore,' he had

continued excitedly.

'Liferods, eh? But Orrion, our troubles are not with life, we are all living and living and living, it's the dying, or lack of it that's causing all our problems,' Tarramore said in a rather exasperated tone. 'We cannot sustain things as they are for very much longer. The restrictions on the birthrate have made a small impact, but it's not enough. Our land is turning to baked desert as we speak; other areas are now completely underwater. It's not an easy task being a Leader at this time Orrion. Now, I must go and discuss solutions next door with the others.' He pushed his chair back, placed the Liferod he held back onto the table and made to stand.

'I had hoped for more,' Tarramore said in a quiet voice, almost to himself.

'But, I have brought you more Uncle Tarramore,' Orrion blurted again, 'Look.' As he said this he grasped up one of the Liferods and thought for the internal release. All at once, in a smooth motion, a flame appeared and he continued in an earnest way, 'We all know we are too many Uncle. These Liferods are designed to determine our qualities and make us all believe that we belong to something worthwhile.' He placed the extended flame onto his arm and it glowed brightly for a heartbeat. He removed it and the mark of a flame had been tattooed onto his forearm. It both looked and felt special.

Picking up another Liferod he released the catch and a wing appeared. 'Trust me Uncle, do you want one?' The look in Tarramore's eyes convinced him that he did. 'Feel for yourself,' he offered.

Tarramore's forearm was almost twice the size of his own and was covered in course dark hair. Not put off by this he pressed the wing onto Tarramore's arm. Again, there was a slight flare, the smell of singed hair, and the wing was majestically displayed on Tarramore's forearm. He was an air sun sign so the wing suited him as much as the flame sat right on Orrion, being a fire sun sign.

Tarramore drew a deep breath into his lungs, exhaled slowly and agreed, 'It certainly does give a sense of worth and belonging and that could prove useful in the times ahead Orrion. Thank you.' He had stretched out his hand to shake Orrion's own, but Orrion didn't take it.

'There's one more thing Uncle.'

'Yes, what's that Orrion?'

'Anyone who has a tattoo will cease to live if they have a second branding,' he said in a quiet voice.

Tarramore lowered his arm and sat down again. Finally, a solution he thought.

'My father told me it will be painless and that person's last moments on this Earth will be the best they have ever had. It's what we need. Isn't it? Anyway, that's why I am giving them to you.'

Tarramore's mind was racing. He knew instinctively these Liferods could make the difference they needed to make for population control. His smile lit his face. 'Why didn't you tell me that first Orrion, I could perhaps sell that concept to the Twelve?' he mused.

Tarramore hadn't questioned that they would work exactly as Orrion had outlined, a factor that helped to build his admiration for the man. Tarramore always believed him, and this was strong feature of Orrion's love and trust.

'Ok Orrion,' he said 'I want you to tell no one else about these, especially not your mother,' he said pulling a face that showed fun distaste. He continued though in an altogether more serious tone, 'You will be rewarded well… very well for these, but now I must go back to my meeting.'

It had been precisely 15 minutes, almost down to the second and he had left through the side door and was out in the street, with an empty backpack, a spectacular flame tattooed on his arm, which he both admired and needed, and an excited feeling in his tummy, tinged only with a very small wisp of doubt.

He had heard nothing more about the Liferods for four long years…

Chapter Two

BABES

Time turned all too quickly and Melody could feel the babe was growing stronger within her over the passing weeks and months. She had taken to talking to this one in her belly the way she had no other.

Trying to explain why? Why she had to do what she had to do for the sake of her family. She also talked about the laws of the Fire Clan, the good things about her other children; how strong and vital were her big sister's to be. Ayesha with her flaming locks and vivid green eyes. The soft skin that dimpled around Maria's knees and the earnest way in which she thought she helped with the everyday chores of the household.

She even tried to explain away the change in her love's behavior to her unborn child. A child she could never know.

Her heart broke at the thought of that particular fact.

What was even more upsetting to her was that they had never really talked about what was to happen to the child growing within her now when planning their need for a son. She still didn't know in fact. She had tried to broach the subject with Viktor, but he turned away from her more often than not. She felt that she couldn't reach him anymore and he was withdrawing from her company more and more, avoiding the inevitable conversation she knew they needed to have. There was never a right time for that though it seemed.

Since the night he had visited with Seraphina he could hardly look her in the eye, and his touch was no longer the loving touch it once was. She explained to the babe in her womb that it was because they would have to give her away, that they could never know her. But, she knew that was a lie.

Melody still secretly longed for the return of her husband's feelings for her. That he would let her know he still loved her no matter that she had been unable to give him the son they all needed and wished for. However, she was not a stupid woman and Viktor's absences of late, coupled with the faraway look she caught on his face when he didn't know she was watching, on top of the restless nights he had when abed with her, made her anxious.

Unable to find the right time to talk to him about it, she realised that they were both suspended in the everyday, scared to scratch the surface with any real conversation. It was just too big and too hurtful what they were doing.

What she really wanted to do was to get on her knees and beg him to take the lonesome path with her. That they could go back to being happy with all of their girls, including the one growing within her, but somehow, she just couldn't bring herself to ask it of him. The wall between them grew ever thicker.

Once more she turned to the mound in her belly, 'It will be over soon. I will lose you Rose, but it's for the best. I'm so, so sorry; I will never forget you, no matter what! It's tomorrow babe, we have to go to see Seraphina tomorrow.' she spoke on quietly to the babe within her.

Viktor twitched the flap of their tented home and watched Melody as she caressed her tummy, muttering to it. He caught his breath at this vision of his lovely wife. He so wanted to run towards her and take her in his arms and say to her that all would be well. But, deep inside he knew it would never be the same again.

Why had they been so cursed? Perhaps if he had not been so possessive of her she could have had a better life with Derrik? The anguish he felt at that moment tightened his throat and burned his eyes.

So, instead of entering their home, he turned around again and walked back towards the base of Mount Sepit Mhor, taking up his now well-trodden path towards Seraphina's home. The walk was quiet save for the twittering of birds and he startled numerous butterflies as his stride took him into their settled resting place. As he walked, he felt his anguish begin to lesson and his desire begin to mount.

He just couldn't get the woman out of his head. He hadn't said two words to her since that night and yet she was always there, floating in his mind. He almost felt he was tied by an invisible thread to her and knew instinctively that there was nothing he could do about it.

Mid way to Seraphina's abode he stopped. There was a great rock just off the path to the left and he crossed to it and sat down. The anguish and longing were still there though, tickling at the back of his mind like a forgotten secret, always.

Why was this happening to him? He questioned himself again. He knew that he loved Melody. 'I love you Melody,' he said it out loud to confirm this to himself, to the air, but it didn't diminish his feelings of longing for the other woman.

He hadn't set eyes on her since the night they had conceived his son, but he longed to. He longed to gaze into her blue, blue eyes and run his fingers through her long silver hair until they caught and he could pull her towards him in a strong embrace. Being closer to where he knew she was, somehow helped him to feel closer to her.

Knowing this was irrational, Viktor never allowed himself to go more than half way to Seraphina's caves. The rock marked the spot where he stopped. No further, his mind screamed at him. His sense of duty to Melody, his family, his Clan, coupled with his fear of Seraphina and all that she represented, stopped him from venturing any further.

Of the son he would soon have, well he didn't know what he thought of that any more.

He sat on for a time.

'Ayesha come here,' Melody said as she pulled her strong-willed daughter towards her in an awkward embrace, separated as they were by the babe in her belly. 'It's time for me to go to Seraphina and keep the ACCORD. The babe is coming soon. You will have a brother.'

'I don't want a brother,' Ayesha replied flatly.

'Of course you do sweetheart, and when you meet him you will love him. He will look up to you, you know. You can teach him so much,' she encouraged, hopeful that she could strike the right chord with her eldest daughter. 'In the meantime, I will need you to be in charge of everything until

I come home.'

How do you prepare a ten-year-old to accept the inevitable changes to her world? She needed Ayesha to be in her corner. This was going to be almost unbearable for her to give up her baby and take charge of another's. Her husband's son, yes, but not belonging to her. Not like baby Rose growing within her at all. She belonged to both of them and they would never see her together. Melody wasn't even sure if she would get to see her at all, or if Seraphina would just whisk her away before she could hold and comfort her as she had all of her other girls?

Pulling away from her mother's embrace which was getting tighter by the minute, Ayesha was well mannered enough to reply, 'Of course Mother. Don't worry, everything will be fine here.' But she couldn't resist adding, 'Hurry home.'

Melody smiled at the earnest look on her daughters face and wished, not for the first time, that she could have been the son that she so obviously desired to be. It was time for her to go though, so she had to put her faith in her eldest, still a babe herself, to look after her home and her siblings. A task she knew that would not sit well with Ayesha.

Stepping out from behind the tent wall of her home, Melody held her head high and walked towards the 'animal dance' arena where she knew her husband would be waiting. It was important to set the right tone and atmosphere in front of the Clan. She had hoped for a moment alone with him before she had to leave, but that was not to be. He had left earlier with a mumbled goodbye and warm luck wishes.

Oh, she knew it was hard for him too, but did he not know how hard it was for her? She couldn't recall the last time he had even properly held her. She just couldn't be sure they were doing the right thing anymore. In fact, she might just decide to come home with their daughter and see what he thought about that. Her thoughts were random and ever changing like the four seasons compressed into one day and more latterly from minute to agonising minute.

Anger was building within to help her through these next few days, or so she hoped. She knew it was a futile attempt at defiance though. She was up to her neck in this rouse. Had helped to plan it from the outset, but that didn't mean that she had to like it. In fact, she freely admitted to herself that she hated it. As the weeks and months had passed she had grown to loath herself and her part in the lie.

As she walked towards the center of the clearing, many women gathered and moved towards her, walking with her, shouting their support. The other mothers making comments and light humor about the childbirth experience. All in all, there was a hint of festivity in the air. A festivity she had to pretend to share.

On reaching the 'animal dance' arena, she looked up to find Viktor smiling down at her. Their eyes met and locked. Foolishly she coloured like a lovestruck youngster as her heart skipped a beat. And she was reminded that she would do almost anything for him in that moment.

Viktor boomed out loudly for all to hear, 'Clan, before you my wife stands with child. She is more beautiful today than on any other day. Look upon her and be proud she is your Leader's wife. She makes me happy in all ways and now she goes to bring forth a new life to join us. To ensure our continued prosperity as a Clan.'

Men flanked him on all sides. A great cheer went up. The men patted his back and shook his hand then he was swallowed up into their midst.

The women broke into song. It started with young Brigid, who had the voice of an Angel, and then Little Maria started to harmonise. Others joined in, their words becoming a chant. Melody's feet moved to the beat, away from all of them, towards Seraphina and despair.

And then she was alone, bereft of husband, family and friends. She should be happy, but all she wanted to do was cry, or act and run away. Her feet were on the trail though and they followed it, one after the other, diligently.

At the halfway point, marked by the rock her husband had sat upon the previous evening, she came upon Derrik.

'Melody, please don't do this. Come away with me. We can make a good life, you, me and the babe.'

His voice was desperate and pleading, grating against her fear. She rounded on him, 'Derrik, you should not have come here. I am with my husband's child and we have an ACCORD that cannot be broken on any man's whim.' Then in a more considerate tone, in response to the crushed look upon his face she went on, 'Derrik, you are a good man, a great man perhaps, but we were never meant to be. I am honored by your attention and care, but, as I've told you before, we can never be more than friends.'

Downcast, he replied, 'If that's what you want Melody. I just had to be sure. Just had to try one last time,' his voice which was filled with emotion, trailed off.

'There is one thing I would ask you though,' she half pleaded, 'Can you please look out for Ayesha while I'm away this month. Being the woman of the house doesn't sit easy with her. Try to find an excuse to let her hunt with you if you can?'

Wounded again, he replied, 'Of course Melody, I'll do that for you, although I'm a bit surprised you didn't ask this favour of your husband.' With that final sarcastic remark, Derrik gathered his feelings back inside, turned and walked away.

She watched him for a time, wondering. He didn't turn again as he had so often in the past. Feeling really alone now, she made the remainder of the journey with mixed emotions.

Winter had turned to spring and summer had arrived while the babe grew within her. The forest which hugged the edges of the mountain was busy with life, but she hardly noticed as she neared Seraphina's cave.

Seraphina waited under the boughs of a large Olive tree. When she saw Melody approaching she said, 'Melody, welcome. It is time, come.' Turning, she began leading her to a cave entrance that was in tune with the mountain. The entrance would not easily be identified by a casual passer to the area covered as it was by trailing vines.

Later, Seraphina busied herself, in an efficient way, making her preparations for ministering childbirth. Eventually she said, 'Here Melody, drink this. Just relax and get some sleep, we may have a busy night ahead.'

'Thank you, Seraphina,' Melody murmured back, 'For everything.' She left the details of 'everything' unspoken.

'Huh, you're a strong one Melody, you may even get through this and be happy,' Seraphina observed ruefully.

Throwing back some skins, she indicated to Melody that she should lay upon them. Surprisingly, all at once, Melody felt tired and snuggled down to sleep.

Seraphina watched her rhythmic breathing for a while before leaving. She would be back soon enough she knew, when the potion took affect and the contractions began.

After a night of bewilderment and pain, Melody sank once more onto the skins and fell into an exhausted, drug induced sleep.

Seraphina scooped up the babe and took it to the 'other one', the term she used to describe her reluctant, pregnant house guest.

'What did you do to that woman that she screamed so when bringing out the new life?'

'That was none of my doing and none of your concern,' Seraphina replied. 'Here, it's a bit early for you, but I want you to try and suckle the babe,' she said handing the child to the 'other one'. 'You can name her, she's yours.'

'You cannot be serious,' the 'other one' replied. 'My son grows strong within me, even if half of him is wrong.'

'There you go again making assumptions,' Seraphina spat back. 'The half that is wrong is your half. He doesn't belong to you. He is my gift to the Clan Leader. You can have the girl.'

She watched as the 'other one' composed her strange, beautiful face, and put the girl child to her breast to suckle without another word. She was learning so much about this 'other one'. She had suspected that she could nurse a child at any time, pregnant or not, and she was right!

Over the next few days, Seraphina busied herself caring for her two lodgers, for which neither was grateful. Melody kept crying loudly for her babe and had to be regularly sedated, while the 'other one' watched her every move, and said nothing. Eventually the boy was birthed and she took him to Melody.

'Your son Melody,' she said as she attached the boy to Melody's nipple.

Immediately the babe started to suckle strongly, but Melody left Seraphina holding the baby as it drank her milk. She didn't know this child, he wasn't hers. Tears leaked from the corner of her eyes.

A week of hard work followed for Seraphina, with many sleepless nights.

Melody cried on.

‘Enough Melody!’ Seraphina exclaimed. ‘Do you want this babe or not? Think on what he means to you and your family. You need to pull yourself together.’

Melody only wept more and Seraphina was beginning to suspect that the whole plan was no longer going to work. The potion she concocted for sleep that evening was a bit stronger.

Melody faced a new day in a zombie like condition. This continued for a further week with no improvement as far as anyone was concerned.

This new silence from Melody began to grate on Seraphina’s nerves almost as much as the crying had the previous week. Meanwhile, she was using the ‘other ones’ milk to feed both babes now. Something had to change!

Melody could not seem to get over the loss of her girl and was listless at all times. The potion she had given her wasn’t that strong, there was just no will from Melody to get back to herself she thought. So, she increased the strength of the potion she was giving to her once more. She knew the risk, but felt she had no other options open to her. It will help her recover she thought. I’m sure it will…

Two days later she could no longer rouse Melody although she tried hard. Thumping her chest and breathing her own breath into her mouth, but nothing, no response at all.

Melody had passed.

Seraphina knew she had been giving her too many drugs to help her get through the pain of loss, but she didn’t think she had given enough to kill her. The 'other one' was chained though so she couldn't have done it. Could she?

Feeling exhausted herself, she had no idea how she was going to break the news of his wife's passing to Viktor? She had practically guaranteed that nothing could go wrong with their plan. But it had gone very, very wrong though and she would now need to invent a new plan.

Could she do that? She was flexible she acknowledged to herself, ever one to see the way through an issue. Well it was more than an 'issue' she knew, but the principal was the same was it not, she mused?

The next evening, she made a trip to the tented village and sent a scout to summon Viktor to meet with her at the rock. 'He will know which rock to come to,' she said to the scout cryptically.

Viktor did know to which rock Seraphina referred. The one he had agonised at for many nights of late, telling himself he could go further and then not daring to. He approached swiftly and silently, but she didn't startle. He bent to one knee in one easy motion and began the welcome, with head bowed.

'Get up Viktor, get up,' she instructed him immediately.

A million questions whirred through his head as he watched her stern features struggle to contain emotion. What emotion he couldn't be sure though. This was unheard of and a sense of foreboding started to form in the pit of his stomach, gripping like a vice.

She paused long enough to make sure he wouldn't blurt out his questions and in a considered tone said, 'Viktor, I have news for you. I'm afraid there has been a complication I'm sorry to have to tell you. I'm afraid that Melody has passed, she died last evening Viktor.'

Viktor stared at her, trying to comprehend what it was that she was saying. This was not how it was meant to be at all. What had she done to his Melody?

Before another heartbeat, he had her by the throat and coming up real close to her face, he snarled 'You said it was safe, you said it wasn't like a real ACCORD. You said she would be fine.' No louder than a whisper he continued as he shook this little woman, 'What did you do to Melody?'

Struggling to release herself from Viktor's mad grip, Seraphina thumped her small fists against his broad chest. When finally, realising what he was doing, he let go of her throat.

Both were now struggling for breath.

'Viktor sit down' she ordered.

He half collapsed onto his favored seat of late. 'How did this happen Sun Mother?' He used her honorific title, feeling a bit like a babe himself in that moment.

'I cannot fully explain it Viktor, it makes no sense to me,' she replied in a seemingly confused and flustered manner.

TWO BEATS.

'You have a fine son. He is strong and healthy,' she continued.

He stared at her in response and said nothing, feeling nothing.

TWO BEATS.

'I have to get back so I won't mince my words now. Viktor we all make choices, you made yours, I made mine and Melody made hers. You're right to think this wasn't meant to happen, it wasn't. But in the end, it was Melody who didn't want to go on.'

TWO BEATS.

Her words washed over him. He felt nothing, numb, like

a small bit of rock tumbling from the mountain to scatter into oblivion. He drew in a deep shuddering breath.

TWO BEATS.

Seraphina considered the broken man before her and felt some pity. She ventured to share her new plan. 'Viktor you are still a man, and a man has certain needs. You will need more than children in your life from now. You must remember that you are Clan Leader.'

Pausing for breath, still feeling the remnants of his grasp on her throat, as she picked her words carefully, she continued, 'The Clan needs you to be strong. We all need you to be strong. Melody has sacrificed to give you the son you need. It was her choice remember? I will bring your son to you one month hence. You and the Clan need time to grieve and celebrate Melody's life before welcoming him I think.'

Viktor howled like the wounded wolf, the sound extending far beyond this dirty little spot. Finally comprehending. Finally allowing the loss to register, as her cruel conniving words released pent up fury.

TWO BEATS.

'I will also arrange for you to see the 'other one', not close mind, but seeing her will help you I think,' she continued trying to reach for a calmer reaction from him.

TWO BEATS.

It was too much! Bile rose to his throat and he again wanted to choke the life from the small emotionless little woman who stood before him. Simultaneously, his loins responded to the prospect of being able to see the other woman he could not remove from his head, even now.

He felt beaten. Both empty and full at the same time. Hanging his head in disgust at himself, now bereft of his

Melody, he could not contemplate life. He also now recognised and acknowledged the compulsion he could not control. Something had happened to him that night when his son was conceived. He couldn't fathom it, but would now have to live with it.

The pity was he knew he had neglected Melody before she left. Feelings of guilt threatened to overwhelm him then. He had promised himself that he would make it up to her when she got back. But, she wasn't coming back and he no longer knew how to deal with releasing the guilt he felt in his very core.

One month later to the day, he collected his son and learned of the place he could go to watch the 'other one' bathe. Life was unbearably cruel. What a fool he had been.

He just couldn't help himself though, as he counted the hours until he could go and watch his new fascination, already thinking to himself that he would leave the boy with Ayesha.

Prologue Part Three 'Anew'

Orrion had known he was different from others as soon as he was able to form the thoughts that he was a being and that there were others sharing his space. Living close to the point where the two worlds were thinnest, his mother had enjoyed one sublime day and night with a being from the second level. A Fairie so beautiful and overwhelmingly passionate; his father.

He had never tired of hearing his mother talk about his father as he grew into a strong, intelligent and almost unbearably handsome boy. He had met him of course, just once, the day he had been offered the Liferods and brought them into his own world.

He had thought that he had the answer to the worlds growing problems in the Liferods. He recalled the look in his mother's eyes when she discovered what he had done though. And that he had given them to another without so much as asking her opinion. But, at 16 years of age he had placated her absently, only to watch her later volunteer to be one of the first to be subjected to the branding ceremony.

'Mother, oh mother why did you do it?' But, he knew deep down inside, she had wanted to show him first hand, the horror he had unleashed on the people of their world.

His mother, Iris, had been gifted from birth with empathy for the land and environment around her. She had devoted her life to measuring and monitoring the effects of pollution and in particular the fine balance between the use of the earth's resources and the intensity of the sun. It was the 31st century and still no solution had been found to stop the mutilations on people that were required to resolve skin cancers and burns caused by an ever-increasing intensity in the sun's rays, relentlessly bombarding the earth.

She had campaigned long and hard. Continually promoting the use of energy saving devices and outdoor suits. The sheer numbers of people living on the remaining earth space, the waters now covered around 85% of whole planet surface, still persisted to think of themselves first and the planet second in her view. Plastic surgery was excellent and there was no real chance of dying from anything as trivial as cancer, or indeed heart disease. Consequently, people were living longer and longer.

An agreement with the population had been reached whereby each woman was only allowed to have one child. But, the population still grew, even as the earth space flooded and reduced.

Iris had decided reasonably early in her life to devote her energies to her career as an environmentalist and had no desire to add to the growing population problem, as she saw it. That was until her 'one special day' where she was transported to a space and time with a being from another world, where she lost herself; her beliefs; her cares; her worries; and consequently, ended up contributing to an increase in the population after all. She had given birth to Orrion nine months later to the day.

Orrion had grown up with the knowledge, imparted by his mother, that population control was paramount to the survival of the human species. Surely, he couldn't be blamed therefore for finding a real solution. A solution that everyone had so desperately sought?

Straightening up, he sighed and crossed his small quarters to his viewfinder. These memories always made him feel restless and uneasy.

The viewfinder was an elaborate affair, given his status in the community. It was a fine gift from the First of the new Order of the Twelve - Tarramore.

Concentrating hard now on the viewfinder, he decided it was time to delve deeper and release his memories. The device had a flat, mirror like surface that appeared to have no density, yet supported objects that were set onto it. It was held up by strong wooden carved legs that were polished to a high gloss. He was extremely familiar with its use and channeled his thoughts to run the memory card he sought.

An image immediately appeared on the surface... his mother walking tall and straight towards a podium in a square. The square was crowded with people and enclosed by buildings on three sides. Towards the back of the square a podium had been erected and that was his mother's destination.

Orrion had watched her walk those three hundred steps

innumerable times on his viewfinder, but his heart still ached as if it were the first.

Of course, he had actually been there and his memory of the rising excitement of the crowd as they clamored to see, even although there were large screens all around depicting in satisfactory detail the events transpiring on the podium itself, was both profound and undiminished.

The crowd was hungry to witness the real thing. Millions were watching on the screens that had been strategically placed throughout the city. Some had even invited friends and family to their homes for a personal viewing. Throughout a kind of perverse carnival atmosphere had pervaded the city, but those 'lucky' enough to be at the center, in the very square, were eager to witness at first hand, history in the making. This was evident in the way fathers put children upon their shoulders, the press of the crowd and the eager, almost fanatical expression on many faces.

There were of course those who were opposed to the way events were transpiring; ironically, he was now one of them. Reliving the memory through his viewfinder, he tried to press on through the crowd, which was not easy as people were trying to maintain their position. He payed them no heed as he struggled forward, ignoring their curses and open animosity.

The viewfinder showed his mother walking forward, proud and head held high. The crowd murmured and parted for her, a kind of quiet hush coming over the closest to her and her fellow volunteers.

He could see Tarramore standing front and center on the podium. The background music stilled, and an expectant pause gripped the square's occupants.

'Welcome Iris,' boomed Tarramore as his mother

mounted the steps to the podium. 'Welcome Simon, welcome Julius and welcome Parton.' The four were now standing alongside Tarramore, facing the crowd.

'We are gathered here today to make a new history,' he continued. 'Our world is endangered, not by war or famine or disease, but because we have triumphed over these possible fates. Finding solution after solution to the killers of our fore fathers, long since passed from this world.'

Pausing for effect, he then continued, 'The four people you see before you now are proud, brave people make no mistake! They will be the first. Living proof that they believe in a future for all of us.' At this point he had brandished his arm in the air and his wing branding was revealed, in all its glorious detail.

The crowd responded by revealing their own essence: flame; mountain; wing; wave. Everyone had one, needed one and wanted one to show that they belonged. In four short years, Tarramore and the Twelve had branded the population of the world with the Liferods.

It had been reasonably easy for them. Word of mouth and the sight of the brands brought on a longing that quickly shifted to a must have, and in the end, a need to belong. The marketing campaign that The Twelve had devised was hardly necessary, but Orrion knew Tarramore had a grander plan; he himself had given it to him when he had revealed the true nature of the Liferods. It was all focused on this moment in time.

Never in his darkest moments could he have imagined how terrible the consequences of his actions would be though! His own mother, one of the first four to die!

Orrion's attention was once again focused on the podium. Tarramore had been leading the crowd in tumultuous applause, directed to the four who now stood in anticipation on the platform. Simon shuffling his feet and puffing hard.

Tarramore raised his arms and fanned them above his head in an effort to restore quiet once more.

The crowd obliged and continued to watch with barely contained excitement. He was going to give them a show to remember.

'Fellow Citizens,' Tarramore boomed. 'The time has come for us to cast aside our selfish, individualistic behaviour. We must now strive together to maintain our standards in this life. Each and every one of us has a deep responsibility to preserve our world for our future generations.'

Pausing again for effect, Tarramore looked around triumphantly and continued, 'We have tried to do this for many years. Our learning and knowledge are unsurpassed…' he orated. 'and yet, we cannot sustain our planet because the real truth is that there are just too many of us. Our children are precious to us and deserve a future. A bright possible future,' he was nodding his head now, 'And they now have a chance of that future because of these four brave people and the many more brave people who will follow them.'

Tarramore drew in a long breath to make sure everyone understood that this would be for all of them, him included.

The silence was deafening.

'It is my greatest wish that we will all find a way to face our own end with such dignity and care,' he softened his voice while bowing his head respectfully.

Continuing again, he acknowledged, 'As a people you have voted. We asked you, 60 years and lift the restrictions on our policy of 'one woman one child', 70 to maintain the earth's resources for a further century at best and 80 in the hope that we could strike further out into space to find another sustainable planet that could support our way of life.' He looked around trying to make eye contact with everyone in that square.

It had felt like Tarramore had achieved that Orrion recalled.

'You told us 60, that is what we heard and that is what we now start to do.' Tarramore looked around the gathered crowd, like a powerful predator. 'Like me, other members of the Twelve each have four volunteers. In this way, all of the world's Member States will go through the same process we do here. We will say goodbye to our most treasured loved ones and thank our Lord that they had the courage to stand... and to fall, before us all, to lead our way into the light.'

Orrion watched himself struggle on through the crowd in his viewfinder, people shushing him as they now stood enthralled by the lilt in Tarramore's deep melodic voice. Enthralled by his words and mesmorised by the spectacle they were about to witness.

'Therefore,' again Tarramore paused for effect, and cleared his throat in an attempt to sound humbled, 'It is with no small measure of regret that I take up this new duty of mine.' He gestured towards a table.

Orrion thought it would have been a fitting point for a roll of drums. Instead, there was a slight gasp from the crowd, as they simultaneously sucked in a collective breath.

Four chairs had previously been set up and the four volunteers, Orrion now thought of them as victims, took their seats. Each faced directly into the boxes just below the podium that had been especially reserved for their immediate family. His own mother's box was empty, but she showed no emotion at that fact.

Struggling onwards through the crowd, Orrion had become increasingly desperate in his attempts to reach that box.

Tarramore crossed to a table bedecked with a white shroud and picked up the object of his desire, his Liferod. He held it above his head and a hysterical cheer rang out from those in attendance in the square.

Orrion took this opportunity to close the distance to his mother's 'Friends and Family' box. So close to the podium now, he could read the excitement, bordering on lust that crossed Tarramore's features as he watched himself lower the Liferod on numerous screens around the square.

He had made it into his mother's 'Friends and Family' box and at once felt light, freed from the press of bodies and the grip of the crowd, like a butterfly newly emerged from its cocoon. He looked up into his mother's face. Her eyes met his with a steely determination and he knew that he had lost her.

Iris had turned 60 years of age only last week. Would have, should have had several more years grace before the decree needed to be met, but she had been the first to volunteer. She had told him that she didn't want to be part of a world that condoned euthanasia. That she was ashamed her own son had brought them to the point that made such a thing possible. She saw it as her duty to be one of the first to die.

Oh, he had begged and pleaded with her to no avail. She was determined in the will to die equally as much as she had been determined to live a full life.

As Tarramore crossed the short distance to her with full strides, her eyes softened slightly and she smiled, albeit briefly, demonstrating to him that in the end she still loved her son. 'I love you no matter what' had been her mantra throughout his life and he felt her love keenly, like a physical presence in his gut, as he stood in that box about to become bereft of his only known family.

Unable to help himself or stop what was about to happen, he shouted out as loudly as he could, 'I love you mum… I'll fix it, I promise.'

Their eyes had locked then and love flowed. A deep understanding born of a shared encounter with another species, in addition to the bond between mother and son.

Then, without further ceremony, Tarramore held his mother in his strong arms while he pressed the Liferod to her temple. His mother's eyes closed, a look of rapture crossed her face, and in the space of a heartbeat, she was gone.

It wasn't until much later that Orrion had been able to see anything beyond those last moments of communication between himself and his mother. The memory tape ran on and he was semi-conscious of the same fate befalling the other three volunteers. But, he had been caught up in his own bubble of grief.

When he did eventually really look beyond his grief to the crowd, to the other 'Friends and Family' boxes, and to Tarramore himself, that he realised that the taking of life from his mother and the others had resulted in a profound change in Tarramore.

At first, he had thought that it was a consequence of his having performed the death rites, but he grew to realise that Tarramore had gained something of the essence of the life that he had extinguished in others.

Then, Orrion was really scared.

Switching off the memory card with his thoughts alone, he sought out a present view in his viewfinder. Channeling his thoughts, he was immediately rewarded by a sharp picture of a man on a white horse. He had what appeared to be short hair at first, but Orrion knew it to be tied back in a severe ponytail, the ends of which were braided and beaded with charms. The rider wore a lose fitting tunic of soft cotton in a deep green, over trousers made of a thicker riding material, with black leather boots, the cuffs of which were sneaking just beyond his knee in the fashion of the day. The rider was surrounded by green hills which were splashed here and there by the purple of the heather that grew naturally around the Highlands.

So, it was to be The First himself who would carry out his own second branding. Orrion wasn't surprised by this, given that Tarramore alone knew he was half Fairie. Tarramore was probably looking for a big hit of life-force from him, he thought bitterly to himself. Tarramore was at best a day away if he chose to stop for the night, a matter that Orrion couldn't be sure of.

As he looked on the viewfinder's screen, The First drew on his horse's reigns to bring the animal to a halt, and then turned, with the deepest of brown eyes, stared directly at Orrion through Orrion's own viewfinder.

Startled by this new trick employed by The First, he moved his thoughts away from the viewfinder. However, instead of winking out as it should, the picture held, albeit not quite as focused.

Now mesmerised, Orrion looked on as The First brandished the Liferod, reared his horse and then coaxed it into full gallop, off in the direction of Orrion's own home. The viewfinder didn't fade until both rider and horse rode out of the picture circumference that he had previously set in his viewfinder.

Finding that he had been holding his breath, he now

pushed it out of his lungs. Deciding there and then it was probably best not to count on The First stopping anywhere for the night. Not even to rest his mount. He could almost feel the minutes ticking away. Did they know? How could they know? He had been extremely careful with his work. Secretive in the extreme.

And this new… thing… What was that all about? Two-way communication through a viewfinder! It was tuned to his thoughts, was heavily pass protected. How did The First breach it? Orrion had a feeling of being hunted and then he thought he understood. Tarramore was coming for him, would take him like so many others before him. But, he alone knew that he, Orrion, was a special prize and would likely give him more power, or lifeforce, or whatever it was he got, as a result of the killing brand. He was a half-blood Fairie and The First was the only other living person who knew that.

It was now past time to move and put his plans into action. He had one more thing to do here first though. Focusing his mind again, he tuned in once more to the viewfinder seeking the release.

It was important to him that The First wouldn't be able to unlock his memories, both conscious and forgotten. If that man was able to do that, he may be able to undo all of his efforts over the last thirty-five years. Thirty of them spent right here in this mountainside.

He found the release with his mind, knowing it to be a slippery thing. He had made it so to ensure that he could not erase his memories from himself easily, most especially the painful ones. After a bit of a mental struggle, there followed a gentle whirr and the top of the viewfinder put forth its offering, a slim black cartridge, his memory box. Picking it up, he put it into his pocket. Now feeling somewhat calmed by the presence of the artifact, he crossed the room and surveyed his surroundings one last time.

This place had been his home for the best part of thirty years and he realised that he would miss it. Especially his armchair by the fire. The fire itself was designed to mimic a real log flame fire, but without harming the environment. He had enjoyed many a night in that very chair with his whisky and his thoughts dancing in the flames. The quiet times had helped him to realise his dream of building a machine that would save the world. This was his grand plan. He also believed that it was achievable. Well he guessed he would find out soon enough.

Moving through the door he touched a side panel and was rewarded by the dull clunk of not two, but six deadbolts hammering into place. Let The First think he was hiding something in his living quarters. It would take him out of circulation, if only for a few hours which could only be a good thing in Orrion's humble opinion.

Turning from the door, he walked down a dimly lit corridor. It had no windows and a steep gradient descended to his workshop which was completely encased within the mountainside. After around 20 minutes walking he emerged into the workshop proper. It was a huge cavern contained within the mountain itself and was the prime reason he had chosen to live in this remote part of the world, cut off as it was from the amenities of the twelve states and city life. It afforded little in the way of communication links and transport was rustic to say the least.

Many of his long-ago friends had said he was crazy to even consider living in such a remote spot. He supposed they thought of him as a bit of a hermit. They were most probably right he mused. To be outwith the city was to be outwith the reach of all things that served to make humankinds existence easy, pleasurable and protected.

People had come to accept the concept of the Liferods and their use, some seeking to benefit financially from the disposal of the remains following second brandings. There had never been such a good time in the whole history of the world to be associated with a funeral director's involved in the disposal of 'ancients', as people above the age of 60 years had become known.

But, his thoughts were wandering today. Not surprisingly really, Orrion acknowledged to himself. It was a big day for him too after all.

Surveying the cavern opening up before him, he could see that two thirds of the floor of the workshop was raised above the outer edges of the room, in the form of a gigantic circle. The radius of the circle was as large as the length of a football field and at the center of the circle stood his life's work. A tall cylinder-shaped machine, that was dull grey in colour and reached up powerfully into the roof space of the cave like a phallic symbol.

It was a sleek machine, with dart like protrusions emerging at the lower end, which were supported by tethers running off the circle at right angles, and disappearing under the outer lip of the main platform. He knew that the tethers were attached to a huge bolt fastened securely into the rock below, at the center of the circular floor. This bolt provided the balance required to support 'Anew' while she was being built.

He had made it his business to know everything about this machine. 'Anew' was his masterpiece after all.

Several figures were at work up and down the length of

the machine he called 'Anew'. They were completing the polishing and checking for any imperfections in the surface. He called out to the foreman, a stalky fellow who was gruff and usually extremely concise, to the point of rudeness. This fact didn't bother Orrion in the slightest as he had no need for friendship, only excellent craftsmanship, and this man was a fine crafter. 'Hi, Stannous, can you come down for a moment?'

'I'll be down when I've finished this,' came the reply.

Orrion wasn't exactly sure what Stannous had to finish or how long it would take him, but knew that for these forty men, their work was nearing completion.

Stannous eventually lowered himself on a pulley type rope made of the finest leather and dropped to the floor. 'Nearly done now Sir, we're just finishing the polishing, shouldn't take more than a half hour. We'll be leavin' after that.'

Orrion regarded Stannous. The muscles in his arms, back and shoulders were strongly defined. A smear of grey powder marked his cheek, a sign that he had been working alongside his men on the polishing. Orrion possibly respected this quality of working alongside his men, more than any other the man possessed.

Deciding then to confide in the man after all, he had argued with himself about doing that, but in the end decided that someone ought to know what he intended to do. He tentatively broached an opening with the man, 'I want to thank you and your men for the work you have done. I could not, by any stretch of the imagination, have achieved my dream without you.'

Stannous regarded this handsome man standing before him. He had no time for his kind for sure. But, he paid well and that was why he and his men had agreed to take on this job, leaving their families for too long now. He was eager to get finished and had struggled to keep his men on the job, if the truth be told.

Stannous had nothing to lose now though so just replied, 'I'm not sure where your dream is going to take you Sir, other than down those undertakers either way. You can't run from being an 'ancient' you know and no fancy machine is gonna take you anywhere but to your death. That's what I think anyways.'

Stannous had the decency to look down at his feet while delivering his assessment of Orrion's intentions.

Stannous coughed and spat, 'Anyway, you can thank us properly by payin' us like you said. Me and my men don't want any part of where your goin' or what you're goin' to do to yourself, so we will leave directly as we are finished.'

Orrion was almost dumfounded. It was the longest speech that Stannous had ever made in the last five years that he and his team had worked here. However, overcoming his surprise he said, 'Of course, your pay in full,' and taking a paper he had prepared pledging all his wealth and worldly goods to Stannous from the breast pocket of his shirt, he tried to hand it to him.

Stannous looked at the paper in his outstretched hand and replied bruskly, 'Like I said, we have about a half hour or so to finish the polishing, you can pay us then.' And with that he turned, ran and pulled himself up by his leather rope in one smooth movement, as it was counterbalanced to propel him up or down as he required.

As Orrion walked over to a small desk in the bottom corner of the room, he knew that Stannous was still watching him. He placed the paper on the desk. It was everything he owned pledged to Stannous and his men. In his youth he had amassed a small fortune from the 'sale' of the Liferods, and some wise investments served to ensure that he had been much more than comfortable over the years. Placing a bottle of his best malt on top of the paper was the best he could do. He had hoped to share a parting drink with his workmen, but Stannous's 'speech' had demonstrated that he would be crossing a line that they would not allow him to cross.

Thinking the better of it, he opened the bottle and poured a small amount into a glass and toasted himself and 'Anew'. 'To 'Anew' and all those who sail in her!' He tossed the neat warmth down his throat and replaced the small glass on the table beside the bottle. He poured another. Let them partake or not. It really didn't matter to him now.

In any event he was back on schedule with some time in hand. The camaraderie he had hoped to share with the workmen in his finest hour, a mere glitch in his greater plan. It was clear they were more than eager to leave, judging him to be trying to escape his life hour - his 60th birthday.

It was an early retirement age by anybody's standards, but the fate of all the Nation's citizens. If he were trying to escape he would be considered the lowest form of life. The sustainability of the earth for future generations depended on everyone taking on this mantra and believing it wholeheartedly. At least that's what the Twelve had proscribed, and then vigorously marketed, so that now most people both expected and accepted the fact that they would only live until their 60th year. No wonder the men didn't like him if they thought he was trying to avoid his death hour.

Orrion shuddered to think of his part in achieving the current state of affairs though. The irony was that the money he was using to create 'Anew' and pay Stannous and his team, had come from his bringing of the Liferods to this world - a fact he could never run away from, no matter how hard he tried. But, he was still determined to make amends. He had promised his mother as much before her death. So, make amends he must!

Orrion seemingly waited patiently and was finally rewarded when Stannous and his men dismounted from the surface of 'Anew'.

Stannous himself was the last to descend, having completely circled the structure numerous times on the way down, his keen eyes finding no blemish and, satisfied, he lowered himself catlike onto the floor of the cavern. His men had gathered to one side, close to the exit and were awaiting a nod from Stannous prior to their departure.

On silent feet, Stannous crossed to the place where Orrion had left his payment, tapped his cap towards him and nodded to his men to leave at the same time crossing the floor to follow them. Of the whisky, Stannous didn't partake, and it was left lonesome on the table where Orrion had left it.

After Stannous and his men had left the underground hideaway, Orrion began his final preparations. He knew that it would take some time, probably in the region of an hour, for them to clear the area sufficiently. But, of one thing he was sure, it was that they would not dally in their exit from the mountainside. They would be more than happy to cash in their hard-earned bounty.

One more sip of whisky for him though, and he had drained his second glass. Setting the empty glass on the table to his side, he crossed to the wall, where a control panel was set. It was a fairly straightforward panel with three main switches. It operated remotely, but he took some comfort from the seemingly unobtrusive and accessible manner in which he had left it hanging on the wall.

Pressing the blue button, a stairway slid noiselessly from its outward position to connect with the face of 'Anew'. He had specifically requested that he always be the one to operate the stairway.

This was another factor that Stannous could have found either fault with, or just plain weird. But, to his credit, he never commented about this request, even though Orrion knew that this had held up work at times. And that Stannous's men had cursed at Stannous and told him to just bloody well get on with it and press the button himself.

However, Orrion did have his justification for this seemingly odd behaviour, he just chose not to share it with Stannous or his men for that matter. 'Anew' was his machine and his duty. He certainly wasn't going to risk any mishaps before she was launched.

Climbing the stairs reasonably quickly, he opened the door of 'Anew' with the remote, using the yellow button. It slid open noiselessly on well-oiled hinges, and he entered his cabin.

The cabin was his domain. While Stannous and his men had built the outer fabric of 'Anew', he had masterminded the development of the cabin. Oh, he had designed the whole structure, but he had both designed and built the interior himself for which he was immensely proud. It was a small cabin really, but then he wouldn't need much space where he was going, he told himself for the hundredth time.

No time now for regrets…

A lifetime of work and ambition about to be tested for the first and last time. He had one choice, one hope, one life to give, for the good of all to follow.

Orrion knew that he had only one choice left open to him

really and that was to take the risk. It was a big risk for sure, but a well calculated one. He secretly suspected it was brilliant!

Completing his final checks, he inserted his memory card into the mini viewfinder he had installed in 'Anew'. Satisfied with the responding whirr and click, he moved the screen to his mother's last day with his mind. As the noise of the pressing crowd began its eternal symphony, he watched his mother make her last walk towards the podium. When eventually their eye's met on screen for the last time, he pressed the third and final red button…

The explosion was enormous as 'Anew' was catapulted out of the mountainside.

The world rocked, as the sky changed.

An outer layer began to form in the upper atmosphere, rapidly building out from what had been one man in a relatively small space craft.

In the space between here and now, he had found the strength. Surely it had to be his finest hour as he became one with 'Anew' and left his earthly body behind.

The earth now had an outer protection from the immense, destructive heat of the sun. The earth and its inhabitants would survive…

But, at what cost?

Two worlds crashed together as the atmosphere changed. The world of man and the world of Fairie. Surely, they would now remain together for eternity.

There was a great shuddering as the earth opened its maw and greedily consumed the structures of man, while shouting its wrath through spewing's of lava and steam from the great mountains that appeared on its surface. Transforming its very pock marked face to store the tiny efforts of man that it now gathered to its bosom and claimed within its very core.

Those who are left in the aftermath are few. Life is tough now. Food and shelter hard to come by, but worst of all, the very worst thing of all, is the grey. Constant grey! Oh, how the brightness is missed.

We hide and we band together. Few have anyone they can call family. We are a people bereft.

There is one small thing that brings us together though. That makes some kind of sense to us, in this senseless world that we still call home. Our essence! Each has the brand. We recognise our kind and seek them out. Because, even at the end of time we are born to survive, long to do so, unable to comprehend anything other than survival. Even although inside we wish with every breath for it all to end!

What of hope? There is little of that left in this forsaken place. But you just never know, just never know!

We have lost so much. When will it end?

An extract from a survivor's journal of unknown origin but marked by Air.

Chapter Three

Twelve

Standing out in stark relief against the grey sky, Amador scurried across the open ground towards the cliffs, cloak billowing behind him. It was no duller than any other day, just grey like always. He sighed and sought to firm his balance, as he walked closer towards the edge of the cliff.

It was his favorite spot that he aimed for. His lookout. What he saw from that spot stretched out as far as his eyes could see, a great expanse of grey green water, peppered with white where the wind played amongst the waves. Foaming, brilliant droplets of water were jettisoned into the air, and the water then meeting the earth below, before crashing against the red cliffs with a roar. Then once again propelling droplets of water to fly out across the vastness and mingle with the air, like a temporary intruder.

Reaching out to touch the cliff face with one hand, he pulled his robes closer together, one side with the other, and made his way along the ledge to reach his destination, a natural cocoon on the outer edge of the cliff. The wind stole his breath away, freezing his ears, but he battled against the force and was rewarded by the calm of the fissure, along with the fresh feeling in his face, as he found his favoured spot.

The great expanse of water was, he knew, not a suitable companion. But, the sense of air, space and oneness here in this particular place always helped to provide him with the balance he sought. The elements as one, the earth, the water, the air and, if he strained hard enough, occasionally a glimpse of a far distant sun, shrouded as it was.

Believing his thoughts were most pure in this place, he once more he turned to considering the dilemma he faced. He was well aware of his like for puzzles and riddles, in fact a large proportion of his life he had given to the service and the solving of just such. Riddles amused him, but in the most part, it was for the pursuit of knowledge that compelled him to solve riddles. He was also aware that he excelled at it, his intelligence cutting through all that would fool the cleverest of men.

The question which was posed to him by The Order of the Twelve was 'Why was the weather'? It was an altogether fundamentally stupid question Amador thought and missed out on the basic principles of life.

He would give it a go to answer it for the Twelve, but he suspected the question, which was on the surface straightforward, potentially had a sting in the tail. I mean, why was the weather, he thought - What? There? Fine? Altogether bothersome! He would get to it though. He had already decided to answer this riddle with a riddle of his own and was feeling rather clever with himself about it, but he would have to be careful.

A slow smile spread over his face as he contemplated the tricks he would present. He could shape the air after all. Forbidden it may be, but his daring use of it would remind them all just who was aspiring and worthy. And, who was not, he felt sure. There were other supplementary questions about the sun and that was an area of questioning that perplexed him even more.

The question he posed for himself was more interesting he thought. Why were the races separate? He meditated on the latter; here in his secret place where all four of the elements were presented to him.

As a waiting member of the Order of the Twelve, he knew that his time was growing ever shorter to answer their question, but he still favoured his own. He had been called by the Leader of The League of Twelve to make his case and he intended to give it his best effort. Feeling it was both his duty and his right to respond.

He knew that he would have only one chance to fill the vacant space within the League as they did not come around too often. Which was curious in itself, he thought, given the dangers that the League were often exposed to.

His thoughts were jumbling over each other today and he silently admonished himself for this.

Amador wanted to become one of the Twelve desperately; in fact, he had deduced that he deserved just that, based on his own personal commitment to the Twelve. But it was not an easy question to solve or to answer, and he had already arrived at a hundred more questions than coming anywhere close to an answer.

Was the question always the same? He sighed and spoke

to the wind his friend. 'I think I glimpse the heart of it, but it makes no sense. I am left with trickery and illusion rather than fact and results. Tomorrow I will leave for Lorrianlee to try my hand at becoming a full member of The Twelve. I'm as ready as I'll ever be.'

Amador remained in his fissure though, gazing out over the water, oblivious to the growing dusk and the change in the tide. Eventually, shaking himself from his revere, he gathered his robes together again and once more stepped into the breach.

The wind reached out to him, taunting him with its gusts and whispers, whipping at his clothing in an attempt to lay him bare.

That night he slept restlessly and went over in his head the presentation that he would give to the Twelve in his wakeful moments. Perhaps he was not ready after all? Perhaps he was meant to devote his life to his own studies? He sighed again, a bad habit he had grown all too familiar with of late. There was definitely more than one riddle puzzling him at the moment.

The Conclave of The League of the Twelve was five days hard travel by horse from his home which was nestled in the Cliffs of Pyree. It was essentially due west and was situated on the outer perimeter of the known lands, although the Lands of the Fire Clans lay to the south, and also occupied a westerly position, albeit separated by mountainous terrain. On the whole Lorrianlee was an isolated place and after his five-day trek he was glad of the shelter and the comforting bed awaiting him at Outer Reach, the Conclaves most easterly outpost. From there, he knew that he still had a two-day treck on foot to reach Lorrianlee, the Conclave proper.

As he climbed down from his horse, Amador asked the

stable lad to prepare the tackle he would need to care for his companion, instead of leaving the job to the lad. 'I always find that my friend here likes me to care for him after a journey. Nipped another lad once and from then on till now, I do my best to see he's alright before I see to myself.'

The lad smiled and replied, 'You're welcome to him, he's a big beast,' as he handed Amador a bucket with towels, brushes and combs.

'You can be of great help to me though,' Amador said 'And get some tasty oats and water for him. Oh, and he'll love you forever if while I'm away, you can rustle up a carrot or two.'

The lad nodded, not used to being given so little to do, and scurried off to see if he could purloin a carrot from the cook's kitchen. It was always wise to listen closely to the ones who wore the robes the lad had come to realise.

Later, when refreshed himself, Amador relaxed in a corner seat in the sitting room. It was a large, but cozy room, with a full fire in the grate. He drank in the atmosphere of the place and noticed a couple of young lads having an earnest conversation. He could hear snatches of their talk and it was all about how they would prove themselves worthy to study with the League. The tall skinny one with the bright blonde hair was saying that one day he intended to serve in the League of the Twelve. The other looked suitably impressed.

Amador left them to share their dreams and sighed. It was not so long ago that he had sat there himself with such a dream. The road to learning had been long and hard since then. Indeed, joining the League wasn't an easy task in itself, and might explain the deep frown on the face of the smaller of the two lads.

He considered that the frowning one might not make it

into the League, never mind The Twelve. He knew from personal experience that more often than not it was the people with confidence who pulled through. The lad didn't look like he had much of that quality about him, hanging on every word the other said. Probably just as well for him, Amador mused, as there was a lot to fear in the learning.

He himself had had to face up to his own fears, living with the sacrifices demanded of him in severing all ties with family and friends, giving himself over to the learning, and the protection of the League and the Leader.

It had been tough at first, but now he barely gave it a second thought. His thirst and his being were for the pursuit of purest knowledge. Protection came in many forms he knew and his own was a preference for learning. The learning had helped him to feel like he mattered, or at least what he said mattered, making him feel like part of something worthwhile and therefore protected.

Having been removed from his family at such a young age, he had reached out for the feeling of protection somewhere. His protection was in learning, nothing strange about that at all, but deep down he knew it was strange alright.

And now, here he was with an opportunity to realise his own boyhood dream and actually become one of the Twelve. Did he know enough? Was his hypothesis sound or would they tear it asunder? He had been over it so many times, but it all seemed so simple. The day after the morrow would tell one way or another.

He sighed again.

The question that he had been tasked to answer specifically was about the weather and the sun. How they both influenced the balance of life on the planet. His own interests lay elsewhere, with the peoples of the earth, not its resources. He knew that the Leader also had an interest in his preferred study, so Amador was a bit surprised by the question he had been allotted to investigate. The Leader never was one for making things easy though he mused.

Time to retire though, he thought, and rising to his feet he nodded his head towards the lads, before thanking the bartender for his hospitality that evening. The food had been warm and welcome, although he was now being constantly reminded of it through his indigestion. His stomach was not supporting him that night and he felt sure it was just the thought of upcoming events that were regurgitating in his mouth as well as his brain, as the fare had been fine enough.

His room was directly along the corridor and up two flights of stairs, to the right of the sitting room entrance. Climbing the stairs in an absent-minded sort of a way, he didn't fail to notice the small group of seniors assembled in the chairs, just off the first landing. These particular seniors were the men assigned as assistants to the small group of men, currently anyway, who were aspiring to the League of the Twelve.

He had chosen to forgo this particular asset, but others gathered seniors to them like bees to their honeypot. As if by doing so, it would somehow elevate their position. No matter. Amador knew that he had competition, but felt sure that his studies would prove to the League that he was the best placed to ascend. By the look on the faces of the seniors when they saw him climb the stairwell, they knew it too. Smiling inwardly at that particular thought, he continued on towards his senior free room.

Thoughts sobering though, when he reminded himself that there was another who was not only clever, but also very devious. He couldn't count on this being a done deal. No, he must concentrate, remain calm and go over his findings once more. You can never be too prepared he told himself, not for the first time!

The meeting two days hence was his opportunity to be heard. He wouldn't waste it. Amador knew that being one of the youngest aspiring to the League didn't necessarily put him at a disadvantage, as there had only been one other placement in the past 50 years into the Twelve. There was therefore, no great turnover amongst the Twelve, and so only ten of the twenty-four aspiring to the League of Twelve had actually had the benefit of being tested before.

The weather is what? The sun and the balance of life on the planet? Sun and the balance of life on the planet? Had he prepared enough? His thoughts whirred in circles in his fine mind.

The next two days were marked by the sounds of his walking. The rustling of the pack he carried and the slapping of his wet robes against his legs. It rained a lot in these parts. His breathing was measured in time to his strides, stretching out on the flatlands and shortening on any assent he encountered.

The land he walked across was mainly flat, but teamed with life. The plants were abundant and often delighted him with their aroma as he walked by brushing against them at times. Some just shouting their scent out to him from a distance. Possibly in the hope he would brush against them and help spread their wonder further down the trail he followed. The birds and the bees had that job well in hand though from what he could tell.

As he walked, he comforted himself with the fact that he had only himself to worry about, and consequently made excellent time towards reaching the Conclave.

Amador caught glimpses of the structure as he crested minor hills. It never failed to take his breath away. Not that he had visited often, only twice before in fact. Once as a small boy with a petition from his mother, and again as a worthy student being tested to becoming one of the aspiring candidates. Both times the League had found favour with him.

There was nothing private about the building itself, it rose majestically from its base a full thirty stories. He could not envisage how such a structure came to be placed in what was a hugely isolated location. It was like something from another world.

There were four blocks that each towered to thirty stories, which provided the cornerstones to a massive courtyard at the center. Each block represented the four peoples of the lands. The most southerly represented the Fire Clans. To the west lay the Earthlanders, the north represented the People of the Air and the east building represented the Water Peoples. At the top of each building, the emblem of the four lands was displayed: a flame; mountain; wing; wave. The whole of the structure was surrounded by a massive wall that could only have been built by giants, so great it was. The effect was a minor city in an otherwise barren landscape, with flatlands for a two-mile radius from the site in all directions.

He had reached the outer edges of the flatlands, approaching from the southeast as it was the only accessible avenue to the Conclave, cocooned as it was by treacherously high mountains. It was an amazing sight viewed from this vantage point. The clouds clung to the mountainside in the distance in puffs, hovering below the peaks like soft white pillows, adding to the surreal atmosphere of the place.

It was late morning of the second day of his travels since leaving his horse at the Inn. As he drew closer the sounds of training began to reach his ears.

'Move your boney ass man, come on, you can do better than that.' The voice continued from afar, 'What a waste of space you are man, you will never make it past the initiation stage.' And then, 'I'm wasting my time trying to teach you lot.'

Ah, Inspector Willmott. Amador had his own memories of the man. Initiates moved on to become cadets and this was when the mountains became the training ground. It was expected that all cadets would make it to the top of a mountain, while being given near impossible tasks along the way.

The years melted away as Amador's eyes sought out the craggy knoll of the southernmost mountain. He had been told to rescue a little girl who was lost on the mountain. Had climbed down a scary precipice to reach a small cave from which he had been sure he had heard a whimper.

A stupid Earthlander child Wilmot had said, 'Gone and got herself lost in these here mountains.'

Amador could still hear the taunt in Willmott's voice when he recalled the moment.

'Anyone brave enough? She's not that important, but are you brave enough to go into the mountain and get her out?'

Apparently, he wasn't. He had been left by his fellows, and of course there was no child. He hadn't even bothered to question why there would have been an Earthlander child anywhere near the mountains. It wasn't his finest hour, he knew, but there was learning to be had from the experience for sure.

After two days down the hole in the mountain he knew that they wouldn't be coming back with a rope to help him out. So, bit by tiny bit, he had made his way back up the sheer precipice he had more or less slid down in his haste to prove himself. On the fourth day he had reemerged, hands and feet a bloody mess, as they had sought, time after time, to find a hold that was not there to be found.

Eyes now moving back towards the Conclave proper, he wondered what depraved tests he would have to endure to become one of The Twelve? One thing he did know for sure though was that he wouldn't be climbing down a ravine again anytime soon. Once bitten twice shy.

Willmott's voice carried through the air to his ears again, 'Come on man, a fit body hosts a sharp mind. If you can't control your body, you will never control your mind.'

Amador finished the sentence along with Willmott in his head.

It was strange. He hated the man, but he still kept himself super fit and often, when stretched to his physical limit, he would run the man's awful sayings in his mind, and they helped him to finish what he was doing. Amador understood the training method now, even although he didn't always agree with it.

Although it got results with some people, he had seen others broken. Thinking back to the heavier lad from the Inn, he felt sure that he wouldn't relish Willmott's style of training the body to sharpen the mind.

He approached the gates, which were standing open. A protective portcullis was drawn to the halfway position, but would still allow a giant to pass through without so much as bending his or her neck. The gate was guarded to the front by two men in brown robes, who stood gazing serenely at a fixed distant point. There was a further four brown robed guards stationed two at each side of the portcullis, and two more monitoring the other side of the wall. They were eight deadly weapons. Amador knew this only too well. Their serene demeanor belied their training and killer instincts.

His own test to become one of the Ascendant's in waiting had involved a near death experience with a brown robe wielding a staff. He still practiced forms with his own staff to this day. It helped him to maintain control, speed and power. In fact, it was now his preferred method of hunting.

What would the test be? Wondering about the test was beginning to overshadow his fear that his presentation wouldn't come up to scratch.

Crossing the square, he made his way to the northernmost tower. He was one of the people of the Air. Unfortunately, so were most of the other candidates at the Conclave, and consequently the room he was assigned was small in nature. He had no need for grand comforts though, so was quite happy with the arrangement. On the bright side, it was clean and he didn't have to share. Another benefit of doing without seniors.

Looking out of his window which faced to the north and the greatest of the mountains surrounding the conclave, he could appreciate why no one had ever managed to conquer that monster. Not to his knowledge anyway. It was strictly eagle territory.

On that thought, he watched the circular path of the Golden one, and sighed. This evening he must endure the pomp and ceremony of the opening event. Tomorrow would be the crux, for both test and presentation. He didn't know which would come first.

Deciding to take a look around in order to mentally

prepare himself and to try out his presentation in the room in which he would give it, he left his room behind. You can never be too prepared, he thought to himself again. Taking his staff along with him, just in case he was to be tested with a brown robe on route though. Prepare for the worst in this place and hope for the best, he reminded himself.

The meeting area was at the top of a long flight of stairs. He alternated between taking these two at a time, three at a time, and quick pace, one at a time, until he reached the top. It was a long way up, but he emerged into the meeting space with breath to spare.

Cold emanated from the stone walls he had passed and the air inside the stairwell was still. His breath started to huff before him as he climbed higher to the top of the tower of Air, but this open space felt ironically cozy.

The meeting room was vast and set out at one end with a raised dais. The First would sit at the center of the table that was placed on the dais. There was to be no seat for him or his colleagues, but this didn't surprise him. There was instead a podium with a lectern situated to the right of the dais.

Moving towards it, he tried to imagine the main dais filled with The Twelve, well, minus one. The seat he hoped to fill. He tried not to get too excited at the thought of it, but his mind had a way of taking him there anyway it seemed.

'Amador, you're just a tad early, its tomorrow I'm expecting to see you here,' boomed The Leader of the Twelve.

Amador started; surprised at being found coveting the position he had not yet won. The Leader, sometimes referred to as The First, had entered the room, but from where Amador didn't know. He hadn't used the stairs, his girth being too massive for such an undertaking.

Amador thought he looked well though. He was a tall man in the region of about 6ft 4'' and at least half that again in his width. The robe covering his bulk was multi coloured. It had no hood, but was exquisitely cut and tailored to a small v at the neckline. He was smiling as he crossed the room towards him.

The First's smile was always so reassuring Amador thought dropping his guard and training for a moment. Quickly catching himself, he hurried towards The First and with a flourish, bent to one knee and bowed his head. 'My First, it is an honour. Please forgive my untimely presence in your Great Hall.'

'Oh Amador, friend, stop fussing so. I expected that I would find you here. I came to ask for your help.'

Amador came to the only logical conclusion for the Leader's ask for help and said, 'Of course, let me get a seat for you.'

'Not that kind of help,' replied The First, 'Although, if it's not too much trouble,' he let the sentence hang while Amador rushed to the dais to retrieve a seat and bring it down for The First to sit in, who let out a long weary sigh as he eased his bulk into the proffered chair.

'Thank you, Amador, thank you. Ahhh, I grow so old and weary. It's a comfort to me to see one such as you, full of youthful vigor and promise.'

The First smiled and nodded as he heaped these words of praise on his loyal subject. 'I'm afraid I do need your help and I do have to ask you to do something for me. It troubles me to do so, but I truly believe you are the best man for the job.'

Amador felt slightly taken aback but replied, 'Anything

you request, I am here to serve.'

'Ah, you're a good boy Amador, a credit to your mother and your family.'

Amador was beginning to wonder where this was going, reference to family was forbidden in the Conclave, with all allegiance being given to The Twelve. But, it was The First so he said, 'My mother and my family Sir?'

'Yes, yes, I know of them. Here let me show you something.' The First took a baton from within the folds of his robe and pointed it towards the large screen situated to the left of the main dais. He swished the baton this way and that until the picture of a family tree appeared. 'You see, my sister was your mothers, mothers, mother's mother etc.' He flipped through what looked like centuries of names and completely lost Amador with the point he was trying to make. The First continued, 'So, you see, we are related from way back.'

Amador didn't see exactly, but stood waiting expectantly.

'Not that relatives matter here, oh no. They usually just get in the way Amador, in the long run. You mark my words,' he said pointing his baton at him. 'Anyway, to clarify what I am saying, I don't think of you as a relative of mine, but you are and I wanted you to know that.'

Amador was at a loss for words. The First was looking for a reaction, and although his mind was racing, he steeled his face to remain impassive.

'Good, good,' said The First. 'I am telling you this because I wanted to ask you to do this thing for me that I can trust no other to do.' The First paused for effect. 'It has come to my attention, through certain reports that I get, you know.'

Amador didn't know, but smiled encouragingly at The First. This was highly irregular, him being here alone with

The First at all, never mind being the only one that could be trusted. Mind reeling, he held onto his position of showing no emotion.

'There are reports of goings on within one of the Fire Clans. Seems one of the Clan Leader's has got himself a new son. Well not so new now, he's nearly ten. Normally I would ask a senior to carry out the branding ceremony, but I think it would be best if you do it for me. The Fairies have taken an interest for some reason.'

'The Fairies?' Amador asked.

'Yes, the bloody Fairies, that's what I said,' the First boomed back at him.

'Of course, Sir. Sorry Sir,' he said trying to recover his oblique position.

'Anyway, the ceremony is in a couple of days so you will have to leave now. Hold the ceremony, do the branding and then return here.' The First rummaged in his colourful robes and produced a stick which he held out to Amador. 'Here You will need this though.'

'Leave now Sir?' he enquired.

'Will you stop repeating everything I say to you? Yes, leave now! Think of it as your test Amador. Come back when it is done and we will hear your presentation.'

'Oh, can you wait so long before making the choice?' Amador blurted. Immediately aware that he could have asked a thousand questions, but as usual the 'what's in it for me' one had bubbled to the surface and was out of his mouth before he could stop it.

At least he had managed not to repeat what had just been said, he was feeling foolish about that approach now for sure. Amador knew he was way out of his depth and was feeling flummoxed by the highly unusual behaviour and words from

The First. He had no choice but to go along with things now though. The word test had been used and he would not let himself, nor The First down.

The First responded positively, 'Of course, of course,' he laughed, 'I can hold it off indefinitely if I choose to. But, we'll wait for you Amador.' He held out the stick again and signaled for Amador to take it. 'It's kind of special you know. Hold it and think of fire Amador.'

Amador took the stick from The First. It really was spectacular and he let out a gasp as he raised it.

'Nice eh?' The First encouraged.

'Beautiful,' he breathed in reply. Amador thought about fire as instructed, and an inner section emerged, carved with the familiar flame emblem of the Fire Clan.

'This wood feels alive, and the carvings… I've never seen anything like them,' he enthused.

'They are the Fairies son,' The First said patiently.

Looking up in awe, he said reverently, 'For a moment earlier I thought, I thought, oh no matter.'

'You thought I meant real Fairies, and that I was losing my marbles?' The First enquired whimsically.

Feeling his face flush with colour, something he hadn't felt for many years. But, in this quiet time with The First, holding this stick, he felt like the boy he had just been called, again.

'It is called a Liferod Amador, but I don't want to make a fuss about this. You should go now and leave directly from the West Gate.'

'From the West Gate?' Realising he had just repeated what The First had just said again, he quickly added, 'But it's never open.'

'That's right and therefore no one will see you leave.'

'Right now?'

'Yes, I think that would be best,' said The First authoritatively. 'Here, take this too, I think you will need it. It's a crystal globe filled with the light of a distant sun. It will help you to see your way through the caves at the other side of the West Gate. Turn south as soon as you can though, you don't want to get lost in the West mountain, it's not a place for one such as you Amador.'

Taking the globe, he said, 'All right Sir, it shall be as you ask of course.' With that he wrapped the Liferod in its pouch again, and placed it in his deep inside pocket, picked up his staff, bowed to The First and left.

'Oh, you are priceless Amador,' The First said to the now empty room. He stood up and moved with an agility and grace that belied his large bulk, replacing the ornate chair effortlessly back onto the dais. The same one that Amador had tried not to struggle with when bringing it down for the weary First to sit upon.

The First whistled for his senior assistant who immediately appeared in the room. The man must have waited nearby so quick was his entry. 'Boric, please ask Faldo to attend me here as soon as possible.'

Boric rushed off to do as he was bid, all the while hoping that Faldo would move quick. It was not good to keep his master waiting, and he didn't want him to think that he, Boric, had delayed.

Faldo arrived in the Great Hall while The First was still content. Things were going to plan. 'Faldo, Faldo, well met,' said The First with a smile.

Faldo bent on one knee before him. 'My First, it is an honour,' he said as he bowed his head.

'Yes, yes, you can stand Faldo,' said The First. He wasted

no time, 'I have decided that you Faldo will be the new member of The Twelve. What do you say?'

'You honour me so Sir and I have yet to give my presentation,' Faldo countered.

'That answer is precisely why you are the best man for the job Faldo,' the First said stroking the man's ego. 'Your presentation will not be needed now. I will inform everyone, and we will seal it at the celebrations tonight.'

Faldo replied, 'Thank you indeed, and celebrate we will. And Amador?'

'Yes, you always see the heart of a matter quickly, don't you Faldo. He was your competition to be sure, but he has stolen something of mine. Something that is important to me, this very afternoon.'

The First held up his hand to quell any response from Faldo. 'Yes, he has taken a Liferod that belongs to some friends of mine. My friends will not be happy, and I must have it back, you understand?' he elaborated, 'Amador turned up here early, must have run half the way, so early was he, craving my attention and indulgence. To try to curry favour no doubt,' the First mused aloud, 'I showed him the artifact, the Liferod actually, as a way of diverting him from making a grave error in trying to capture my attention and enhance my opinion of how clever he is.'

Faldo looked suitably shocked The First thought.

'Ah, but I will not let him take away your honour. Tonight, we celebrate, tomorrow you can go to find him and bring my Liferod back to me.' Then turning to touch the man before him on the arm, he asked, 'Will you do that for me Faldo?'

'Of course, Sir. I don't believe it! I never would have thought. Still I am honoured to accept the position you offer me. But, we can postpone the celebrations and I will go after him immediately?' Faldo asked in the hope of a negative response.

'No, we will not. He won't get too far. I had a report he left by the North Gate. Tomorrow will do, and you will have your seniors to help you. Amador is only one man. You may go now Faldo, I will see you tonight.' he said dismissing the man who would be his new bloodhound from now until the end of time.

Alone again, the First smiled a genuine smile that reached his eyes. He was happy, happier than he had been in a long time. The Liferod was in Amador's care, on its way to carry out a proper branding that would probably kill the boy who was causing all the fuss. He hoped so at least. Those half breeds were too dangerous to live anyway in his opinion.

It was also going to get those damn Fairies off his back for a while too. If necessary he could tell them that Amador must have had the Liferod all along, and that was why he couldn't find it.

'Excellent!' He was sure Faldo would get it back for him, of that he had little doubt. Underneath the calm demeanor the First knew that Faldo was ruthless. He would do it, although it would be an annoyance to him, but would get the Liferod in the end and return it as asked.

Yes! He would watch the action unfold. He hadn't had this much entertainment in a long while.

Yes! Tarramore, The First of all men, was happy.

Journal of the Living

Oh, happy days. I glimpse your face in my memory. So dear to me, but gone this long while from me, so that each time I have to reach harder through the blurring edges of my memories to find you. Sometimes the effort is beyond me.

Other days, like today, you surprise me with the memory of your smile and I truly recall the days before time changed everything.

Oh, those were happy days.

What would it be like to reach out and find that the last change at the end of time was undone? To feel the warmth of the sun's embrace on my skin and to have to shield my eyes from its brightness? I did that once without thinking. Now, I would feast my eyes on its yellow visage, until black spots occurred to swim in my vision, so that I would never, ever forget the beauty of that light!

An extract from a survivor's journal of unknown origin, but marked by Air.

CHAPTER FOUR

HUNT

Ayesha and Orrison emerged from their tent and silently walked towards the 'Animal Dance', where they had arranged to meet Miele. Dawn was just breaking and the camp was beginning to stir, carrying the sound of muted voices to their ears, as families gathered to break their fast for the new day.

They had agreed to hunt a big cat with Miele as their mentor. This was part of Orrison's moving on ritual, but Ayesha couldn't take him alone to oversee the transformation from boy to man. The Clan's rules said that only a man could bear witness to the right of manhood, but as usual Ayesha had managed to get her own way and was allowed to accompany the two on this trip.

Orrison didn't have to make the kill in the hunt today, that would be next week before the branding ceremony, but he had to observe and learn. He was to become the future Leader of the Clan and big cats didn't come along too often. When they did, as Leader, he would be expected to hunt and kill the beast.

Ayesha was taking Viktor's place as he had said he was unable to go. Ayesha knew her father couldn't bear to be around Orrison, so she didn't have to work too hard to persuade her father to let her go in his stead.

She had been following the big cat's progress over the winter months, but it was now starting to roam closer to the camp and as such presented a problem to the Clan, as they were competing for kills. The small array of cattle, farmed by a few members of the Clan, were also at risk of becoming easy slaughter for the big cat who was hungry from poor pickings over the winter period.

Ayesha's father's closest advisors, The Flames of Sepit, had decided that the cat must be killed and she now wanted the skin for her new chair in the 'Animal Dance'.

As she looked around the 'Dance', her first kill deerskin seemed out of place and was just too 'soft' for her liking. A big cat skin would show her hunting prowess to the whole Clan and remind them of her abilities, even although she was a girl and not a boy.

Ayesha knew that Miele, the Huntsmaster, liked to remind the Clan of the fact she was a girl on a regular basis which irked her immensely. Come to think of it, Miele was a problem for her whole family. He had spent the years from her mother's death taking every opportunity to undermine her father and to throw doubt on Orrison's right to Lead the Clan. It was small, well placed, seemingly innocent comments at first. But, as some listened, and others didn't threaten, his snide remarks were becoming more and more open.

She was torn. She valued Miele's knowledge. He had taught her more than any other, including her father. The skills she had developed under Miele's experienced tutelage she knew that she couldn't have gained elsewhere to the point she now respected and grudgingly admired the man. He had been the first to teach her that hunting wasn't about masculinity, but good observation, planning, cunning and courage.

Given her small stature in comparison to the men in the Clan, she had listened carefully, learning fast and well. Hardly any of the others her age had made the kills she had, and yet she kept pushing herself further. She knew Miele wasn't keen to let her try for the cat, but Ayesha was determined nonetheless.

Her family and its place in the Clan came first, and Orrison being there provided the subtle reminder needed to Miele of her heritage.

'Well met Huntsmaster,' said Ayesha, which was quickly repeated by Orrison.

Miele grunted in response, eyeing the lad with barely masked contempt. 'Let's away then,' he said, 'The day is wasting as we stand here.'

Walking to the outer edge of the encampment, they each then broke into a light jog. Each carrying a spear and a bow, together with a set of quivers at their back. Ayesha also liked to carry a light sac, the strap of which crossed her chest, leaving her hands free for weapons.

Not far from the camp they began the assent, gradual at first, but becoming steeper as they moved into the higher reaches of Etive Mhor and her sister hills. All three were accustomed to the hunt and they moved forward with ease, barely making a sound. They all knew that the big cat was likely some distance away and so they jogged at an even pace, in a purposeful manner.

Ayesha cast a glance at Orrison. He was keeping pace well with both her and Miele so well, she was sure that he wouldn't falter. He was in his manhood year now and would be ten at the turn of the moon. It was strange, she thought as she jogged, our Clan measure day to day time by the sun and the light, but months and years by the moon and the dark.

Her thoughts turned back to Orrison. His branding ceremony was next week and, as heir apparent; he would be given the full ceremony with one of the 'Wise Ones' performing the rights at the 'Animal Dance'.

There had been much activity amongst the Clan and the preparations were well underway with a festive atmosphere beginning to brew. Most notable by the high spirits of the children and the relaxed jibes of the older members of the Clan. This, coupled with the bustling activity of the adults meant that the preparations were in full swing.

Ayesha wanted this cat. Needed it like she needed the air to breathe. She wanted her chair to be right for the ceremony at the 'Animal Dance'. The branding for Leadership was never to be for her, but she at least wanted proof of her hunting abilities to be there for all to see. She had never been to a ceremony when one of the 'Wise Ones' had been called upon to attend, so she was beginning to feel really excited about it.

Orrison ran along beside her oblivious to the thoughts running through her head and she wondered what he was thinking about it all. He didn't appear to be phased. When she asked him about it he just smiled in his lopsided, endearing way and said he was fine.

Ayesha had cared for him like a mother in these last ten years. Trying to be the mother he never had. The awful thing was that mostly she had to be the father too. A bitter thought. She adored her father and he clearly loved her back. But, since her mother's death he was a different man and he found it hard to care for Orrison. At the same time, Orrison tried everything to gain his father's attention and approval. So far that approach hadn't worked for him, but she had to admire Orrison's spirit to keep trying.

Ayesha knew that her father liked to go to the lake to watch the strange woman. She didn't know the woman to speak to and nor did it seem did her father. But, if she needed to find her father, she knew on which path to wait. Her father also drank a lot of firewater in the evenings and made soft sounds at night that she didn't even want to think about at all. His eyes told their own story, as they were always bleary and red rimmed these days.

For all that, the Clan was still happy to have him as their Leader. Even despite Miele's whisperings about Orrison.

Sometimes she wondered herself. She had seen the woman with the long silver hair bathe too, just once when her curiosity had gotten the better of her. She had hidden in the bracken close by where the woman came into the water and she had a full view. The memory that stood out most was the colour of her eyes. They were so blue… just as Orrison's were. She also always had a young girl with her who was as dark as the woman was fair.

Ayesha shook her head and tried not to think too hard about it. Orrison was her brother, she loved him and as of next week he would enter his manhood years then be confirmed as the next Leader of the Fire Clan. That was all there was to it!

As he lopped along beside her, arms and legs already too big for his body at ten, but beginning to show the promise of the man he would become, Ayesha was content.

She wanted this cat though!

It wasn't too long before they found some evidence of the beast they hunted. All were expert at reading tracks, but it was Orrison who was first to speak of the signs.

'It's pretty clear that the cat has been here. Look here and here,' he said pointing. 'My guess is that she waited on that cliff above the tree line and came down quickly through the edges of the trees, through the long grass, then, circling her prey, came up behind for the kill.'

Orrison's voice hadn't broken as yet, but due to the solemn, hushed tone he used, neither Ayesha nor Miele denied him the moment.

'Aye,' said Miele, 'Seems you be right boy. We're in her territory now, take care; it's been a longer winter than most. She could still be very hungry.'

'Is that why she's been coming to our lands, because of the winter?' Orrison asked earnestly.

'Aye,' replied Miele. It was enough.

They shifted their spears, and Ayesha, who preferred the bow, knocked an arrow. They set off into the forested area with her taking point, Orrison in the middle and Miele protecting the rear. All were watching and listening vigilantly now and they moved forward as one. Prepared.

Tracking the big cat was relatively easy as they had each assumed that the cat would have returned to the shelter of the rocky ledge from where Orrison had rightly said she likely would have started her hunt.

As they ascended to the ledge, it was clear that the cat had favoured this spot. She had obviously fed on her kill, sheltered in the lea of this particularly big rock, albeit some time ago from the look of the remains.

Miele signaled to Ayesha with two fingers to his eyes then pointing both outwards. She knew he was reinforcing the need to be watchful by this gesture. One of the few prints they had followed on the climb up to the rock was very large. This was a big, big cat.

She felt her adrenaline begin to rise. They were on the hunt proper now.

In a similar gesture Miele signaled to Orrison to move up to the top of the rockface. Once Orrison had scrambled up top, they began to advance.

Ayesha was again, taking point. Orrison was up top, and Miele was covering the rear.

All was silent, another sign that the cat was close.

Then, with no warning, Miele shouted out as the beast broke from cover. In a matter of seconds, it had closed the gap between him and it. The cat muzzled and bit through Miele's hamstring in one smooth motion then proceeded to pounce on top of him.

Miele screamed. A piercing sound.

The cat had been hunting them as they had hunted it.

Ayesha turned whip quick and loosed an arrow that sailed through the space where the cat's head and throat had been only moments before. In a heartbeat she had another quiver in her bow as she ran forward to ensure success with her second shot. She had to pull up short though as Orrison dived from his higher perch to land upon the beasts back.

Ayesha just couldn't get a clear shot as Miele lay pinned beneath the beast and Orrison clung on top. She watched, breath caught, waiting for the right time to release her arrow.

She watched Orrison's hand come high into the air, bloody. And watched as he plunged it down again into the waiting throat of the big cat.

The cat rolled off from Miele and her arrow found its mark. But, not before the cat's front paw raked Miele as it fell, with Orrison continuing to stab at the now dead animal.

As the cat fell, its momentum carried Orrison with it, and it landed on top of his leg pinning him to the ground.

Rushing towards him, Ayesha hefted the still warm cat to and fro to help free Orrison's leg. Once he was freed, she ran to Miele's side.

It wasn't good. He was unconscious and it was pretty clear that his stomach had been opened by the cat's front paws. His leg was bleeding badly where he had been bitten, and this Ayesha began to bind with some rough grass to stem the flow of blood.

Miele was ashen but beginning to come to awareness.

She said, 'Miele, it's all right, you're going to be alright.' Then she shouted, 'Orrison get over here I need you to hold this for me.'

'It's my leg Ayesha, I'm trying,' he replied as he shuffled towards them dragging his injured leg behind him.

Miele half grunted, half gurgled.

'It's all right Miele, you're going to be alright,' she said as calmly as she could muster, but even to her own ears her voice came out a few decibels too loudly. She took a breath to try to calm her mind.

'Hold this tight here Orrison, we need to stop the blood flow.' Then she shouted at Orrison, 'Give me your belt.'

Wrapping Orrison's woven belt around the pads of grass she had placed on the bite in Miele's leg, she pulled it tight.

Miele slipped into unconsciousness again as she pulled the belt even tighter.

Next, she cut his skins at the shoulder and pulled his top skins down to reveal his belly. Two gashes split the flesh. Muttering to herself as she worked on.

Ayesha had twine in her sac but she knew that sewing was out of the question. She tried to see inside, but there was just too much blood, so she grabbed up her sac, upended the contents unceremoniously onto the earth and placed her sac on top of the open wound that was his stomach.

'Here now Orrison, hold this in place lightly for Miele.' She hadn't noticed she was crying until a drop splashed onto Orrison's hand as she guided it towards her sac. She wiped the tears away with her arm and made herself stop crying. Crying was for girls.

Orrison was staring at her with his mouth slightly ajar and then said the most stupid thing, 'You have the skin now Ayesha.'

She didn't reply.

Eventually she said, 'Right, you need to get in close to Miele and try to keep him warm while I go to get help.'

'I said you have the skin now Ayesha,' Orrison insisted more loudly.

'I heard you the first time Orrison,' she spat back at him. 'It's your kill Orrison, your skin and you're welcome to it.'

Ayesha wanted to scream at him, shake him and punch him. Miele was lying there dying and all he could think of was the cat skin! She wanted to yell at him and blame him for jumping down onto the cats back which meant she couldn't save Miele with her second shot, but her face burned because she had missed with her first shot. Likely the second shot would still have been too late anyway. There was no way that anyone could know that now.

She shouldn't have brought Orrison, he was really still a boy, a boy with no mother and a father who didn't like him. She had tried to fill the gap, but she just couldn't do it. Tears were flowing down her face now, unchecked.

No, she tried to pull herself together, she needed Orrison now. She was glad he was there. He would keep Miele warm while she ran to get help. She said, 'Keep Miele warm Orrison, that's the best you can do.' Her voice was flat now, but there was nothing she could do about that either.

Orrison looked hurt, but he ran his slim body along the length of Miele's and pulled his head in towards his own shoulder.

Quickly considering, Ayesha said, 'Good. I'll be back with help as soon as I can.' With that said, she turned and ran off, back in the direction of Etive Mhor and home.

Orrison's leg throbbed and Miele's shallow breath on his shoulder was the only sign that he still lived on.

Time stretched out.

'That you Orrison?' Miele breathed. 'That was some big cunning cat huh. Guess you killed her good and proper.'

Despite himself, Orrison felt pride surge at the praise he was getting from such a great man who was an honoured hunter of the Clan, and he tried to get closer to give him some more warmth because Miele was starting to shake a bit.

He copied Ayesha. 'You're going to be alright Miele, yes you'll be alright. Ayesha's gone to get help. My father will come and everything will be alright, you'll see.'

Miele coughed and blood trickled onto Orrison's shoulder. He could feel the blood's slow journey to earth as it trickled from his shoulder, into his neck, and from there dropping bit by bit onto the ground, like a reminder of what belongs on the inside.

'Your father's a fool Orrison. That was a brave thing you did today lad and no mistake. Aye, brave or foolish, but I think brave first.' Miele coughed some more. 'You'll be a man soon eh, a man to lead our Clan. Do it well Orrison. Be brave. Brave when you know for sure what your father did to your mother. Brave when you eventually know your own mother. Brave when you know who and what you are. Yes, you will need to be brave.'

Orrison couldn't help himself, he pulled away and said, 'What do you mean Miele, what are you talking about?'

But, as he moved he had taken his hand off Miele's stomach wound. Miele's whole body spasmed and then relaxed.

Orrison tried to get the right position again. His leg really ached now. He pulled Miele's head back to his shoulder, but it fell away. Three times he tried this. Three times Miele's head rolled back off his shoulder.

'It's all right Miele, everything will be all right. You'll see. But, what do you mean; I don't know what you mean? It'll be alright. Ayesha will be here soon with help and everything will be alright. You'll see,' he recited.

When eventually Ayesha, Viktor, Derrik and Isaak arrived, they found Miele where he had fallen to the big cat. He was quite dead.

Orrison was almost finished skinning the beast, which he continued to do. No one spoke.

Ayesha eyed Orrison.

He pulled the last of the skin free and hobbled towards Ayesha. 'This is your skin my sister.'

'No brother, it is your skin;' she replied 'A skilled, brave hunter died for this skin today. Do not shame him or me by not claiming what was hard won,' she continued in a more heated manner to help stem the pain inside of her.

Orrison both felt and looked small. He lifted his eyes perhaps seeking guidance or acknowledgement from Viktor, she couldn't tell. There was neither.

'What happened here?' Viktor asked. Between them they told the sorry tale.

'The skin is yours Orrison,' Viktor said flatly. 'Perhaps though, you should have thought before jumping. You stopped Ayesha getting a clear second shot. Miele might still live if it wasn't for you.'

With that pronouncement, he gestured for the men to lift Miele's body onto a makeshift stretcher to bring him home, so that the Clan could properly celebrate his life.

Following behind, Orrison hobbled along carrying the skin with Ayesha's support.

Both were lost in their own thoughts.

I often wonder why I keep going, but try as I might, I am unable to end my misery. It is a constant battle in which to live is the only possible outcome. I crave survival against all odds. I stoop so low to make sure that I do survive. I'm not sure that I can ever be called a rational person anymore? I am sure though, that I am a survivor.

It's dark these days. My mind grows dim of memories and my pencil, my precious pencil, is but a stub. My pencil keeps me sane I think, in the madness of this new world. What will I become when it has gone I wonder? Best not to examine that too deeply...

I will build a capsule. I must build a capsule. Like the ones prepared by the school children for future generations to find. I remember the millennium capsule being reported on the news. We had found it and opened it a whole Millennia after it had been buried. I wonder if anyone will ever find my writings and what they will make of them if they do? I have nothing else to put inside my *capsule other than my pencil, my stub, and I don't think I want to put my stub into it. Come to think of it, I don't have a capsule! Thank goodness for that, I can keep my stub.*

An extract from a survivor's journal of unknown origin but marked by Air

CHAPTER FIVE

PYRE

Amador lost no time as he moved through the Conclave proper, stopping only to gather enough food and water for his hoped-for short journey through the western mountains. Storing his hoard in a makeshift sac that he fashioned from his robe, by pulling up the bottom of his robe and tying the ends securely at the shoulder, leaving his legs and hands free. He would need the freedom of movement in his legs, clad in his undergarments, for the climb ahead.

It wasn't uncommon for a member of the Conclave venturing into the hills to be dressed in this manner, but he prepared himself in secret and slipped unnoticed towards the West Gate. The First had said that he had to make all haste, and he intended to do just that.

The conversation he and The First had shared had

unsettled him though, and he would be able to reflect on it as he walked. It had occurred to him that perhaps this was part of his test and so, ensuring he was not observed by his fellows, he considered his options for speed of travel.

The First had told him that the caves in the mountains were not a place for him. He had only ever investigated the outer limits of the caves while training for the Order. He wasn't even sure that there was a clear way through. Equally, he didn't know that there wasn't. He had the strange globe given to him to light his way. Why would The First have given it to him if he expected him to take the circuitous route?

Amador tried to consider what the weight of the mountain would feel like if he were to become lost inside? It wasn't welcome speculation, but haste was also required.

He had decided. He would climb up a good way and then descend through the network of caves that he had heard did exist. Deciding then to ignore the warning; he would take the globe as the sure sign of what he must do, and thereby shorten the journey. Speed will likely be as important in this task as in others that have been set for me before, he thought.

He scouted around the western mountain where bracken covered the base, mapping the path he would follow with his eyes. Always deciding in advance where he would walk. He was a fit man who could easily climb the bottom reaches of the mountain, but he knew it would become tougher as he climbed.

This didn't deter him from the fast pace he set himself. As he climbed he listened to the gathering silence, but he didn't stop to admire the view. At last he reached a point where the rockface was almost vertical. He hadn't been able to see this obstacle until he was almost upon it, and to go back around would mean that he would lose valuable time.

He didn't have a rope he could use, so he removed his footwear and placed his sandals in his makeshift sac. He used his belt to fasten his staff so that it strapped across his back and began to climb properly. Finding the finger and toe holds, he made his ascent, again, mapping out his route in advance.

Amador knew he was an efficient climber and his rhythmic movements gave him the momentum for the extra push or pull he needed from his limbs. Reaching a ledge, he pulled himself up. There was a cave opening just to the left of where he sat. The rockface stretched on above. He had hoped to go higher before entering the mountain, but the cave presented an opportunity that he decided he had to take.

'Well, I don't want to look a gift horse in the mouth,' he said aloud to himself. He knew that he could climb higher still and possibly end up having to climb back down again to this very entrance.

Having recovered quickly from the climb, he moved across the rockface, swung his body and dropped in a controlled way into the entrance of the cave. He could see a little way in, but thereafter darkness took over, cloaking his path.

He knew he would have to be careful, but thought it would be better to use his senses rather than the light of the crystal globe that The First had given him. It would dull his other senses with its bright light.

But, first he decided to stop at there at the mouth of the cave to eat a light meal of bread, ham and cheese and to drink some of the water from the container which was belted at his waist, knowing he may not get another chance to get the sustenance he would likely need inside the network of caves.

Resetting his makeshift sac, he unloosened his staff, which he intended to use as his guide. Satiated, he moved into the cave and darkness descended.

'What is that click clicking sound from above? Wait, there is a man coming, I can smell him,' Boeson thought to his friend.

'*Be still Boeson. He is on the other side from us.*'

Boeson grunted and stooped to gather a huge boulder in his massive hands. The two unlikely friends waited.

'*What does he do in our caves with his click clicking? He is like an ant waiting to be squashed Elm.'*

'*I don't know yet, but there is a protection, I can feel it.*'

'*Phaa, let's see if it works, then shall we?*' And with that Boeson threw first one boulder, and then quickly loosed a second.

'*Enough! Boeson! I said there's a protection,*' Elm thought to his friend. Boeson wasn't the easiest to stop from a course of action though. He always acted first and thought later. Elm laid a hand on his friend's massive forearm as a further restraint. '*No. Boeson no. Enough*!'

Boeson just grunted again.

Amador could smell the water more strongly now. It hung in the air and smelled dank. He thought he had heard a noise and pulled the crystal globe out. Thinking quickly, he uttered 'Spark' and the enormous cavern he found himself in was bathed in light. His eyes were at once drawn to two boulders hurtling towards him and so he started to run down the scree slope that he stood upon hoping they would miss their target, as he felt sure they were aimed directly at him.

His reactions were fast. His last vision was of two boulders hurtling over water towards him. BANG. The first struck the place he had been only moments before. He was thrown into the air and lost his footing and began to tumble and slide within the belly of the mountain, all purchase lost. BANG. The second boulder struck to his left. Again, he was thrown into the air and tumbled, pall mall.

Groping about in the dark Amador fell fast. Uttering, 'Spark.' The crystal globe woke to life on his right; he reached for it, and just missed. He was anxious now and falling. And the crystal winked out.

Glimpsing the drop below, he knew he had to slow himself, and steadying his mind, 'spark.' There was a trickle of light, and then nothing. The bauble was caught in the slide, as was he. He grasped to his left and his fingers found his staff, not a moment too soon. Forcing the staff into a gap in the cave wall, it held fast and luckily, he with it, while the landslide moved below him and dropped into the lake far below.

Eventually the slide subsided and Amador caught his breath, his mind racing. Again, he said, 'Spark.' A soft glow at his back reassured him that his globe wasn't lost and he dug carefully through the scree to retrieve it. He looked around as he knew a death ledge was extremely close, and he shuddered at the thought of how close he had come to going over that edge.

The light from the crystal now also revealed a set of stairs carved into the side of the cave. He was both amazed and relieved to find them there.

Miraculously he hadn't broken anything in the fall, but he knew that he would be both bruised and cut. Thanking the air for the breath in his lungs, he made his way towards the stairs. His makeshift sac was torn at one shoulder and he had lost most of its contents in the fall. Tucked against his belt, both the Liferod and his water container were intact, and he breathed a sigh of relief.

How would he have explained the loss of the Liferod to The First? He was sure he didn't know. The Liferod felt warm to the touch and gave him an immense sense of reassurance.

As he made his way down the carved stairs he marveled at them even being there. If he was being tested, surely the worst must be over? However, he had an uneasy feeling that he was being watched, so he proceeded in his descent very carefully.

'*Come Boeson, we must leave this place,*' Elm thought to Boeson. '*We must go to get the last Liferod from the man of a thousand years.*'

'*But what of Fern, she is trapped with no wings. She is nothing more than a slave and her keening hurts Elm.*' Boeson thought back.

'Don't you think I don't know that! She is my sister Boeson and I love her more than life. But she has her own journey, as retrieving the Liferod is mine,' Elm replied. *'We have to undo what my Uncle started if we are to have any hope of surviving on our own. Since the clash of the worlds and the shrouding of the sun there are too few babes who survive and we hide in the mountains instead of playing in the sun as we once did. You are the last of your kind Boeson. Do you not feel regret in your blood? Can you not hear your own keening, for it is so loud? No. We must leave Fern and this place. We must retrieve the last Liferod. If we must die out, then let us do so wisely.'*

'I just don't want to leave her. I want to smash these little men to pieces.' Boeson's angry words were not matched by the water gathering in his large eye.

'I know, I know,' Elm comforted, '*but you know it really*

is for the best.'

The two friends watched the little man climb down the stairs of Iho and waited for him to pass. Two unlikely friends, one grotesque; the other quite beautiful, hidden in the shadows.

Emerging from the caves Amador blinked to adjust his vision to the brightness of the day. As he started to walk he came across a small woman gathering herbs.

'Who passes my abode and walks the caves of Iho?' Seraphina challenged.

He replied, 'It is Amador, aspiring to The Twelve. I have come for the branding ceremony of the Clan Leader's boy.'

Seraphina stood, cradling her full basket on one arm.

He thought that she looked like a child by her size, but her eyes were sharp and focused directly on him, with an intensity that made him feel slightly uncomfortable and truly scrutinised.

'Welcome Amador, aspiring to The Twelve. You come in good time, the boy will reach his majority on the morrow,' she said. 'I am Seraphina, Sun Mother to this Fire Clan,' she continued, bowing to him.

'Well met Sun Mother. May the sun always shine brightly on your hair,' he replied and was rewarded by a wide smile.

'You know our ways Amador. Have you before been met by a Clan Leader?' she enquired.

He replied, 'No, no, never before. Only in the parchments I read Sun Mother. I am a student of the peoples of our lands.'

'An interesting study I think, but made better by the experience, I hope. Let's walk Amador.'

Together they struck out across the meadow, stopping now and then to retrieve an essential plant for her basket.

'It's a fine day Sun Mother. I can tell you that I am most happy to be out of those caves.'

'I'll bet!'

She was obviously a woman of few words he thought.

'Alas, we have recently lost our Huntsmaster and are now preparing to celebrate his life this night.'

Considering the small woman before him, Amador noted the determined look on her face.

'You will know to be happy and not sad at this celebration Amador?' she enquired.

'As you wish Sun Mother,' he responded.

'But of course, I wish!' she replied with a smile. 'Although I see Iho did not let you pass through his domain unscathed,' she said taking in his torn robes, tangled hair and beard.

Stopping again, Seraphina tugged on a particularly stubborn plant with extremely long roots. Noticing his watchful gaze, she said, 'Mint for tea, I'm rather partial to a good pot,' she chuckled. 'Come, I will show you where you can refresh from your journey.'

With that, she led him to a fresh mountain lake, where he washed away his aches and scrapes with a swim.

He remembered the stories of Iho that he had read as a child. They had frightened him then, but he never thought he would ever get to walk his caves and come out alive.

The story said Iho was a mad dwarf who stole children away to his caves where they were never seen again. As he sat to dry himself on a rock, he mended his torn robe with some twine that Seraphina had given him for that purpose. He could hear a child playing happily nearby. A boy he thought given the fighting nature of the game he was playing. He smiled a bit and again thanked the air for the breath in his lungs.

With his robes patched as well as could be, his water carrier and the Liferod hanging from his belt in the folds of his robe, he carried the crystal globe and his staff as he made his way towards the Clan's encampment.

He wanted to know more about the boy he would make a man on the morrow, so he took his directions from Seraphina and went to find Viktor, the Clan Leader.

As he rounded Sepit Mhor, he could see the whole of the tented village spread out before him. It was larger and more settled looking than he had thought it would be from his reading of the parchments. From this vantage point he could see the formal setting of the tents. They were arranged in a semicircular fashion from what looked like a plateau at the base of Sepit Mhor. The spacing between the tents allowed passage into three main arteries that led from the plateau to the outskirts of the village. This was interspersed with semicircular pathways between each row.

There must be at least a thousand tents here, he thought to himself. He was most impressed. The largest of the tents were on the outer rim of the camp. From his studies he knew that these belonged to the Clan Leader and his most trusted men. His Flames. Placing them on the outskirts created a sense of safety for the Clan, but also meant that the Leaders would be seen walking amongst members of the Clan as they went about their daily business.

Just beyond the camp he could see that a large pyre had been erected and the Huntsman's body was being winched to its summit.

Amador began his descent hoping that he would be able to find footwear to replace his lost sandals before meeting with the Clan Leader.

As he reached the village proper, his gaze was drawn to the plateau and the strange seats covered in animal hide. They were both monstrous and graceful at once he thought to himself.

Noting that many of the Clan's folk had stopped what they were doing and were openly staring at him, he smiled and pointed at himself. 'Amador, I am Amador, I've come for the boy's branding ceremony,' he said to all watching. He smiled a bit more, but not one of the Clan's people approached.

He tried again, 'I am Amador. Can anyone tell me where I can find Clan Leader Viktor?'

Amador thought he knew exactly where to find Viktor, but he hoped asking for help would break the silent looks. And sure enough, a lass stepped forward.

'Amador, I am Ayesha daughter of Clan Leader Viktor. I will take you to my father. Come.'

The young woman standing before Amador was a beauty, even with her serious expression. She was slim and clad in furs, cinched at the waist, emphasising the narrow lines of her slim figure. She had long auburn locks that were tied loosely together at the nape of her neck. Some shorter ringlets escaped and framed her face.

'Ahhh, well met Ayesha,' he said bowing, but she had turned her back towards him and was already walking away. He hurried to catch up.

'Ayesha, is there somewhere I can…'

She stopped and turned, regarding him with her green eyes, missing nothing. 'Shoes, you have no shoes,' she said in a soft voice.

Quickly tucking his toes beneath his robes, he said, 'Yes, I was about to ask. I'd like to purchase a pair, if I may? I seem to have lost my own in the caves of Iho.'

'The caves of Iho, you say. I'm thinking you were lucky not to lose yourself Amador.'

The frank manner she had about her was both unsettling and refreshing he decided. His brief encounters with those who knew he was an aspiring to join The Twelve held him in great esteem and talked to him with awe in their voices. This was a whole different experience for him.

'Come, I will take you to Fiamma,' said Ayesha, 'She is making the best shoes for the Clan.' And she strode off again.

He had no choice but to obey her instruction and followed her direction with a light step.

The moccasin booties Fiamma made for him were a joy for his tired toes. 'Fiamma, these are just perfect, how may I repay you?' he enquired.

Fiamma was an ample woman whose many children had played around her while she had worked. 'A blessing for my family Sir,' she replied hopefully.

He set to work and very quickly bestowed the blessing she had requested. A flurry of wind always impressed and was easy to conjure for one such as him. Each of her children had their hair ruffled in turn. His booties were indeed worth the small price.

Fiamma was obviously delighted, and by the look of her watchful gaze over her brood, most appreciative too.

Following Ayesha again, they eventually found Viktor, staring up at the pyre now holding his dead Huntsmaster.

Ayesha said, 'Father, I bring you Amador, who will brand Orrison on the morrow and make him a man.'

'It will take more than a branding to make Orrison a man,' Viktor replied. 'Still, Amador, well met, and thanks to you for travelling so far,' he continued, as he regarded Amador in a very similar manner to his daughter.

Once more, he felt totally scrutinised.

He thought that Viktor looked strained, and assumed it was likely related to the loss of his Huntsmaster at such a momentous time for his son.

The sarcasm in Viktor's voice when he had mentioned his son was not lost on Amador, but he smiled anyway and gave the Fire Clan greeting. 'Viktor, I am Amador, aspiring to The Twelve, may the sun always shine brightly on your hair.'

'Amador, you are a wise one indeed! Welcome to my Clan. What is ours is yours, just ask,' Viktor replied. 'You will join us in this evening's celebration?' he enquired. Our beloved Huntsmaster will dance with the sun for the last time,' he concluded.

'I would be most honored to celebrate his life with you Viktor. I have heard tell that the Sundance is something to behold. I confess, I have long hoped to see it for myself,' Amador enthused.

He thought that he had conveyed the right amount of respect when referring to both the celebration and the Sundance, but Viktor still looked a bit wary, so he changed the subject.

'Orrison is your son, and the morrow is his special day. May I meet and spend some time with him?' he enquired.

'No, that's not possible Amador,' Viktor replied. 'He left a short time ago. Our custom requires that he walks the lonesome path for a night and collect the stone found only at the summit of Sepit Mhor. Before he can become a man, he must chase the boy away.'

'Forgive me Viktor; I had thought that he would be here for the celebration. I heard of his part in the hunt for the big cat,' Amador said.

Viktor's eyes darted to Ayesha.

Holding up his hand, Amador shook his head and said, 'I was having some shoes made,' he pulled back his robe to reveal his new booties. 'I tend to gossip a bit. You see, I am so interested in the study of our peoples,' he emphasised, stretching out his arms encompassing the camp, 'and I'm afraid the opportunity to talk to people overwhelms me. I do hope I haven't caused you any offence?'

Viktor stared at him and Amador tried his very best to keep his face looking contrite.

'Ayesha here will tell you of our customs and our people and how we like to do things around here. You can join us for the fire dance this evening. Here at the pyre,' he said, 'Until then Amador!' Viktor turned and walked off in one direction, while Ayesha turned back towards Sepit Mhor.

'Come Amador,' she beckoned, 'I will tell you everything you want to know about our Clan.'

Amador was still unsure if he had caused any offence, but he turned to follow her, his mind full of questions. There were undercurrents at play here, and no mistake. He longed to discover the whole of it.

Orrison looked down from his position in the heights of Sepit Mhor at the camp that would one day be his to Lead. It looks so small, he thought to himself. I always thought it was bigger.

Orrison had climbed up the mountain before, but never quite so high. He was to be alone for the night, but he could still see the camp. There were lots of little people scurrying to and fro preparing for Miele's celebration. He could make out the pyre and he had decided that he would watch the sun dance from his lofty location.

Orrison knew that he had to retrieve a rock from the

summit, but he wanted to see the dance. His father could have allowed him to do this task last evening, freeing him to be at the celebration, but he had refused him again.

It was always the same, no, no, no, but he couldn't tell him to move on now and not watch from here. It meant that he would have to climb to the summit in the dark, but that didn't bother him as much as not seeing the dance.

Orrison wanted to see Miele burning, maybe then he would be able to get his voice out of his head; over and over his last words. Who is my mother? But my mother died and that's why my father can't look me in the eye. But Miele said I had to be strong when I find out who my real mother is, he thought. I know who my real mother is already. It just doesn't make any sense.

Over and over he had tried to make sense of it, but came up empty time after time. He resolved that when he became a man on the morrow he would seek guidance from Seraphina. If he still heard the voice in his head after Miele was burned and gone.

Knowing that Miele hadn't liked him, in fact, he was acutely aware that he wasn't much loved by anyone, he thought; except Ayesha. Ayesha loved him, even if she shook her head, shouted and stamped her feet at him, he knew she still loved him. But, he thought, I don't care about Ayesha, she's just a stupid girl. He didn't really like girls. They giggled and squealed and did girly things. At least Ayesha could hunt.

Father, why must everything be so hard for me? I try and I try to make you proud. Why are you not proud of me? I'm good at what I do, he thought. You say that you don't like my blue eyes, that they're not natural. Do you think I don't have the fire in me because of my blue eyes?

And there it was again, Miele's voice in his head questioning his mother, his real mother.

Feeling frustrated and confused, Orrison thought on. Maybe if I get the stone and the brand father will treat me like a man? He could live in hope at least he guessed.

But, I'm still going to see Miele burn first though he thought. And yes, I'll celebrate. Celebrate that he's gone. I'm glad he's gone!

Like a broken doll, he huddled down and waited for the sky to change and Miele to burn.

Journal of the Living

We scurry furtively like rats across an open space. There are many of us in this band. We plan together and strike against our enemies, devouring their food, sampling their water, leaving their carcasses behind for the animals to find. It is good to be part of a band. We are the people of Air and we live beyond the end of all time. I have eaten well this day.

An extract from a survivor's journal of unknown origin but marked by Air.

Chapter Six

Celebration

Having spent an excellent day with Ayesha, meeting lots of the Clan and hearing firsthand about their history, Amador's interest in the ways of Fire was piqued.

He had also heard all about Orrison and the loss of his mother in the birthing of him and had started to appreciate how hard it must be to find solace for both him and Viktor. He reflected that it may have contributed in some way to Viktor's earlier words.

Ayesha clearly enjoyed hunting. He had been told the tale of the latest hunt for the big cat and why Miele's life would be celebrated that evening. The skin now adorning Orrison's chair looked fearsome, even without its owner. Amador struggled to comprehend how a boy of ten could best such a beast, and surmised that he must have had more help than he had been told about.

Feeling like he now knew all about the 'animal dance' and who had killed for each skin and the tales behind the hunt, he hummed to himself as he started to anticipate the evening's mysteries.

He hadn't had the opportunity to visit with any Fire Clan before and was relishing every minute. There was something to be said for experiencing things for oneself that was missing from the papers he read. He would have travelled here before, had he not been so caught up in the environmental puzzle that had been set for those aspiring to The Twelve.

Anyway, he had thoroughly enjoyed himself today and was appreciating the fact that he knew that there was more to come.

In fact, he was beginning to enjoy himself so much that he was no longer sure anymore that this was part of his test. Indeed, the journey through the caves hadn't been necessary. The branding ceremony wouldn't be held until the morrow. But, he had bought himself some time among these people and for that he was grateful.

Ayesha was looking at him and he shook himself out of his musings.

'Come Amador. We go now,' she said.

Looking around he noticed that most of the Clan had already departed from the 'animal dance' and were making their way towards the outskirts of the camp. Both he and Ayesha hurried to follow in their wake.

'It will soon be time for the Sundance Amador. You will love it. I love it,' she said reverently. 'It is very special and no more so than when we are celebrating the life of one of our own Clan.'

By the time they reached the outskirts of the village, everyone had gathered in a large semi-circle facing both to the west and the pyre. Ayesha pulled him through the crowd to a position at the front.

Then the drums started to beat, a slow rhythmic tune, deepening and quickening.

A line of men dressed in paint and animal skins began to dance, miming a hunt to the beat of the drums. The crowd began to chant and clap in time to the beat.

The dance continued.

When the drums and the chanting reached a crescendo and the beast was killed in the dance, a great cheer went up and everyone stamped their feet as they clapped on. Ayesha turned to look at him and Amador noticed that her eyes were bright.

He found himself stamping his own feet and clapping and she gave him a huge rewarding smile. Next the dancers took up torches, and circling the pyre in time to the drumbeat, they took up their allotted positions.

Amador would never forget what happened next for his whole life. He had read about it, but could never have imagined anything so beautiful. The firedance! A whole patch of sky turned red and orange and pink. His breath caught in his throat and he could feel the tears start to form in his eyes. It was spectacular.

As the fire danced in the sky, the pyre was lit and Miele was celebrated. His spirit released to dance with the fire in the sky for the last time, as was the custom of the Fire Clan.

There was feasting and merriment in the camp that evening, but Amador remained detached as he had felt truly humbled by the fire in the sky.

Amador could never have imagined such a mass of

colour, painted, and changing as he watched, in the sky above. The sky was grey. Everyone knew that. It was always just darker and lighter shades of grey. What he had witnessed though drove shards of glass through his knowledge and ripped it asunder.

Astonished also at his own reactions, he felt sure that this was his test laid bare, before his very eyes. He thought of his presentation on the environment. It seemed to be a hollow nothingness in comparison to this mighty wonder, knowing that he would now have to give it much more thought.

He wondered why, only here in this place was it possibly to see such a thing? He had travelled amongst the earth peoples and dwelled for a time with those of the Water. He grew up in the wings of the Air people. Nothing in his whole life experience could have prepared him for seeing the sun set in the evening sky though.

He felt truly small.

Next morning, he awoke early and went back to the lake Seraphina had shown him to refresh himself and make his preparations for the branding ceremony. Walking back towards the camp, he looked up at the sky. It was familiar grey again, if a lighter grey than in some areas of the land, he thought.

He still felt both astonished and humbled by the events of the previous evening. The firedance would have been spectacular on its own, but the pyre's flames dancing in the dark later, made the whole experience even more memorable.

The branding ceremony was to take place at the 'animal dance' at midday, so he spent the rest of the morning wandering and chatting, and found himself bestowing many blessings on his travels. Word had spread that he could make the air move and children followed him around squealing with delight as he ruffled their hair from afar.

It was nearing time for the ceremony now though, so he sought out Ayesha. He found her in the thick of things, up to her eyes in preparations for the big feast. The second celebration in as many days had kept all of the Clan's women busy he knew.

Rough made wooden tables were strewn with all manner of culinary delights. Each of the Flames of Sepit had a specialty and the tables groaned under the weight of so much food.

Surmising that there were a lot of mouths to feed, as he knew the Clan had made short work of the previous evening's offerings, it was likely there wouldn't be much going to waste today either.

Spying Ayesha, he walked over to her. 'Hello Ayesha, I guess it must be about time for the ceremony. Should I go to the 'animal dance' now?' he asked.

'Oh, Amador. Well met. I hope everyone has been looking after you?' she enquired. 'I got a bit caught up here helping out. I guess I'm filling in for my mother.'

Ayesha gazed around the array of food set out on the tables and said wistfully, 'You know, I really think my mother would have been happy to be here on this day. The day Orrison will become a man and begin his proper training to become the next Clan Leader.'

Amador considered the young woman before him and replied, 'Yes, I'm sure she would have loved it too, but she would be so proud of you Ayesha. What a lovely girl you are,' he said, knowing it was probably the worst compliment he could give her at any other time, but right now she looked grateful.

‘You should go and meet with my father and the Flames of Sepit now Amador. You will find them over at the ‘animal dance’,’ she said gesturing with her arm in the direction. ‘This is man’s business now. I’ve helped him as much as I can; it’s up to him now.’

Ayesha’s face was closed as she said this and he could tell that there was a part of her that would always look for more responsibility in the Clan, likely to no avail.

So, he said, ‘Thanks to you Ayesha. The branding ceremony won’t take long and then everyone can enjoy this wonderful food that you have arranged for us.’

Walking over to the plateau he easily vaulted onto the structure that held the ‘animal dance’. He had noticed Viktor talking to a group of men. They were gathered around Orrison’s seat, covered in the big cat skin, and Amador approached them, coughing slightly to alert them to his presence.

‘Amador, well met,’ said Viktor. ‘I want you to know the Flames of Sepit. They will witness the branding. Derrik, my right-hand man,’ he said clapping Derrik on the back.

Derrik nodded his head in acknowledgement.

‘Dougal, John, James, Isaak, Douglass, Gordon, Andrew and George,’ he said as each man in turn nodded his acknowledgement as his name was spoken. ‘We haven’t appointed a new Huntsmaster since Mieles’s passing,’ he said as if this fact would be obvious to him and it was of the utmost importance.

‘Well met, Flames of Sepit,’ Amador replied, nodding his own head in their general direction.

The group seemed to echo Viktor’s concern for the Huntsmaster in their body language, so he thought he would throw in an observation of his own. ‘It seems to me that you have a potential candidate for Huntsmaster in Ayesha. She seems very interested in hunting. I think I now know the history of every skin here in the 'animal dance,' he suggested half laughing.

There was a mixed response amongst the Flames of Sepit, but mainly one of disapproval. Although he had tried to keep his suggestion light and jovial, it wasn't received like that at all he noticed.

'Huntsmaster is an important position in our Clan Amador, but I understand that you are not from here and don't know the dangers involved,' Viktor admonished. 'I fear that I have been too soft on Ayesha and have exposed her unnecessarily,' he concluded.

Douglass interjected, 'The Huntsmaster is also a member of our ruling group. His words carry great importance in our way of life. That's just not a woman's place.'

Knowing that he probably shouldn't have suggested it in the first place, but he had met great women leaders in other lands, and thought it would do no great harm to introduce the concept to these men. A bit presumptuous on his part, but it was the one thing he just didn't understand about their way of life.

Amador was a teacher at heart, so he always felt the need to point out areas of life that he thought could improve people's lives. Perhaps it was just a stretch too far for these men of Fire though. He had tried, but a stray sigh emitted from his tight lips.

However, Derrik said, 'That's an interesting proposition you make Amador. Ayesha is indeed interested in the ways of men. You are wise indeed to have observed this in so short a time amongst us.'

Viktor rounded on Derrik. 'That's for me to care about

Derrik, she is my daughter.'

Lowering his gaze, Derrik submitted his position.

Amador watched the scene play out before him. Isaak looked like he was fit to burst. His whole face had turned bright red, clashing with the orange of his hair.

Unable to contain himself Isaak burst out, 'Preposterous Viktor! I can't believe that we are even having this conversation. Huntsmaster is for all the Flames to decide, not just you. It affects all of us.'

'I wasn't the one suggesting putting her forward for the position,' Viktor retorted, as he regarded first Amador and then Derrik coolly, like the bite of wind that smells of snow.

'We don't have a nomination Viktor,' Derrik said meeting Viktor's fierce gaze again. 'I think Amador makes a good observation about Ayesha.'

'And what would you know about it?' Viktor replied heatedly.

'I would know,' Derrik replied, 'that Melody asked me to look out for Ayesha before she went to meet the ACCORD for you Viktor,' he finished in an altogether too quiet tone.

'So you keep reminding me Derrik, I am all too tired of you reminding me of Melody's words. She was my wife. My wife, and don't you ever forget that. Ayesha is our child. Our first born. Would you have me put her in harm's way Derrik?'

Amador hadn't intended to provoke such a heated dispute, but wasn't sure he should intervene. It seemed that there were a lot of difficult issues that this Clan was trying to deal with.

Derrik said, 'Of course Viktor. It's as you say. It's your choice to put her forward or not. Ah, here comes Orrison now. Your own and Melody's youngest son,' he said emphasising his last word.

Turning towards Orrison, Viktor half shouted, 'Orrison come here. Where have you been? You should have been here an age ago. Did you gather the stone? Are you ready to become a man or not?'

Viktor was clearly still angry, as was evident in the way he addressed his son.

'Apologies father, for being late. Sepit Mhor was much higher than I had thought and it took me some time to find the right stone. I had to climb down to reach them as a great hole has opened up in the top of the mountain. I got the stone though,' he said as he offered it to his father.

Amador noticed that the stone was about the size of a man's fist and looked like black glass.

Viktor took the stone from his son. 'You have found a large piece of Obsidian Orrison. It bodes well for the Clan. Your protection amulet will be special if you work the stone right,' he said softly.

Orrison flushed with pleasure at his father's words.

Taking his eyes away from the stone, Viktor said, 'Well, you're here now; let's get onto the next stage. Orrison, this is Amador, he is aspiring to The Twelve and he will complete your manhood journey with the branding.'

Amador returned Orrison's gaze as he regarded him in the way both his father and sister had previously. He thought the boy looked exhausted. There were dark circles in the pale skin under his eyes.

Orrison dropped to one knee. 'Amador, aspiring to The Twelve, may the sun always shine brightly on your hair.' He looked up from under his locks of hair with vivid blue eyes and flashed Amador a perfect smile.

Amador was taken aback by his eyes and the look of the

boy. He could tell just by looking at him that he didn't 'fit' with the Clan. Many had Auburn or red hair, brown or green eyes. Orrison just didn't fit in the picture. His blue eyes most especially.

'Ahhh, yes Orrison, well met and thanks for your blessing,' he replied, hiding his observations with a serious tone, while gesturing to Orrison to sit upon his seat.

'That's a big skin for one so young,' Amador continued. 'I'm most impressed Orrison. Do you always do things on such a grand scale?' he enquired.

Orrison stood as tall as he could and replied, 'There was a little luck involved Amador, but I always try to honor my father.'

Orrison took his seat, and the Flames of Sepit gathered around him.

Amador drew out the Liferod that had been comfortably sitting within the folds of his robes for the last day or so.

Viktor moved to stand before his son. 'Orrison, today we make you a man and you stand to inherit the ruling of the Clan in your time. You will have the Flames of Sepit for good guidance and counsel, but decisions will be yours and, on your shoulders sit. Are you ready?'

Orrison's small face looked up reverently at his father, the Clan Leader. 'Yes, I am ready father,' he replied.

'There are many journeys that a boy must make before becoming a man,' Viktor continued. 'I see your skin, the cat on your seat; I see your stone from which you will make your protective amulet. Is there anything more you need Orrison?'

'Yes father, I need my flame. It will burn bright, guide me and see me safe in its essence. It will watch me and the Flames of Sepit will know that my blood is their blood.'

Orrison had hesitated only briefly on these last words, but

Amador perceived the hesitation. He wasn't sure if any of the others had though as there were smooth faces all around him.

'So be it Orrison' Viktor said, moving to stand at his son's right shoulder.

Taking this as a cue, Amador moved forward to stand before Orrison.

The sense of anticipation in the air heightened and although this ceremony was for the Clan Leader and the Flames of Sepit to witness the boy's branding, he could feel the silence gathering at his back where the rest of the Clan watched and waited.

'Orrison. This is a big job you take on. Not that of Clan Leader just yet, but that of moving from boy to man.'

The lad was dwarfed by his seat covered in the cat skin and looked anything but a man to Amador. 'Are you ready?' he asked anyway.

'Yes, I am ready Amador,' Orrison replied, eyes shining with intent as he said this.

Satisfied, Amador continued, 'A man is many things Orrison. He is brave, strong, loving and full of knowledge. If he is a good man he is also humble, when he needs to be humble. Are you ready to become a man Orrison?'

'Yes, I am ready, although I must learn to be better at all of these things,' he replied lowering his gaze in a seemingly humble manner.

Satisfied again with Orrison's response, Amador turned to Viktor.

'Viktor, do you stand here as Orrison's father, secure in the knowledge that he is ready to become a man in his tenth year?'

'I do and I am,' Viktor replied solemnly.

'Is there anyone here who would dispute this?' Amador enquired of the Flames of Sepit.

There was no response, so he continued. 'Are you ready to receive the flame Orrison?'

Orrison visibly swallowed and Viktor suddenly looked tense. 'Yes, I am ready,' he replied again.

Amador paused. It was the first branding he had ever done and he wasn't exactly sure where to put it. He recalled having seen the crest of a mighty wave tattooed on the arm of Merson, the Leader of the Water Peoples, but he had to be sure so he said to Viktor, 'Reveal your own flame Viktor.'

Viktor obliged by lowering his skin to reveal a splendid flame above his heart on the left-hand side of his body.

It seemed there was no set placement for the brand, so he looked again at Orrison. He was such a skinny lad. His arm would take the brand, but only just. In this Clan a boy became a man at a much earlier time than the Water People, so he thought that was likely the reason Viktor had been branded on the chest. He had made his decision.

Amador thought of fire as he had been instructed by Tarramore. The Liferod pulsated in his hand and released its emblem.

He asked again, 'Is there any man here who challenges Orrison's right to the flame?'

Silence again.

Amador moved forward and pressed the flame to Orrison's chest, just above his heart. Orrison's eyes flew wide as he touched him with the Liferod. A few seconds only, and the brand was displayed on Orrison's chest for the Flames of Sepit to see.

Viktor exhaled a held breath with some notable relief.

The Flames of Sepit moved as one to the edge of the

platform that was the 'animal dance', with Viktor and Orrison. They now had to present themselves to their Clan. Their decision to support Orrison's claim to be Leader marked by all of them each standing side by side with him on his branding day. A fact that could be handed down in stories within each of the Sects within the Clan.

But, Orrison stumbled as he stood and shuffled towards the edge with the others. Viktor frowned at him and for once Orrison didn't notice.

Viktor shouted out, 'Here is my son, once boy, now a man. See his flame! Feel its heat! He will grow to be your future Clan Leader.'

The Flames of Sepit started to chant, 'Orrison, Orrison, Orrison, Orrison.'

The chant was taken up by the Clan who were gathered around the 'animal dance'. There was clapping and stamping of feet and the chant continued.

Amador noted that people were happy. Their future as a Clan was secured for many long years to come, barring a fatal accident, was evident in their response to the branding ceremony.

Then, without warning, Orrison fell over and began to writhe on the ground.

Those around Orrison stopped chanting immediately, as did those who could see what had happened, but the chanting continued for a while longer until everyone in the whole of the Clan knew that something had gone wrong.

Those who couldn't see directly, the people filling the three main arteries leading to the 'animal dance' waited to discover what had happened.

Meanwhile, Viktor stared at his son writhing about on the ground looking both distant and horrified.

Ayesha leapt up onto the rock and tried to hold Orrison. 'Give us some room,' she shouted, as all around tried to press in to see what was happening.

Viktor visibly staggered backwards, tearing his eyes away from the writhing boy. Derrik grabbed Viktor by the arm and pulled him around. 'By the fire man, what have you done?' he asked accusingly. Disgust was evident in his voice. 'I was there when you were branded Viktor, nothing like this happened. I am asking you now, man to man Viktor, is he Melody's son?'

With the exception of the thrashing noise Orrison was making, the silence was palpable.

Viktor pulled his arm free of Derrik's grasp. 'Do you challenge me Derrik?' he said quietly. 'Here and now while my son writhes on the ground before us?'

Derrik was beside himself, long held suspicions and hurt flowing to the surface. 'Come on Viktor! What else could it be? The branding is good and yet he is having some kind of seizure.' Derrik saw the look on Viktor's face which was closed and full of anger and backed down saying, 'Look, of course I don't challenge you, I just don't know what to think. Melody…' his voice trailed off as her name caught in his throat.

Ignoring Derrik now, Viktor shouted 'Seraphina, where is Seraphina? She will know what to do.' He stooped and picked up a now limp Orrison in his arms.

Ignoring Ayesha sitting back on her haunches and the shocked disbelief apparent on her face, he ordered, 'I will take him to the tent. Someone must find Seraphina and send her to me!'

Then Viktor bounded from the platform, Orrison's limbs flaying from his strong arms as he did so. And those who had squashed forward to see what had happened, now hastened to clear a passage through the crowd for him.

Amador watched as the scene unfolded before him in a kind of haze. Clearly his intuition had been right about Orrison. Something didn't ring true about his heritage. He admonished himself for not digging deeper before the ceremony. He wasn't sure what was happening to the lad now, but had a sneaking suspicion that Viktor had possibly broken the cardinal rule. The rule of fire with fire, earth with earth, air with air and water with water.

This was the way for all and known by all. It ensured the survival of the human race. If Viktor had mixed!

He found this too hard to comprehend though. With the breath in his lungs he fervently hoped that Viktor had not been so foolish. But, the evidence all pointed to him having done so.

One part of Amador was morbidly fascinated, the other horrified, as the branding emphasised the essence. If it wasn't fire with fire, what was it, he wondered? There were only three other possibilities, each with its own dangers. His mind flew.

He watched Ayesha stand and try to call for Seraphina. To try to gain some semblance of order over the watching crowd.

The Flames of Sepit weren't helping her, so he stepped in. He moved the air about Ayesha and her voice was at once magnified and carried far. She glanced around, startled herself, and then catching Amador in her sights, immediately continued.

Everyone listened.

'We don't know what has happened to Orrison. He may be fatigued by his manhood journey. But the flame is burning in him, and we need Seraphina,' she shouted.

She then turned to the closest people beside her and tasked two of the fastest runners to go and fetch Seraphina from her caves.

Continuing, she said, 'Everything that can be done is being done. I will come back here every hour and let you know what progress is being made. Until the next hour, we women have worked hard to provide for this day, don't let it waste. Eat and drink, I'm sure everything will be fine,' she finished rather flatly.

Turning to Amador she said, 'My thanks for the loud voice. It certainly helped. Perhaps another time you can teach me how to do that for myself?'

But, she was obviously distressed and she pleaded 'Can you help Amador? Can you try?' Her voice was anxious and she waited for his response.

'I'm not sure Ayesha? There's more to this than meets the eye I think.' He immediately regretted his choice of words that were drawing attention again, in his own mind at least, to the blue of Orrison's eyes. He had observed their colour and known they were out of place in the Clan. He really should consider his choice of words better though before he opened his mouth.

Moving to action he said, 'Take me to your father and Orrison and we'll see.'

So many words link to eyes he thought and couldn't believe he had made the same mistake twice in as many sentences! He continued more thoughtfully, 'When we get there I think you should leave though, otherwise I suspect that there will be pain in the heart for you.'

'There is always pain in my heart Amador, but I can cope,' she replied bravely.

He followed her small back to Viktor's home as she ran ahead of him, clearing a pathway through the anxious crowd.

Arriving at their tented home, Amador looked at Orrison and was immediately concerned. He was aware of Viktor, distraught, speaking with Ayesha. Asking about Seraphina. And also, of Ayesha seeking comfort from her father, that did not appear to be in his gift to give at the moment. However, Amador was concentrating more on the air around Orrison. It was hot.

Amador had the strangest sensation of being physically pulled towards the boy, so strong was the pull of air. Swallowing, he acknowledged to himself that at least there was both fire and air at play.

The boy was unconscious and his breath was shallow. He looked so pale lying against the colourful skins where Viktor had placed him. He was clearly fevered and Amador thought he might just burn himself from the inside out, if he didn't act quickly.

However, he needed to be sure of his suspicions, and it was a delicate matter indeed that he had to broach with Viktor.

Turning towards him and Ayesha he said, 'I think I may be able to help, but is there more I should know before I start Viktor?' The look of despair that crossed Viktor's face told him everything he needed to know.

'I ask that you leave now Ayesha, while I talk with your father. I need you to fetch me some fresh water.'

Ayesha was obviously undecided about leaving, as she hesitated.

'It will help Orrison Ayesha,' he encouraged.

At these words, she turned and hurriedly left the tent.

Amador regarded Viktor, who was clearly unable to make

eye contact with him. He said, 'Viktor, here's what I think. I think you have somehow been led astray, by whom, I'm sure I don't know, but your son is burning up in a mixture of fire and air.'

Viktor looked like he was about to interject so he held up his hand and said, 'No, don't say anything, just listen and let me finish. I think you have been with a woman of the Air, and Orrison is the result of that union. I really don't know how or why this could have happened and right now I don't want to know any more than if this is true?'

Viktor moaned and said, 'I don't know if she was of Air. I don't know anything about her, except how lovely she was. The fire in my heart knows this to be true. My head tells me something different. I am a broken man Amador, but the boy doesn't deserve to die for my mistakes.'

Viktor looked both tormented and tortured and was clearly distressed. He continued, 'Seraphina was…'

He was cut off mid-sentence as the tent flap was pulled back and in walked Seraphina.

'Seraphina was what Clan Leader?' she asked as she strode in.

Viktor mumbled, 'Helping.'

'You're right I was helping, I'm always helping and I'm here to help you again. You need me Viktor.' It was a statement rather than a question.

'Yes, Sun Mother, I need you,' he replied, immediately contrite.

Amador noted Viktor's broken nature and stepped in.

'And just how have you helped Seraphina? It seems clear to me that you have condoned a great wrong, and it doesn't matter to me for whatever reason.'

His manner was commanding and left Seraphina in no

doubt that a response was required, and that a response right now was in order.

But, she was not to be intimidated easily.

'What do you know about real life Amador, aspiring to The Twelve,' she spat back at him. You and your kind sit in your lofty places, practicing little tricks to entice children and amuse yourselves by gathering all your knowledge from books. You know precious little about the real world. The hard choices that have to be made to keep people safe and well here in the real world, so don't stand there passing your lofty judgments on me. Or on what I do to help these people,' she finished passionately.

Taken aback by Seraphina's bitter response and intuitively knowing he was treading on dangerous ground, Amador tried a different approach. He had been so shocked by what he had discovered, he wasn't handling this in his usual smooth manner.

Orrison was burning up and likely to self-combust if something wasn't done soon. The very air around him was being drawn towards him and becoming hotter by the minute. He could feel it, sensitive as he was to his own element.

He tried again, 'Look at the boy Seraphina. The air around him is heating up. He is using it to fan his flame. He is burning inside, he will soon burn outside if we don't do something,' Amador said as calmly as he could muster at the moment.

'I don't know what you think happened here Amador,' she replied. 'It must be his fire that is drawing the air, nothing else.' She shot Viktor a look. 'Melody had a difficult birth with the boy, that's true. He had to be helped out on the cusp with earth. He may have suffered because of that, although it's unlikely. It's the fire you have branded him with that's causing the problem. He was perfectly fine until you did that. See how it writhes like a real flame on his chest. Viktor's doesn't do that. You have made a mistake Amador. Do you know what you did?'

Amador's mind reeled. Earth. Earth was good. If anything, it would help to dampen the fire down without putting the flame out completely. The boy could yet live. Seraphina had openly accused him of doing something wrong though. True, he had never given a branding before, but he was still sure that air was at play here and in a big way. His elemental senses were being hit by it.

Wondering for a moment if he could have passed some of his own air essence into the lad unconsciously, but immediately dismissed that as a foolish notion. He was sure Seraphina was accusing him of doing something wrong to cover up her own part in this sordid affair. But, whatever that was, he couldn't know right now?

Ayesha returned carrying fresh water supplies.

Amador glared back at Seraphina but didn't rise to her challenge by protesting his own innocence. Now was not the time. He knew Orrison was burning up and he had to help first. Instead he said, 'Ayesha, I need you to sponge Orrison down to help cool him.'

'Once you have finished sponging, you can apply my special salve,' Seraphina interjected.

Ayesha looked first at one and then the other, before resigning herself to follow orders from two people.

Amador said as mildly as he could muster, 'Seraphina, I don't think you should put a salve on Orrison. He is burning hard.'

Seraphina visibly bristled and replied, 'I think you should

mind your own business Amador. In fact, it may be best if you leave. I am the Clan healer. I am the Sun Mother.'

Reeling, he withdrew, but he found he couldn't leave. It was a truly impossible situation he had managed to get himself into, but he had to try to help.

As Ayesha began to apply the salve to Orrison's hand, blisters erupted. She became frantic and said, 'What's happening Seraphina?' Ayesha almost wailed, 'Amador's right, he is burning. Oh, the fire is too strong.'

Amador turned to Viktor. 'Let me help him Viktor. Seraphina is Sun Mother, but you are Clan Leader. Please let me help him, he is your son,' he begged.

Viktor replied, 'Alright, alright!' He said this in an authoritative manner, somehow finding the courage to come out of his wretchedness.

In that moment, Amador could see why he was Clan Leader.

'You may help for now Amador. Seraphina, he was right, your salve isn't working. Move over and be happy that Amador with his knowledge of the world is here to help us.'

Without a further word Seraphina left the tent, clearly put out and most unhappy, muttering under her breath all the while.

With Seraphina gone, Amador moved back into the fray.

'Ayesha, keep sponging. I will cool the air around him and hopefully between us we can bring Orrison back to consciousness,' he instructed as he sat down next to Ayesha to begin his work.

The air around Orrison was too hot. Moving it only caused the heat to swirl, making both himself and Ayesha perspire.

He had to extend his reach and pull cooler air from ground

level from as far away as possible. Simultaneously he had to push the hot air upwards and away from Orrison. This was a continuous struggle as no sooner than cooler air replaced hot, it was heated again by Orrison.

They continued their vigil into the night.

After what seemed like a very long time, he could see that Ayesha was becoming exhausted and he felt tired too. What was worse was that there was no real impact from their combined efforts, just no deterioration of Orrison's condition.

At least Viktor had stopped his pacing and the other children were being looked after elsewhere, so it was just the three of them now with Orrison.

Another hour passed by. 'Spark,' he said, startling the others with the bright light from his crystal globe.

All three squinted past the darkness.

'Sorry, I need to see better how Orrison is fairing,' he said. There was a light sheen covering Orrison's skin and Amador was now wondering how best to replace the boy's lost fluid.

'Viktor, I need you to find something that can soak with water that can be dripped into Orrison's mouth. We need to try to give him back some of the fluid he is losing.'

Viktor managed to find leather that had been stripped of its fur which soaked up water very efficiently.

'Ayesha take a break while your father gives Orrison a drink.' Amador instructed her again.

Ayesha stood up and stretched. Glad for now to be offered a bit of respite. 'I need to move my legs for a bit and breathe some fresh air,' she replied. 'I better go and give a report to the Clan too. I won't be long.'

He could see the concern etched on her face as she turned

to leave. When she had gone, he took the chance to speak with Viktor alone.

'Viktor, Seraphina speaks in truths that she would like others to believe. You told me yourself before she arrived that there had been another woman. I fear for Orrison. I can't go on cooling air forever, and it's not having a huge result in any case,' he asserted.

He watched Viktor's guarded reaction.

'What else can we do Amador? Do I need to call Seraphina back? I know that she will be difficult to manage after tonight. Truth of it is, she has always been difficult to manage. I guess I always thought she had the Clan's best interests at heart, so it's easy to listen to her advice and direction. I need her Amador,' he said desperately.

Choosing his next words very carefully, Amador said, 'I know you need her Viktor. You have a special relationship as Clan Leader and Sun Mother, but, if there is no improvement in Orrison's condition by morning, you know that she will use her position to step back in.'

Amador paused before continuing, trying to impress upon this man the importance of what he was trying to tell him in not so many words. 'Likely she will say you are not thinking straight, not yourself, and she has already accused me of causing this. You heard her. But, only you know that this isn't true.'

He let the silence gather for a few moments giving Viktor time to think through what he had said.

When Viktor made no denial he continued, 'If I stop cooling the air, Orrison will use it to fan his flame and he will burn himself out. Viktor I can't cool the air indefinitely.'

He paused again.

Viktor hung his head and the cloth slipped from Orrison's

mouth.

'Here Viktor, he needs a big drink,' Amador said as he dipped the end of the cloth in water and then put it back in Orrison's mouth.

Viktor resumed his water duties.

Amador returned to the point he was trying to make. 'I know a good man who I think can help Orrison. His name is Merason and he leads the Water People. They are so famous for their healing works Viktor, I'm sure you will have heard of them. I spent some months living amongst them a year or two back,' he said enthusiastically. 'They are friendly, hospitable people, but most importantly, they are healers. If anyone can help Orrison, it is Merason and his Water People.'

Ayesha had just returned. 'You know someone who can help Orrison, then let's send for him,' she demanded.

'I cannot,' Amador replied. 'Merason will not leave the shores of his home. I am offering to take Orrison to him. I am known there and trusted.' He emphasised this last word to Viktor.

Viktor sat and considered the situation for a few moments. Finally, he conceded, 'I agree, you may take him to this Merason. See if he can be healed. If not Amador, on my word, leave him there.'

'No! How can you say such a thing father?' Ayesha blurted.

'Enough! Ayesha, you cannot understand. It will be as I say,' he said strongly enough to brook no compromise.

'You will leave at first light Amador. Here Ayesha, take this cloth and give your brother a drink,' he said handing the cloth to Ayesha and standing to leave.

'I will find you two good horses for your journey

Amador.' And with that he left them, once more a man with a purpose.

Lost in their own thoughts, the silent wall climbed in the small tent and Amador just didn't have the heart to tell her what had really happened.

Ayesha broke the silence first. 'Will you look after him for me Amador? He is my brother, yes, but he is also my boy. I love him,' she said simply.

He replied, 'Of course I'll look after him for you Ayesha. My friend will help.'

'Can you find a cure do you think?' she asked. There was still hope in her voice.

'I will try my very hardest. If anyone can cure Orrison of what he has, it's my friend,' he replied more confidently than he actually felt.

'What's wrong with him Amador?' she asked softly.

Amador blew out some air from his own lungs. 'Well, here's what I'm thinking, but I don't know for sure,' he cautioned.

'I think somehow the natural elements that hold us together and make us who we are have somehow gotten a bit mixed up in Orrison,' he said gently. 'He has plenty of fire in him mind, and that's his true element, but somehow air and earth are in the mix and causing problems with his fire.'

'I see,' she said as if she did. 'So, you're going to mix in some water?'

'Oh, no, no, no,' he half laughed at her simplistic reasoning. 'The Water People are great healers and might be able to sort out the air and earth bits from the fire, that's all,' he said out loud, while thinking that what he had just said was a huge understatement. If only it were that simple.

He continued, 'We all have a bit of the four elements in

us Ayesha. I have read about this a lot.'

'No way!' she responded immediately. 'I'm all fire.'

'Well, I would say you are pretty strongly fire. But are you not clever?' he asked.

'Of course I'm clever,' she responded.

'Now that will be the air in your lungs that feeds your head to make you clever.'

The look on her face suggested she was very skeptical.

'And, are you not stubborn and sometimes sensible?' he continued, warming to the easy camaraderie growing between them. He smiled at her growing incredulity.

'Oh, but I have found a weakness in my argument,' he proclaimed.

'What?' she asked, becoming caught up in the lightness of the moment.

'Water!' he said. 'There's a definite lack of it,' he wrinkled his nose as he said this. 'The air does smell a bit ripe tonight.'

'Oh, how could you!' she huffed and threw the cloth in her hand at him.

Orrison stirred and at once the mood was serious again.

By first light there was no marked change in Orrison's condition, so he was strapped to the horse that Amador would ride.

The horse was a beauty. It was a dappled grey with a small face and strong lines. A second horse was loaded with the provisions they would need. Viktor had explained to him that the horses were Free and should be returned to freedom when they reached their destination.

Amador had of course agreed, liking the wild feel of their haunches beneath his hands.

As he was about to mount the horse, Ayesha stood before

him. She said, 'Amador,' hesitated, and then threw her arms around him spontaneously.

He was rather taken aback, but patted her shoulder in any event, in what he assumed was a comforting manner.

'Look after him,' she pleaded into his chest.

'Of course, I will Ayesha.' Taking her by the shoulders and holding her from him so that he could reassure her by looking at her directly, 'Even if you do smell a bit!'

A genuine smile passed between them and then he mounted the horse and left. Best to be gone quickly before Seraphina arrived back on the scene to gloat and meddle.

The lad felt hot and sticky against his back already, but his heart was light as he left the Fire camp. He knew that he should be heading back to the Conclave and the First, but he had now decided if being one of The Twelve meant he couldn't be amongst the peoples of the land, meeting and talking with them and helping them, he would rather not aspire at all.

Seraphina had scratched a raw edge when she had said that he didn't live in the real world. He had now decided to follow the path that was presented to him rather than do what others expected of him and it felt good.

He still felt slightly guilty about having The First's Liferod dangling from his belt, but he would return it in time. Once Orrison was healed and returned to his people. He cantered on. Alternating between walking the horses and cantering for the rest of the day.

Journal of the Living

I am sad today. Not that I ever feel truly happy anymore. Perhaps content. Yes, content on occasion when my belly is full, but never happy. No, that word has gone from my knowledge. Sad is different. Sad is here every day. My fellow companion in this new world.

Sad, you are so very strong today. I may yet cry.

An extract from a survivor's journal of unknown origin but marked by Air.

Chapter Seven

Intruders

Ayesha decided she had best go to the lake to wash today. She knew that Amador had been jesting with her, but it had been a hot, sticky night. She left her skins at the water's edge and immersed herself in the lake. It was fresh and cold, a pleasurable shock, and helped to revive her tired body. She would need to feel fresh today as flames would likely be thrown, and she knew she would have to support her father in his decision.

She floated a bit on top of the water as thoughts of the previous two days played through her mind, when she was distracted by a noise, half muffled by the water in her ears.

Moving towards the shallows, she stood up, just as three men on horseback came into view.

Ayesha noted that one had a similar robe to the one worn by Amador, the other two had red robes.

On seeing her standing there, they stopped and the man in blue hailed her. He was really quite rude.

'You there, have you seen a man like us in these parts recently? We are looking for him as he is lost and has taken something belonging to another.'

'No,' she lied. Then she qualified her lie by saying, 'There has been no one like you.' That bit was truthful at least she thought to herself.

Who did he think he was? He hadn't even given her the proper respect by giving her his name. And the other two had loose chins and were simply gawping at her.

Unashamed of her nakedness, she began to walk towards them revealing more of her body as she did so, and inwardly laughed at their reactions.

'I am Ayesha, daughter of Viktor, Clan Leader of the Fire Clan. We camp nearby for the moment,' she said to them. He could be rude, but she would not shame herself by forgetting the protocols.

'Ah, yes,' replied the man who was busy trying to look anywhere but directly at her. He coughed. 'I am Faldo, a member of The Twelve. Please forgive my attire as I have not had time to prepare a new robe since my ascendancy.'

The man sounded a bit pompous to her ears and she regarded him in his robe. She couldn't see what was wrong with it and in any event, she was hardly in a position to mind any garment given she had no skins covering her own nakedness.

She looked at Faldo's companions who seemed to have no difficulty looking back directly at her.

'Avert your eyes men,' Faldo snapped as he noticed their

lustful looks. They were then in the position of trying not to look, but being unable to help themselves.

Faldo continued. 'As I mentioned, we are looking for a man going by the name of Amador. We eventually tracked his entrance to some caves close to our Conclave. By my estimation he should have come out of those caves around here.'

She responded, 'There's been no one here, I'm sure we would have met him as our camp is large and not far from here. We don't use the caves around here because they are so dangerous. He could be lost in there or worse. I wouldn't go in to them if I were you.'

'Well, that's not for you to worry your pretty little head about, is it?' he said. 'We are on important business for The First and we will go where we need to go.'

'As you say, of course, it's your business,' she said in an awed tone. 'The best way to find your way into the caves is to go back up this pass and hug the mountain for about a thousand horse paces. You will find a good entrance there.' As she said this she raised her arm and pointed back up the pass.

None looked where she pointed, but instead watched her pert breasts rise with the motion of her raising her arm.

Faldo coughed again and turned to look where she had indicated, but he was clearly affected by her youthful loveliness. 'Thank you,' he blustered.

She smiled up at them and turned back towards the water, giving them a full view of her buttocks, perfectly formed, below the cascade of damp auburn ringlets that snaked down her back.

Diving back into the water, she wondered if she had done enough to divert these men. She really liked Amador and he was helping Orrison. Amador remembered and used her name, unlike the man called Faldo. He was making accusations about Amador that even in the short time she had known him, she knew weren't true.

Surfacing again she watched as they followed the directions she had given them, away from Seraphina's caves.

She was learning that sometimes men weren't always influenced by their head, and continued with her bathing undisturbed.

Faldo and his two companions were immediately detected as they entered the caves.

'*No protection this time!*' Boeson thought to his friend.

'*No,*' Elm thought back.

'These are our caves. Where will we go if these humans keep coming into the mountains? I hunt.'

Elm was dispirited as they had once again failed to retrieve the Liferod from the man of a thousand years, so he replied to his friend, *'I'll wait.'*

Journal of the Living

They came today. We watched from our dark corners, the brown ones who called us out. I won't go.

They may not eat me.

Too late. I have been discovered. I remind myself that I am a survivor.

The brown robed one spoke to me and then pushed me into this pen of stinking humanity. But he didn't see my book. Couldn't know that I am still sane! My pencil, my stub still turns in my fingers.

I am weary. But, I am a survivor. I will break free of these clean people in their brown robes.

An extract from a survivor's journal of unknown origin but marked by Air.

CHAPTER EIGHT

WATCHERS

The Watchers were watching. A collective consciousness, linked by a similar fate. Yes, The Watchers were watching, but they were also waiting.

Waiting for release!

One of The Watchers was no longer content just to watch. It sensed that a new time was approaching and longed for freedom. So, it blew on the wind a small trickle of energy to one who could hear, ‘Call the girl Rose’.

It was a small thing really, on the edge of purpose, but it was as much as The Watcher dared. It would have to do.

The Watchers stirred, no more than a murmur. Care was needed, but it had begun.

***

Amador had paused on his journey to the Water peoples. Exhausted after two day's travelling with Orrison, but he still didn't fail to notice the wild rose bush burst forth with buds, flower, and fade in the space of a few minutes.

Confused by this phenomenon, he glanced at Orrison to see if he was in any way connected. But he dismissed the thought almost immediately, as the heat emanating from the lad had definitely not changed. There was also no sign of his earth ascendancy, which could be the only other explanation for the roses if Orrison was involved.

He decided that he would have to think long on this particular puzzle.

***

Fern listened to the voice in the wind and heard the message. She was not unfamiliar with The Watchers, but had never thought to hear one in this place. She didn't question the instruction, it was clearly meant for her. She wondered why Rose? Rose was a powerful name for a girl of this sort. She also recalled the girl's mother's cries in the night before she passed. Rose was on her lips often. It was curious, but she would do as she had been asked. The Watchers gave good counsel.

The girl was playing in the area they called the garden. It was an enclosure surrounded on all sides by rock, but it was open to the sky. Seraphina grew some of her more potent herbs here, away from possible discovery.

Fern recalled some of the difficult conversations she had had with the girl when she was younger and couldn't understand why she wasn't able to touch or eat any of the plants growing in the garden. She had to resort to using her voice with compulsion to ensure that the girl wouldn't die.

That, together with a good deal of training, meant that she was now sure the girl was conditioned at ten, and could be left for a spell on her own.

Feeling melancholy today, as she missed her home over the mountains, Fern recalled the message her parents had received from The Watchers that one such as she would be needed over the mountain. After thirteen long, lonely years, she still wasn't sure of the path she must take. This wasn't her first rodeo here, but it felt like time was slipping through her fingers as she waited for the right time.

It had been thirteen years since she had seen her family, and time moved more quickly in her own land too, adding to the sense of urgency she now felt. She had felt Elm close by recently and sent her love. Some of her frustration had also accompanied that sending, but she was lonely for her own kind. He was caught in the same time warp as she, and there was no help for it.

Elm had spoken to her and asked her to accompany him on his quest, but she had decided to remain here. She had her own purpose and she also knew there still remained a healthy competition between them. Who would prove the worthier to their parents? She was sure she didn't yet know?

Seraphina had her wings. She had let the woman capture her easily intentionally, but as a result Seraphina thought she was very clever indeed to catch a Fairie woman and this fact fundamentally irked her.

However, it also suited her purpose to remain a captive at present. What she wasn't able to wrap her head around, might never be able to accommodate in her mind, was the birth of a son and having to give him away.

She knew that the Fairie race were finding the mating process more and more difficult and were dwindling in number over the mountains. She often wondered if she was to be part of an experiment of mixing. But then why was the boy taken away? It just didn't make any real sense to her.

Also, what was the purpose of being left with the girl who was all human and would only last seventy or eighty years at best?

Again, she didn't question that she was not intended to have the boy in the first place. She, like her people, believed strongly in the course of destiny. Now she had a personal message from The Watchers and it related to the girl and not her son. It was very curious indeed.

Pondering all of this, she moved lithely through the network of caves that would take her to the garden. At the entrance she paused and watched the girl go through her training. The girl always seemed to want to make her training into a game, as she parried and thrust with her staff shouting, 'die, die, and die'.

Fern watched the girl as she used her staff to lever her body into the air, drop into a tumble, followed by a quick roll and a sharp thrust, 'Die' again!

'Girl, come over here', Fern called.

The girl cartwheeled to her side. 'It's nearly evening, has your training gone well this day?' she enquired.

'Very well Fern. I have mastered better the killing thrust. If I lever my wrist just a fraction more than before it works better. It's just as you suggested, thank you Fern. I am happy with my work today. Would you like a show?' the girl replied happily.

'No, not tonight little one, though your words please me. I have something special for you this evening. Come we will bathe and then I will tell you a story.'

‘A story,’ the girl breathed. She loved to hear a story from Fern. She must have pleased her indeed. It was getting easier to please Fern, the girl thought to herself.

A wide smile graced her face and she took Fern’s outstretched hand to walk with her to the lake.

The girl thought that she must keep trying hard. She was to be rewarded with a story! There was already a bubble of excitement in her tummy at the prospect, but she knew better than to ask any more. The story would come when Fern was good and ready to tell it and not before.

This was a fact that she had learned from an early age. A story was a time to listen and learn. She would be able to ask three questions and have these fully answered. She would think of the best possible questions tonight and she may even get the chance to ask the question she really wanted answered, if the story was the right kind of story.

The girl tried gracefully and quietly to copy the smooth way that Fern moved as she walked quietly beside her on their journey to the lake.

The Fairie woman and the girl washed and returned to the caves as the last of the days light was beginning to fade from the sky. All the while the girl wondered what the story would be. She had been told several stories over the years, but her favourite was still the one about the Fairie queen who had been given the land to care for and the Fairie king who had been given the people to lead. And together how they had loved both, but most of all, how they had loved the Queen’s children and would do anything to make them happy.

The perfect family! The girl could only imagine how wonderful this would be. Perhaps she would hear another story about the Fairie queen and her perfect family tonight?

And how they loved to play and to bask in the bright sun in the days before the sunscreen.

The girl watched attentively as Fern brushed and stroked her long hair until it shone. Then it was her turn. She moved to sit on the skins in front of the chair on which Fern sat with the brush. First the tugs had to come out.

Fern never seemed to have tugs the girl thought for the umpteenth time, but her own hair never seemed to tire of getting them. Her hair was unruly, all curls and springing bits that easily became tangled while she trained.

When the tugs had been tackled, Fern began her story, continuing to stroke the girl's hair as she spoke.

Fern began, 'Well girl, it seems you are to have a name.'

The girl gasped and only just stopped herself from turning and blurting out a question, potentially wasting one of her three valuable questions.

Fern paused in her brushing, but was obviously impressed by the girl's restraint and so resumed brushing her hair.

'Yes, I have been told by The Watchers that you must have a name. It is to be a very special name and you must think on its meaning and then on your purpose. I have decided on the weapon that you must now begin to use in your training as befits your new name.'

The girl couldn't restrain herself, 'A real weapon. What will it be?'

Fern continued in an even way, 'Normally, we of the Fairie race would not name a human child. For one thing your life is not so long for going to the trouble of a naming and for another, a human's name is attached to the person, without the understanding of the importance of the meaning of the name.'

She paused again and the girl, whose mind was racing with a million questions, realised that she had used one that she might need later.

'I will answer your first question girl,' Fern said. 'The weapon of choice will be a knife, razor sharp, hidden on your person and as unexpected as it is deadly. Would you like to ask your second question now?'

The girl considered her options. She desperately wanted to have a name, wanted to understand it and she needed to know what it was. But, she also wanted to know who had given her the name and why. And also, why the knife, and she needed to know the meaning of her name.

The girl suspected that Fern had cut the story short leaving her with so many unanswered questions because she had blurted her first question out in the excitement of learning that she was to be given a real weapon.

'While you ponder your last two questions, I will tell you a truth girl. You ask about your real weapon in an excited way, but the real weapon you have is in your head. The way you reason and think and next in your eyes, nose, ears, taste and touch. Then it is in the way that you use your body. Keep it supple and controlled, for it is your next best weapon. Everything else is only a tool to be learned. A knife cannot be useful on its own. It will just lie where it is put. You use the staff, it is as deadly as the knife girl, but the knife suits your name,' Fern concluded.

'What is my name to be Fern?' the girl asked in a small voice.

Fern half smiled and replied, 'You will be Rose. It is a strong and powerful name and one to be proud of. Think of the roses by the lake. They look and smell beautiful and come in many colours. They have strong stalks on which to grow, but remember that the stalks also have thorns. It is a name that has two faces, one of beauty, the other of harm. The knife will become your thorn Rose.'

The girl was overwhelmed, the name Rose rolling over and over in her head and finally she tested the name on her own tongue, 'Rose,' she breathed. Yes, she liked it, she liked it a lot and said it more confidently, 'Rose, Rose, Rose! Oh, thank you Fern. Thank you so, so much.'

Fern had now stopped brushing Rose's long auburn locks which gleamed from her attention. She replied somewhat absently, 'Don't thank me, thank The Watchers, they have given you the name.'

Rose considered this information together with everything else she had heard and wondered how best to frame her last question for maximum information.

Rose compartmentalised her new name in her head so that she could think more clearly. She wanted to ask who The Watchers were as she had never heard of them before and she wanted to know why they had bothered to give her a name when no one else had.

But, she still burned to ask what her new name meant. There was silence while her young mind reflected on her final question.

Fern waited patiently.

'OK Fern, my last question,' she said. 'Why did The Watchers give me my name?'

'Ah,' she replied, 'that is a question I cannot answer for you Rose because I do not know why they have an interest in a human child. You may ask one more as I could not answer.'

'Who are 'The Watchers' Fern?'

Fern drew in a deep breath. She had not anticipated this question as she had tried to steer Rose towards asking the meaning of her name by shaming the humans who did not know theirs. But, she really should have been prepared for this as the girl's questions were improving all the time. Tonight, was proof of this, with the exception of the first blurted question that she could have had an answer to on the morrow.

However, she had allowed the girl three questions, so replied, 'The Watchers are the souls who have been captured by the Liferods. That is the end of your questions for tonight Rose. Go to bed now. Goodnight and good dreams.'

Rose was confused. Watchers, souls and Liferods, she now had more questions than ever to try to weave into Fern's stories!

But, she said goodnight and good dreams back to Fern and went to bed.

As she waited for sleep to arrive, Rose hugged her new name to herself and whispered it in her head, smiling as sleep arrived. She had her very own name and she vowed there and then to live up to it.

Journal of the Living

I watch what they do. I see them take the people to the enormous one. He has the Liferod still. I can't believe that he also lives. I hear that he searches for those of fire. That is not me. He is the first person I have found who I knew before the end. But perhaps it is not him? He is very big now, though his braids look the same. He was always vain. He will not know me when he takes the life from me. I don't even know his purpose. There are so few left in this place now. And he doesn't even eat the meat.

I'm a survivor. I like my meat blue. I have a mountain of meat in this pile of bodies that the enormous man has built. They are all of fire, although their flames are now extinguished. Some also have the marks. I won't eat the postulant ones. It would make me sick. I am sick, sick in the head. But I'm a survivor. It will be my turn soon. I wonder which pile I will find myself upon?

I've decided that the dead pile is not for me. I'm a survivor.

An extract from a survivor's journal of unknown origin but marked by Air.

Chapter Nine

Water

The horses kept going, although Amador was almost too tired to notice. They had been travelling for over a week now and he felt completely exhausted. He had never had to use his gift for such a long period of time, almost continuously.

The lad was slouched across the neck of the horse that they rode together, no cooler than when they had left the foothills of mount Sepit Mhor.

The second horse followed them, keeping the slow steady pace set by the first. Altogether plodding if truth be told, like the drip, drip, drip of an ice cap as the spring inevitably approaches.

Amador was barely conscious of the dwellings through which they were now passing, as their horse carried its passengers on through the village and down towards the shore. When they could go no further without immersing themselves in water, both horses came to a standstill and blew loudly, as the journey had also taken its toll on them.

Merason had been summoned from his home by a boy who had been asked by his father to run on ahead and alert him to the clearly dishevelled visitors to the village.

Merason could hardly believe his eyes when he saw his friend Amador almost asleep in his saddle. Shocked to the core, he rushed forward to support his friend, to stop him literally falling from the horse.

He quickly asked, 'What's happened friend? Are you alright? Are there others? Who did this to you?'

The questions tumbled from Merason as he tried to assess what had caused this tricky situation for his friend and also if he needed to be worried about any threats to his people.

Amador replied in a husky, cracked voice, 'I am well I think Merason. It is so good to see you.' He managed a small smile and then continued, 'Can you give me a help with the lad?'

Merason acted immediately, issuing instructions for the care of both the boy and the horses. Supporting his friend, they walked together towards Merason's home. He said, 'Come Amador. A drink to fortify you and then it's off to the baths for a revival of your spirit.'

Amador smiled weakly at the thought. 'Don't forget the lad Merason. Keep him cool. That's all I ask, for a little while,' he almost pleaded.

'Amador, don't you worry about the boy. He is being taken to the infirmary. We have the best healers as you know. He will do well with us now that you have brought him. I must admit though that I am wondering about the boy. I saw a flame writhing on his chest. You will need to help me understand why you have brought the fire among us Amador. But, first you must rest. Here, I want you to drink this,' he said as he handed Amador a glass full of green looking liquid.

The drink was a tonic and Amador immediately began to feel somewhat refreshed as he drank down long draughts. He took in the cool white surroundings of his friend's home. His smile was genuine as he grasped Merason's hand and then shoulders in a truly warm greeting. The kind saved for brothers and special friends.

Amador knew he was stretching his friendship. There was no love lost between the Water Peoples and Fire Clans so he enthused, 'It is truly wonderful to be here again Merason,' and then continuing, 'I'm sorry to bring the lad to your door, but I didn't know where else to turn. He is very ill.'

'Yes, well we can discuss that to our hearts content later. You really are a sight for sore eye's Amador. Now go and refresh yourself in the baths, then go directly to the guestroom and get some rest.'

Amador started to protest but Merason interrupted, 'Your words are slow Amador. You are exhausted and it doesn't take a healer to see that. Now go to the baths and then go to bed.'

Wondering why his friend was so reluctant to take his advice, Merason considered that Amador needed some further encouragement so he said, 'I will look after the boy. I have already sent Cody for Finnlach and you know he is our best healer. It will take him some time to get here though, so we will do what we can until then.'

'Thank you, friend,' Amador replied. He guessed that there was no use in arguing and in any event, he knew that he was badly in need of some rest. He would be no use to anyone if he didn't take the offer that Merason was giving him, and he was so very tempted to go to the baths.

Remembering the warm clean feeling of them he almost groaned. He hadn't had much time on his journey to see to his personal care, so he knew that he sorely needed to attend to this. In fact, if he wasn't so tired he would probably care what his friend thought of the smell of him.

Instead he said, 'Please try to keep him cool and send for me if you need to.'

'Don't worry Amador; I will call you if I need to. I understand that the fire in the boy is hot,' he said, and then more jocularly, 'Go now. To the baths with you!'

Amador left Merason's home and headed back along the shore in search of the horses. Old habits die hard he thought to himself. They had served him well, practically finishing the journey with very little direction from him and he secretly thanked Viktor for his choice of mounts.

Heading back towards the grassy embankment on the foreshore where he had been helped to dismount by Merason, he was thankful that it was only a few hundred meters away. The tonic had helped, but he still felt very weary.

As he had suspected, the horses were quietly grazing, having been freed from their burdens. Unfortunately, they were also tethered and became agitated as he approached them.

Noticing that the village Smith was nearby, he called out to him, 'Hey there, can you help me?'

'I'd give those animals a wide berth if I were you,' the man replied as he sauntered over to where Amador now stood. 'Fine they were until we tried to tether them and then all hell let loose,' the man emphasised.

Drawing in a deep breath to try to mask his annoyance, Amador said, 'I'm not surprised, these are Free horses and should never be tethered, it breaks the compact we have with them.'

Moving to the side of one of the horses, he placed his hand reassuringly on the horse's neck, close to the rope that tethered, but not quite touching. The horse nickered and he could feel the nervous twitching beneath his palm.

Speaking quietly, he told the horse what a great service it had provided as he stroked its quivering neck, all the while moving closer to the tether.

Then quickly and confidently he removed the rope from around the horse's neck. The horse's eye widened, but it held onto ground and Amador guessed his companion must be as exhausted as he was. He felt truly ashamed. His own weakness meant that the Free had been tethered and he moved as quickly as he could to untether the second horse.

Turning to the Smith he said, 'Friend, these horses belong to no man, but will provide a service when asked for a time. But, they are as tired as I and will not venture far this night. Can you watch over them for me and let them depart when they are ready to go?'

'Never heard of any Free horses before,' the man replied. 'But, if that's the case, then that's the case, and I guess I can do that for you,' he replied gruffly.

'Put up a real struggle with them there ropes they did. I guess I now know why, but nobody said anything to me about Free horses.'

'It's not your fault. The fault is all mine,' Amador said. 'I think the only reason that you managed to tether them was because they are both so very tired, otherwise you wouldn't have been able to do it. Their spirit is the strongest amongst horses, but I'm afraid I pushed them quite hard coming here.'

'No worries then,' the Smith said. 'I'll look out for them until they decide to leave themselves.'

'I give you my sincere thanks,' Amador replied. 'I should really look after them myself, but there are other things I must attend to. I bid you a very good night.' And feeling a lot more relieved he once again turned towards the bathhouse.

He half walked and half stumbled towards the bathhouse. Knowing what waited helped and he also knew that he didn't have far to go, the bathhouse being at the other end of the cove from Merason's home.

Recalling as he walked on that his last visit to the bathhouse was in happier times, with many men from the village taking the time to wind down after a hard day's graft, before retiring to their homes for dinner. He half chuckled at some of the stories he had heard there of village life embroidered through camaraderie and jest in equal measure.

Tonight, he knew it was likely that he would bathe alone given the lateness of the hour. For once he would be grateful of the solitude.

He wondered if Walker would still be there as he opened the big wooden door to enter. He was immediately reassured as the big man crossed the room and indicated a room where he could disrobe.

Walker didn't use speech and the villagers called him Walker in light of the fact that his strong fingers and hands giving a massage felt like someone walking on your back as his technique was so strong.

Walker was a feature of village life, and spent all but two weeks each year tending the bathhouse and its patrons. No one knew where he came from or where he went for two weeks each year and as he didn't talk, they were all unlikely to find out anytime soon. It was however the source of much speculation and a fair bit of jest, which Walker seemed to take in his stride.

Amador was vaguely aware of the clean hot smell that filled his nostrils and the heat that emanated from the chamber he entered to bathe. The bathhouse was formed around a natural spring that filled the chamber he was now in.

Walking down the steps, he immersed himself in the hot water. It felt so good. And he could almost feel the tension leaving his body as he relaxed into the bubbles created by the water pressure in the spring.

After a few minutes, realising that he was beginning to feel drowsy, he left the pool and lay down on the marble bed which indicated to Walker that he would welcome a massage.

Walker proceeded to give him, what he thought must be one of his gentler massages, as although it was quite painful at times, it was also bearable. He hadn't realised how tense his back and shoulders had become and resolved to return the next day if he could, to try and work some more of the tension out.

Thanking Walker briefly, he dressed and returned to Merason's home. Meeting no one, he let himself into the guest suite and the room he had called home for a good number of months about five years ago. Still feeling tired, he realised it was a good clean tiredness as he climbed into the soft bed for some well-deserved sleep.

Next morning, he awoke feeling somewhat refreshed.

Leaving the guest suite, he climbed the grassy embankment to the infirmary where he knew that Orrison had been taken the previous evening.

He truly hoped that the boy had fared well overnight and that he wasn't too late to help him. Although he did acknowledge to himself that he could have done no more himself, exhausted as he had been.

The infirmary sat at the top of a small hill and commanded a view second only to that of Merason's home. He remembered Merason explaining to him previously that they had decided on that location as it often helped people to heal, having a nice view to look out upon while they recovered, which most did from the expert treatment they received from the Water Peoples healers.

Merason looked up as he entered the room. 'Hello Amador, how do you fare this fine morning?' he asked.

It was a fine morning indeed. Clear and crisp with an uninterrupted view of the bay. Just the kind of morning that he especially liked when visiting here, with the view beyond the bay seemingly stretching to the edge of the known world.

In fact, it was his second most favourite view he thought not for the first time. His own enclosure on the Cliffs of Pyree just surpassed this view in his experience. Then recalling the firedance he had witnessed, what now felt like an age ago, he resolved that he might just have to change his opinion again.

Focussing again on Merason he replied, I'm much rested now. Thanks once again for your kind hospitality.'

Amador's smile faded though as he took in the scene before him. Orrison was still bathed in a sheen of sweat and his hair was plastered to his head.

‘It’s not as bad as it looks Amador,’ Merason said, taking in the worried look on his face. ‘We have given the boy a bed bath to try to cool his temperature as his fever is yet to break.’

When he didn’t respond Merason continued, ‘I’m sure I don’t know how you managed to get the boy here from the Firelands in his condition? It must have been over a week’s travel by horse. Are you sure that he had the fever then or did it develop on the journey?’

Merason was sure that the later must be true and he assumed this as Amador was obviously feeling responsible for the boy. ‘You know five or more days is an awful long time for a fever,’ he said shaking his head in a wondering manner, somehow emphasising his disbelief while at the same time enabling Amador to feel like it wasn’t his fault.

‘Yes,’ Amador began, when more people entered the room. He had been about to explain that it wasn’t a fever, when Finnlach the healer arrived with his son Finnbarr in tow. He had met both on his previous visit and spent long hours discussing the human condition with Finnlach, which was a subject clearly close to his heart, Amador recalled.

Their own story was particularly poignant too, he remembered. Finnlach was the Water Peoples most revered healer and he was now teaching his trade to his son, who was as quick a study, as he was an able healer. He watched and listened well, albeit he was a shy lad.

His mother had died when giving him life, much to the self-chastisement of Finnlach who had tried in vain to save her. A ghost now that was forever etched on his heart, he had confessed to Amador one evening after a rather large round of drinks.

Amador knew that they lived a good day’s walk from the shore which meant that they must have walked all night to have reached them so quickly, and felt profoundly grateful to both of them at that moment. Always setting aside their own troubles to help others took a special kind of person he knew.

There were two other healers in the room which was now beginning to feel rather crowded. The larger of the two men quickly appraised everyone in the room of their care for Orrison over the course of the night.

The upshot of the message was that there had been no change to his condition overnight. They were both clearly baffled, having tried all of the usual treatments for a fever.

Finnlach walked over to the boy and pulled down the light coverlet to his waist. Orrison's flame writhed on his chest just above his heart where Amador had placed it, what felt like a lifetime ago right now.

Merason frowned, considered and then asked, 'Amador, what did you use to brand the boy?'

Amador drew out the Liferod from within the folds of his robe. 'I used this Liferod,' he said. 'It has a special feel to it, but I don't think it's what is primarily wrong with Orrison.'

Merason's eyes widened at the sight of the Liferod, but resolved to save his own concerns until he could talk with Amador alone. So, he just asked, 'Who gave this Liferod to you for the boy's branding?'

'I was given the Liferod by The First of The Twelve. I really should have returned it by now,' he said somewhat guiltily, 'but, I had to help the boy somehow, and here we are.'

Merason also filed this information away for later and knew that he would have to show Amador the Water peoples own branding rod. It was kept in his home and was nothing like the Liferod that dangled from his friend's waist.

Amador was still holding the Liferod up for all to see and Finnbarr reached out to touch it.

Firmly, but not loudly, Finnlach called out to his son, 'Don't touch that Liferod boy!'

Finnbarr grasped his hand back and Amador replaced the Liferod in his robes, slightly concerned with the reaction from everyone. But, there was the need to concentrate on Orrison to try to see if they could help him, so he kept his own counsel too.

'Well, well, well, what have we here?' Finnlach continued as if the previous few moments had never occurred. 'The boy is fevered indeed and losing a lot of fluid.' He pinched the skin on the back of Orrison's hand, which took much longer than it should to settle back down.

Finnlach winced as he was rewarded with a blister on his own thumb and forefinger. 'Curious, very curious,' he said before immersing his hand in a bowl of water which had been placed close to the bedside by the evening healers.

Wincing again, as he pulled his burned fingers from the bowl, he said, 'It's like this Amador, my hands are sensitive and I need them for my work. I reckon that I had better hear all of the background to the boy's condition before I go any further. We don't want any mistakes to happen trying something just for the sake of it. I don't like working blind if I can help it.'

Turning to Finnbarr, he continued, 'But first Finnbarr, place your hand on the boy's forehead, lightly and quickly mind. I want to know what you think too.'

As Finnbarr did his father's bidding, Finnlach said in a proud fatherly way, 'My boy will know and help, as he has the healing hands.'

As he said this he rummaged in the bag he had brought with him and withdrew what Amador thought was a stone at first glance, but then realised it was a crystal he was giving to Finnbarr for the treatment of the small blisters which had inevitably erupted on his palm following contact with Orrison, even although the encounter with Orrison's skin had been fleeting.

Amador knew then for sure that Orrison's condition had seriously worsened overnight.

Finnlach left the bag and its contents at the bottom of Orrison's bed.

Merason had called for refreshments and all four retired to the adjoining room, leaving the two healers with instructions from Finnlach to carefully keep trying to give the boy water to drink and to keep sponging him down with tepid water.

With the need for knowledge clearly paramount to Finnlach, it was the best Amador could hope for.

As he entered the adjoining room, his senses were at once alerted to the smell of warm bread and pastries and his mouth began to water at the prospect of eating them. He hadn't realised he was quite so hungry, and he said appreciatively, 'Merason, this is why I love this place so much. There is always a tasty morsel to be had when you need it, and sometimes, even if you don't!'

Amador beamed a thankful smile at his friend and he tucked into more than his fair share, as he discovered he was famished. Washing the buttered bread down with strong, hot tea.

Merason smiled himself to see Amador relish his refreshments and turned to the young girl who had brought them he said, 'Can you bring some more cheese and bread, oh and some of the special pickle too. I seem to have some hungry guests!'

Turning to Finnbarr, Finnlach asked, 'Well son, what did you feel when you placed your hand on the boy?'

Finnbarr looked slightly embarrassed but, cleared his throat and replied, 'I'm not sure exactly father? Obviously, I felt the heat and it was hot enough to scald my hand, but the quartz has helped to heal it,' he finished quickly seeing the concealed look of concern on his father's face.

Finnlach nodded his understanding and Finnbarr continued, 'It was strange really, but I only had a fleeting moment. It felt like there was a mighty fire burning unchecked within him. I also felt hot air swirling looking for escape. The boy is very weak now, I'm not sure if he can recover from whatever is within him.' Finnbarr cast his eye's downwards as he finished his assessment.

Amador was impressed by Finnbarr's assessment of the situation. He surmised that the lad must be of an age with Orrison, perhaps a couple of years older at most. The coincidence of two young boys, neither having known their mother wasn't lost on him in the moment.

He said, 'Your assessment is a good one Finnbarr. I have been cooling the air around Orrison for the more than a week and yet the fire within him rages on.'

Finnbarr looked up and sought his father's quiet guidance. Finnlach responded, 'You have done well son and thank you. Can you find the smoky quartz in my bag and place it under the boy's pillow? You can tell the others to go and rest now and go and get some sleep yourself as we have travelled long this night. I'll take it from here.'

Amador thought that Finnlach sounded more confident than he looked.

As Finnbarr complied with his father's request, he could hear his father's praise for him, 'Finn will have helped the boy, he always does when he lays his hands on someone, even if only for a short time.'

Amador could hear the pride and love in Finnlach's voice and again wondered what it must be like to have flesh of your own flesh. Everywhere he went there was evidence of this unconditional love. Well, perhaps with the exception of Viktor. There was always an exception to every rule though Amador thought wryly.

Merason interrupted his thoughts as he said, 'I think we need to know the whole of it now Amador. I'd be telling an untruth if I said I wasn't concerned. First, you bring a Fire Leader's boy here in a terrible condition, at no small cost to your own wellbeing it would seem. Relationships are fragile between the races as well you know. Now we have heard from Finnlach's son an assessment that doesn't sound too promising for the boy's recovery. I ask myself what's his father is likely to do if the boy doesn't survive and especially if he dies here among my people? If you weren't a good friend I would be thinking that there was a plot afoot. We haven't had any trouble for a number of years now and that's exactly the way I would like it to stay.'

Amador considered Merason's position. He was clearly both frustrated and worried. And he had brought this dilemma to their door when he arrived the previous evening with Orrison.

But, he also knew that Merason was a strong leader. Yes, he would be concerned, this was natural, so Amador considered his next words carefully before he replied.

'Merason, you have my deepest apologies and I can assure you that no harm was intended in bringing Orrison to you, quite the reverse in fact. It was I who persuaded Viktor, the Fire Clan Leader to allow me to bring the lad to you for help, as I could think of no better place. If there is a cure for the lad, I know you will find it,' he finished hopefully.

Knowing this wasn't enough judging by the concern still etched on his friend's face, he continued, 'I can assure you Merason that Viktor will not seek revenge at your door, nor any of his Clan, nor any other Fire Clan for that matter. No matter what happens to the lad Viktor knows the chances of Orrison surviving are slim and I think he mostly blames himself for this. He is also aware that even if he does survive, he may not be wholesome.'

Amador paused to let this sink in, and Merason moved to sit down shaking his head as he considered what Amador had just said.

Sighing, Amador continued, 'Viktor has instructed me not to bring him back to the Clan until he is fully recovered.' This last statement hung in the air like a death knell.

Both Merason and Finnlach clearly balked at this news.

Trying to understand, Merason asked, 'What of their own healers, could they not help the boy?'

Amador replied, 'Alas, no. Seraphina, the Clans, um, healer, was unable to help at all and indeed seemed to be making a bad situation worse.'

'In what way?' interjected Finnlach.

'Well she seemed to be most interested to apply a salve to the boy and she was pressing Viktor into an impossible situation with his Clan. Politics were at play as Orrison is Viktor's only son you see.'

Merason was visibly shaken with this news. He blurted, 'And he told you not to bring him back until fully recovered? It just doesn't add up Amador.'

Merason was beginning to show his frustration and was clearly at a loss to understand what to do for the best.

Amador knew that Merason's main concern was for his people, but he also knew him to be a kind and generous man with a strong commitment to both family and values. Choosing his words carefully he said, 'It's not that simple in the Fire Clan Merason. They need a son to succeed their Leader or the Leader and his family must leave the Clan. Viktor and his late wife had five daughters before they had Orrison, and his wife died in the birthing.

Finnlach joined Merason and sat down at this news.

Amador tried to send him a look of empathy for his own loss and then continued, 'Viktor needs to stay as Clan Leader with a hale and hearty son, or at least the promise of one to return when healed, or he will have to leave with his daughters. He can't just hand over the Leadership and stay on. It's not their way. I really think that he is trying to protect his girls, even if it means he has to sacrifice Orrison to do so.'

He hoped that the mention of the girls would remind Merason of his own daughter and he noticed with some relief that his friend's features were softening.

Finnlach was keeping his own counsel, but Amador was in no doubt that the story struck a chord with his own situation too.

'I see it's a complex situation that the Fire Clan Leader finds himself in Amador,' Merason said, 'but the trouble still remains at my door unless you or Finnlach can work some kind of miracle together that gets the boy up and out of my infirmary. And soon.'

Finnlach stood and began to pace the room as it helped him to think better. He said, 'I think I might have something worth trying with my crystals.'

'I noticed you giving a stone to Finnbarr and you told him to place one under Orrison's pillow,' Amador said. 'Was it a type of crystal?' he asked, relieved to be back discussing a solution rather than circumstance.

'Yes, smoky quartz,' Finnlach replied. 'It's a good grounding stone and I think he needs some earth energy with all the fire and air at play in him. It's not a cure in itself, but it will hopefully buy us the time to think this through.'

Amador enquired, 'Why crystals?'

'It's like this Amador; I've been working with crystals to aid my healing for some time now. They work through a vibration and can realign energies to heal. I've built up a fair bit of knowledge over the years. Although I know that they're not our traditional healing method, I think they might work for the boy. I'm not sure mind, but I really can't think of any of our traditional methods of healing working. Crystals generally deal with the cause of the problem rather than the symptoms and can have a long-lasting effect,' he concluded.

'I've seen it work time after time Amador,' Merason enthused.

Amador considered this information. He had heard of crystal healing before, but hadn't had the experience of seeing it being used. He also knew that crystals were rare on the whole, except in the Earthlands and wondered how a man like Finnlach had acquired what had looked like such a big pouch of them.

He also wasn't sure that it was the answer for Orrison. However, no other solution was jumping into his head, so resolving desperately to keep an open mind, he said, 'Tell me some more Finnlach, it sounds interesting indeed.'

Finnlach needed no further encouragement. 'I've built up a fair collection of crystals over the years Amador. My wife loved pretty stones and you know that some of the Earthlanders like to use our hospice here for healing and convalescence. They're the people with the money Amador. You know one woman who comes every year always brings a small crystal in payment for the work I do, which is not a lot really, and certainly not worth the crystal payment she makes.

The point is they always seem to be full of energy, the crystals she brings, so I feel I have to take them, to help others of course, not for my own gain. I never really know what they will do at first in the way of healing. But, a bit of time and testing, and I think I know as much as any other man this side of the water,' he concluded.

Interjecting Amador asked, 'Who is the woman, do you have a name?'

Finnlach shuffled a bit and stopped his pacing. 'Why do you need to know this Amador?' he asked rather uncomfortably. 'She is just a woman who comes here to get away from it all for a bit. I'd really rather not say too much about her as she is of no import to your boy Orrison's condition.'

Finnlach was a stout man and Amador could see by the way he placed his feet that he was not for revealing the woman's identity in a hurry. His whole stance said that he would not be moved on this one, but there was also concern and worry in his expression.

Amador was a bit surprised by this, but ever pragmatic he conceded, 'You're right, it's of no great import Finnlach, I was only curious as I know there are several important families in the Earthlands who have amassed great fortune to themselves by mining the land for its precious metals and gems. Please continue.'

Slightly appeased, Finnlach began pacing again and Amador cast a glance at Merason who had retreated to the seat built into the window which overlooked the natural bay, where many of the children were now playing. His face was hidden to Amador as he focussed intently on looking out of the window.

Amador thought he understood that Merason didn't want to be put in a position where he might have to 'compromise' one of his guest's identities, as he knew the contributions from the Earthlanders helped the Water Peoples to survive.

He was also aware that it was a poor life they led in terms of luxury, but a wealthy life in terms of love, caring and community spirit. He thought he knew which way he would choose wealth and it would be with the Water People each time. What was the value of a stone compared to a shared moment after all?

Refocusing his attention on Finnlach, Amador knew he was pinning his hopes on the very stones his education told him would be unlikely to heal the boy who was lying dying in the adjoining room. Sobered by this reminder to himself, he asked, 'Finnlach, do you really think it can work? And how do you use them?'

'Honestly, I'm not sure Amador,' Finnlach replied. 'Here's what I'm thinking though, let me show you.'

Finnlach went to fetch his bag from the next room. Returning quickly, he removed a silk cloth from the bag which he placed on the table in the room, before tumbling the contents of the bag onto the cloth.

Amador didn't know what he was expecting, but there were about twenty to thirty stones of varying sizes and colours. Some were polished whereas others looked dull and, well, stoneish!

Finnlach began to separate the crystals grouping some together and placing others on their own. He talked as he worked, 'You see Amador, these are the crystals I use the most. I only ever have around twenty-five 'live ones' as their energies get used up in the healing.

I didn't know that at first and I'm afraid that some people weren't helped due to my ignorance. Anyway, these ones are the agates. Different kinds mind with different healing properties. These are strong and slow release crystals, whereas these,' he said his hand moving to the shining stones, 'these are kinds of quartz and work much faster.'

Amador noted the enthusiastic way that Finnlach talked about his crystals and couldn't help but get caught up in the moment.

'The others,' Finnlach continued, 'well this group seem to go together, but I'm not sure of their name.'

'Perhaps I can be of some small help there Finnlach,' said Amador. 'I have read fairly extensively and I must admit to a time when I was trying to understand the Earthlanders and some of their ways, I did a little research into crystal lore. This purple lump here is called amethyst, and this yellow stone is called moonstone I think?'

'Of course, moonstone,' Finnlach said with conviction as he slapped his forehead in comprehension. 'It's the perfect name for it! It works best when there is a full moon.' He shook his head, clearly amazed at the discovery of a name that coincided with his own findings.

'Thank you, Amador. You bring music to my tired old ears,' he said, clearly happy.

'It's such a small thing Finnlach, but I'm glad that my knowledge pleases you,' he responded smiling back.

Finnlach beamed and continued, 'I guess it doesn't really matter what they are called or what they all do. We can talk on this another time Amador, if you're interested. I'm sorry, I get carried away sometimes.'

Finnlach picked up one stone from amongst the agates. It was a small stone that swirled with colours from red to orange to brown with luminescent aspects to it. 'This is the one that I think can most help the boy.'

He passed the crystal to Amador and continued, 'This one seems to take the heat out of things so to speak. I think it will help to balance the boy. It will also help to keep him grounded. Most important though is that I think it will help to cool his fire a bit.'

Turning the crystal over in his fingers, Amador did imagine that the stone felt cool to the touch, but the colours looked like those of fire which caused him some concern. The last thing Orrison needed was more fire!

Finnlach broke into his thoughts, 'Do you want me to try it Amador? Of course, it may not work. I'm relying a lot on what Finn told me and he touched the boy only briefly.'

'The crystal reminds me of fire Finnlach, are you sure it won't increase the heat?'

'To be honest Amador, I don't know for sure,' he replied. 'It's a fairly new crystal of mine and I've not had much call to use it till now. I can only tell you that from what I know of it, that I think it's the best option.'

Finnlach looked down in what Amador knew must be a practiced way, very definitely leaving the decision to him with no encouragement or otherwise from the healer whatsoever.

Still tired, Amador knew that he had to take a chance on this man's honest knowledge and healing abilities. But, he remained very sceptical and wary of trying something like this on another man's son. A Clan Leader's son for goodness sake! And here he was with the boy barely holding onto life in his friend's home, needing to decide. Possibly even causing his friend harm in the longer term, although that was the last thing he wanted to do.

Really, it was a fine situation he had gotten himself into this time. He should have left the boy to Seraphina and gone on his way back to the Conclave. Out here dealing with people was harder than he thought Amador realised.

He was also acutely aware there were no alternative options presenting themselves either and that he had to take the gamble. He just wished he knew what the odds were, and if they were stacked in Orrison's favour. He was beginning to seriously doubt this though.

Pulling himself together, Amador reminded himself that he must remain positive, even although he felt so tired again. He could happily fall over and not get up again.

'All right Finnlach, let's give it a try,' he said more positively than he felt. 'What do we need to do?'

Finnlach looked up, smiling confidently and Amador secretly thanked the man for his obvious confidence and conviction.

Finnlach said, 'Well it's not hard really. The hard bit's over and that's deciding to try something different. Come,' he said holding out his hand for the return of the crystal, which Amador duly passed to him.

All three filed into the room where Orrison lay. 'Right, Amador, Merason,' Finnlach said nodding to each in turn. 'I'm going to place the crystal on the boy's forehead. It should begin its work straight away by cooling the fire within him and by adding the element of earth to further ground the boy.

It should also make him feel secure and hopefully rebalance the energies within the boy.'

Finnlach looked to the others for permission.

Both Amador and Merason nodded their agreement, and Finnlach placed the stone on the boy's forehead.

Nothing happened.

Amador didn't really know what he had expected, but nothing at all? He looked at Finnlach who seemed content with this non-reaction.

Finnlach said to them both, 'It may take some time. As I said before agates work slow. We need to leave him for a while. Now if it's alright with both of you, I'm going to pay a visit to the baths and freshen up a bit. It was a long journey and I came as quick as I could.'

Merason responded, 'Of Course Finnlach. My thanks to you are strong. I really appreciate your haste and bid you a good bath. We can catch up later and review the situation.'

Holding out his hand to shake Finnlach's own, Amador said, 'My thanks to you also. We will see each other soon.' He clasped the man's right shoulder with his free hand in a gesture of strong thanks.

'You're both very welcome I'm sure, but let's see how the boy fairs over the next few hours. Now please excuse me.' With that, he turned and left the room headed in the direction of the baths.

Turning to Amador, Merason noticed that he was watching the boy intently, trying to discern any small change, he surmised.

'Come Amador. I can see that you are tired again, so I will send for another tonic for you as there are still some things we must discuss.'

Amador looked at the grave concern etched on his friend's features and acquiesced at once. 'Of course, my friend let us retire to the adjoining room once more, lest I'm distracted from your concerns with my own for the lad.'

On entering the adjoining room Amador moved to the window where Merason had directed his attention earlier. He looked out over the bay and at the children at play in the water, while Merason ordered some more refreshments to be brought, before joining him at the large window.

Merason knew that at heart Amador was a scholar. A scholar who had got himself caught up in the middle of a fine problem. On re-entering the room, he said, 'My friend you have brought some troubles to my door on your journey to learn.'

Turning from the window and feeling somewhat ashamed by his friend's accusation, Amador immediately changed the subject, if only to try to lighten the mood and remind each other of happier times. 'Merason, please tell me that this is not Taye splashing in the water like a fish,' he said gesturing out of the window to the bay beyond.

'Ah, yes Amador, it's Taye. I was watching her and Finnbarr play earlier while you discussed more serious matters with his father. They were both clearly having great fun. He smiled the secret smile of a father who has a bright dream for his daughter's future.

'You know we call her little seal. She is like the creature as life,' he chuckled. 'She can hold her breath for an amazing length of time and likes to dive under for as long as possible. You know Cleon,' he said referring to his wife, 'often panics that she won't come up again as she stays under for so long. I think it's a game to her though,' he finished fondly.

'It's been a long time,' Amador said wistfully. 'She was just a babe in arms when I was last here.'

Merason beamed at him, 'Well there are two more babes in arms for you to meet later. Cleon and I had twin boys just last year.'

Amador was shocked. He hadn't even taken the time to enquire after Merason's family, but was also immensely pleased for his proud friend and told him so in no uncertain terms.

Just at that the refreshments arrived, and he raised his tonic and said, 'To my good friend Merason and his growing family. May good fortune smile on all of you.' And he downed his tonic in one to seal the good wishes.

Now more at ease with each other again, Amador steered the conversation back to where Merason had wanted to go earlier. 'So Merason, I'm truly sorry to have brought the lad to your door, I shouldn't have done that, and I now truly understand your concern.'

'No, I don't think you do Amador. Forget about the boy for now. He will live or die at our door and we will bear the consequences either way. Although, I have to admit that I am most concerned for my people. We don't need a war Amador, but I trust you when you say that the father will not follow, even although I can't understand that for the life of me.'

'Well what are your concerns, if not about Orrison?' Amador asked.

Merason considered Amador and sat down by the fire which had been set in the room and indicated to him that he should take the seat opposite, which he did.

'Amador, I have something to show you.' Merason removed his families branding rod from the sheath that protected it. 'This Liferod has been in our family for generations,' he said passing the rod to Amador. 'I want you to see it, hold it and to consider what we brand our Leaders with, generation after generation. Then consider how it differs from the Liferod that dangles in your robes. The one that you used to brand the boy.'

Amador could clearly see that Merason wasn't comfortable about the issue he was raising with him and when he took the Water people's Liferod into his own hands, he immediately understood why. It was a stick in comparison. Yes, a much used and obviously loved stick, but a stick nonetheless.

Looking again at the Liferod passed to him by his friend, he thought it was really a lovely piece of art, and it was clearly fashioned by the Water People. The carvings were of waves, fish and dolphins, all very familiar to him. At the end of the stick a metal cast had been inserted into the wood. The crest was fashioned to look like a wave and matched the inscription displayed on Merason's arm.

'You see Amador,' Merason said gravely, 'we heat the metal and this gives us the brand. It's nothing like the Liferod you carry.' He took the family heirloom back from Amador, who passed it back to him carefully.

Considering this information, Amador responded, 'I can see why you were concerned when you saw the Liferod I used to brand Orrison, but it was given to me by The First for that very purpose. He couldn't have known about the troubles the Fire Clan were having and the impact that might have had on the lad.'

'What kind of troubles Amador?' Merason asked.

Amador sighed and thought he had best explain what he knew given the circumstances. 'Well I can't be certain of course, but I'm not sure Orrison's mother was actually his mother. Viktor was having trouble having a son. He and his wife had five lovely daughters together, but no son to Lead the Clan into the future. The mother, Melody, died giving birth to the lad, or so the story goes.

I'm not so sure though. The more I think about the fire and air at play in Orrison, the more I think that Viktor may have been with another woman who was not of his kind. Not Fire, but Air. It would help to explain the…'

Merason blurted, 'Surely you can't be telling me that the man was crazy enough to mix the races. It's beyond comprehension Amador, and I must tell you that it makes me feel sick to my stomach.'

'I know it's difficult for you to understand Merason. Your world is not as hard as theirs. I have already told you that Viktor would have had to take his girl's out from the Clan's protection and walk the lonesome path. It would have meant certain death for all of them. Faced with that choice, what would you do?'

'Amador, what you talk of here, about mixing races, how can you even ask what I would do?' he replied. 'You know me well, how can you even think that I would consider doing what you think this man Viktor may have done? I'm gutted Amador, truly gutted.'

He hadn't meant to hurt his friend, in fact he had asked the question in a hypothetical way, and wasn't really looking for a response. He also hadn't meant to share his conclusions with anyone else at all, but he had to admit to himself that he was intrigued with the idea of mixing the races.

And now he was facing another truth. The Liferod he had used to brand Orrison was different in the extreme. He had known this from the beginning really, just hadn't stopped to question The First. That just wasn't what one did with The First; it was all command and be obeyed! He had trusted him like a parent and had taken his word without question.

Bringing the Liferod forth from within his robes, he said, 'I didn't mean for you to answer friend. It was a hypothetical question that I was toying with as I try to understand or find a logical reason for Orrison's reaction to the branding. Now you have given me another solution to consider in the Liferod that I carry. Perhaps it is I who has harmed Orrison right enough, as their wise woman Seraphina had already suggested to me,' he concluded desperately.

'You have your troubles to bear Amador,' Merason responded, slightly appeased by his hypothesis. 'Let's have a look at this Liferod and hope that it provides some answers.'

Journal of the Living

I was brought before the big man today. I was right, he didn't know me. He still talks as if he owns the world. Perhaps he does!

His left cheek has been scarred. He runs his fingers along it often. I told him I need a capsule. He saw my book. Touched it and read my soul. His eyes scorched my face. He reached out and I truly flinched.

He then gave me a pencil. A whole fresh pencil! But he took my stub. It was my only friend, my only friend...

An extract from a survivor's journal of unknown origin but marked by Air.

Chapter Ten

Conclave

Tarramore's plans were in tatters. In his lofty room at the Conclave he thought about what had recently transpired and a feeling of unease was beginning to creep into his thoughts.

Uppermost in his mind was Amador. Well, not Amador exactly, the Liferod! He should have had it back by now. Why hadn't Amador returned directly to him? He had been looking forward to the competition between Amador and Faldo and he just couldn't have guessed who would have won.

Well, that was all in the past now. Faldo and his seniors had just up and vanished off the face of the earth it would seem.

He paced his chamber, constantly returning to the table that contained his viewfinder. He had been backed into a corner by that stupid little Fairie Elm and his ugly giant friend. What else was he to do? He had had to move the Liferod. They would have sensed its presence or at least the protection it gave off. For too long he had been second guessed by those Fairies.

Oh, but, he chuckled to himself, I outsmarted them all when I gave the Liferod to Amador. Sometimes I'm so clever, he thought, but I have to keep one step ahead all the time.

The anger in him vied with the fear. Looking again into his viewfinder he scanned the area all around Mount Sepit Mhor. Nothing! No Faldo, no seniors, nothing. He let out a roar of frustration.

Boric entered and said, 'Did you call Sir?'

'No, I did not bloody call you! You would have known if I had.' He picked up a fruit from a bowl on the table and aimed it at the small man who still stood, half bowed before him.

The fruit was ripe and it split as it hit Boric's cheek, depositing its juice which trickled down the side of the man's face like a burst pustule, as he bent to retrieve the remains of the fallen fruit from the floor least it stained.

Somewhat gratified by the sight of his servant's humiliation Tarramore said, 'Just leave me now. You're dismissed. Go now. GO, before I change my mind!'

Boric scrambled to leave the room as quickly as he could. His master had some nasty tendencies and he hoped not to suffer any further this day.

The First resumed his pacing, muttering all the while, the incident with the fruit already forgotten, as he reconsidered the larger picture.

Yes, he had to acknowledge that Faldo would now never return. He had searched almost constantly for weeks now, for any sign of their departure from the Caves of Iho. That little hussy had sent them there to their obvious death. Did she mean to do that? He did wonder though…

Crossing the room to his viewfinder again he sought out the girl. She was still there all right doing nothing in particular, nothing to bother him at least, he thought. Always wandering about distracting honest men though! Faldo should have been above the lust of a woman's body Tarramore thought not for the first time. Dirty little, naked little girl!

He replayed the image of Ayesha pointing the way to Faldo and his seniors. Watched the lust fill their eye's and then turn like dogs to the slaughter, to do her bidding.

He couldn't hear the conversation of course. He didn't need to. He watched them head into the caves, Faldo trying to look self-righteous, but clearly just as taken with the girl as the other two, who followed him with their dirty tongues hanging out.

Tarramore was beginning to feel angry again and he knew that he was working himself up into a state that wasn't good for anyone, least of all him.

But, Faldo was supposed to bring back his Liferod and if he didn't Amador surely should have! Instead, he was off on some kind of mercy mission with the half breed he had branded.

Tarramore swore loudly, 'One of me!' It was so frustrating! 'I want my Liferod back!' he shouted to the room.

Calming himself again he resumed his pacing. I must think this through calmly he thought. I have time. Yes, I have plenty of time, he now chuckled to himself.

He suspected he was quite mad!

Journal of the Living

The food is charred. It does not taste the same!!!

An extract from a survivor's journal of unknown origin but marked by Air.

CHAPTER ELEVEN

AWAKENING

Orrison stirred in his slumber. He was in that middle state he realised, between sleep and wakefulness. He felt comfortable lying here, listening to the drone of voices not too far away. But, something was different and he struggled towards consciousness to discover what it was.

He felt almost light, like he was floating, the only thing pinning him down was his head which felt both sore and heavy.

That was it, he thought, the voices were unfamiliar, which sent alarm bells ringing in his sore head, as he tried to bring his fuddled mind together enough to wake up.

The smell was unfamiliar too, he realised. Different smells entered his nostrils and he lay upon something soft and warm. Crossing the vast chasm in his mind, he fleetingly wondered if he was now dead. Killed by the large paw of a big cat that had raked over his stomach and spilled its contents for carrion.

Feeling real panic, Orrison willed himself to wake up. Lying there, he took in his surroundings. He was indeed floating above the ground, but on a solid frame that bounced a bit as he moved first one arm, leg and finally his head.

Something fell from his forehead, but he couldn't be bothered to find out what it was, although he did feel startled for a moment.

The voices were louder now in his ears and he sought the source of them with his eyes. Realising that this was no tent in which he slept, but a solid structure, the like of which he had never seen before.

Feeling confused, he realised that he would have to try to find out more, but he felt weak, so he lay and tried to piece together events.

Ayesha! Where was Ayesha? He wished she would come to him now. Hold him and tell him that everything would be alright, just as she had when he was a small boy who had just had a wicked nightmare. Perhaps this is a nightmare, he thought fleetingly, but quickly realised that it was just too real, if unfamiliar.

Orrison thought on, and remembered his journey into Mount Sepit Mhor. He felt for the pouch in his skins, but they were gone, replaced with a smooth cloth. So, his obsidian was gone. Possibly stolen? His mind raced through eventualities. Was he a prisoner here then? Where were Viktor and the Clan?

It just didn't make any sense.

His hand moved to his chest and brushed against the brand. Yes, this was real at least! He remembered the feeling of heat travelling through his body and then he could remember no more, and felt frightened all over again.

The voices were intruding into his thoughts, making him feel drowsy again, so he tried to focus on them and what they were saying. Something about a little seal he thought? Whatever that was?

Realising that one of the voices sounded vaguely familiar, he tried to place it and just couldn't.

Something cool touched his cheek then, startling him. He grasped at it, albeit slowly. It was a stone. It felt smooth and nice, but reminded him of his lost obsidian. Placing it on a nearby table he resolved to investigate.

It took some time to manoeuvre himself to the edge of the structure he lay upon as it moved beneath him. It was then he realised that he lay on a big bag of water. Everything was different, unfamiliar and frightening, so he thought that he must use his skills to discover what had happened to him.

And discover what he must do to get home, hoping fervently that Ayesha was still alive and would come to him to explain everything soon.

The ways of the Fire Clan and the hunt meant that he must also be self-reliant though. Testing his legs, he realised that he was very weak, but he willed himself across the room on hunter's feet, or at least the best he could manage at the moment anyway, which was really quite good considering how weak he felt.

He noted that he walked on flat stone that cooled his feet, but made no noticeable sound. No twigs to concern me here he thought, wondering at the smoothness of the white stone on which he walked. Everywhere he looked was white and clean. Even the cloth that covered him was white. Feeling more and more disoriented with every passing moment, but the voices drew him on, coupled with his own sheer determination.

Reaching a doorway, he leaned against the wall behind it, gathering his strength. He knew he was weak, but right now he felt like he could crumble to the floor and never get up again.

Strengthening his resolve, he noticed an archway at the other side of the room that he hadn't seen earlier. Another exit, he thought, if I need to escape, that's my way out.

Hearing the voices more clearly now, he sneaked a peek into the room. There were two men in the room, one of whom he recognised as being Amador. A feeling of relief flooded through him, something familiar in a mass of unfamiliar. He almost sank to the floor then, but noticed the Liferod in Amador's hand and the other man held one also.

He looks strange Orrison thought. The man was dressed in a white tunic and had lots of big hair that curled down to meet a bushy beard. He was a big man too!

Orrison re supported himself on the wall to listen…

Having heard enough, grief filling him, he stumbled back towards his bed of water and promptly fell into a deep slumber.

Journal of the Living

Washed today! Well, pushed into the river. I feel light. Never thought I would feel clean ever again.

Had to hide my book from the big man! Not many pages left now.

An extract from a survivor's journal of unknown origin but marked by Air.

CHAPTER TWELVE

ARTEFACT

The two friends examined the artefact. It was clearly sentient, as they both had the feeling that the Liferod was aware of them. They examined the carvings together and marvelled at the creatures depicted upon it.

Amador said, 'The First called them Fairies.' He could see that Merason was clearly startled by this news.

'Fairies you say? I have heard the tales of them. We still tell the stories to our children. Perhaps the Liferod is very old Amador, from the beginning of time when creatures such as us still had wings and magic?'

Amador smiled at his friend's fanciful nature that was again evident he was pleased to note. He laughed, 'How so my friend? Do you have a lump on your back where once there were wings? Perhaps we just lost them along the way? And what of this, and this,' he said pointing at other carvings. 'What did they become do you think?'

Merason laughed then too, 'I can think of one or two people I know who may once have been one of these strange grotesque creatures!'

They both laughed so hard at this that Amador could feel the tears running down his cheeks.

Sobering somewhat, he relayed his experience with the rose bush to Merason. 'You know, I had almost forgotten about it, but now I'm wondering if this Liferod had anything to do with it. I guess that's a pretty stupid thought though. How could any Liferod, even one such as this, have that kind of effect? I'm fair puzzled by it though Merason, I have to tell you.'

Merason replied, 'There seem to be a lot of strange things happening around you at the moment Amador, and the only thing that's different is the Liferod. So, it's not so farfetched to be thinking in the way you are thinking.'

The mood had changed again.

Feeling pensive now, Amador lapsed into a comfortable silence. The fire cracked in the grate and he was drawn to the flames dancing across the wood. After a short while he dozed in his seat.

Watching his weary friend, Merason resolved to wait, all the while his mind racing. He could still see the Liferod nestling in Amador's robes. It was a strange thing indeed. Could it have caused a rosebush to bud, flower and fade in the space of a few minutes? If so, what else might it do? The young boy next door was fighting for his life, probably because he had been marked by the thing.

No, Merason didn't like it. He didn't like it at all!

Rising, he collected a blanket from the window box and used it to cover his friend, wondering all the while whether he was more concerned for his friends' comfort, or hiding the Liferod from his view. Yes, he would ask that Amador put it away somewhere safe when he wakes up, he thought to himself. Meantime, he sat in the opposite chair, concerns chasing through his thoughts.

Sometime later Finnlach returned and went to check on the boy. He was feeling much refreshed from his trip to the baths, but wanted to make sure that the crystal had done its work in the way that he had hoped. Amador's suggestion that the look of the crystal reminded him of fire was playing on his mind and he hoped that he had not exacerbated the situation in any way.

Noticing immediately that Orrison was lying in a different position; Finnlach felt a surge of relief flood through him and looked for the crystal on the boy's pillow. It wasn't to be seen, and he walked around the bed to be sure it wasn't there.

Orrison was now lying on his side, with his legs tucked up and was clearly sleeping comfortably. Thinking that perhaps the boy was lying on it, he almost simultaneously reached to check, while noticing the small stone on the table by the bed.

Finnlach became very excited then. Orrison had clearly been awake and removed the crystal himself. Wow! It had worked again this crystal healing! Shaking his head in wonderment he thought to himself that he wouldn't believe it if he didn't see it work for himself time after time.

Feeling immensely satisfied with his work, he crossed the room quickly and entered the adjoining room to find Merason indicating to him that Amador was sleeping and that he should go quietly.

'The boy has been awake did you know?' Finnlach whispered.

'No,' replied Merason, 'How do you know?'

'The crystal has been removed from his head. Did either you or Amador do this?'

'Perhaps he has moved and it has just fallen off,' Merason suggested helpfully.

'Fallen onto the table by his bed?' Finnlach replied with a smile on his face. 'The boy is clearly just sleeping now.'

'That's wonderful news Finnlach. We didn't hear a thing,' Merason said more loudly than he meant to.

Amador stirred and wakened. Looking around he found both Merason and Finnlach beaming at him. 'What's happened?' he asked, coming fully awake instantly.

Merason replied, 'Finnlach said that the boy's been awake and placed the crystal on the table beside his bed. Come, let's have a look.'

All three returned to Orrison's bedside. It was clearly true. Orrison was asleep and the heat in him had subsided.

Feeling the weight of his responsibility lift a bit, Amador breathed a huge sigh of relief and was tempted to wake Orrison from his slumber, just to make sure he wasn't damaged in any way from his ordeal.

Resisting the temptation, he followed Finnlach instead, who was gesturing for all three to return to the adjoining room.

'Do you think I should try to wake him? You know to make sure that he is really alright?' Amador asked the two men standing before him.

'Let him sleep Amador,' Finnlach replied. 'It's the best thing for him. Really!' he emphasised the last word when he saw the concerned look on Amador's face.

‘I know you’re right Finnlach,’ Amador replied, ‘but I just want to make sure he hasn’t damaged anything inside his head with all that heat exposure for such a long time.’ He knew he sounded desperate, but he just couldn’t help it.

Merason broke into the conversation in a fatherly way, ‘Amador, we share your concerns, but Finnlach has said that sleep is the best thing for the boy now, so leave him to sleep. We’ll find out the rest soon enough. I mean, even if Orrison is damaged in some way there’s not a lot you or anyone else can do about it now, is there?’

Knowing that Merason was right didn’t help. Thinking wryly that this wasn’t the first time or likely the last that he would be right. So, he smiled and offered his hand to Finnlach, who took it. All three had a mini celebration of hope, right there in the front room of the Infirmary.

Eventually Finnlach said, ‘Why don’t both of you take yourselves out for a bit of fresh air? I’ll stay and watch the boy.’

Amador was clearly about to protest, so Finnlach interjected before he could, ‘Go out Amador. This is what I do. I’m good at watching over people who are ill. I’ll let you know as soon as he wakes again, if you’re not already back before then.’

Merason agreed with Finnlach, ‘Yes, come on Amador, I want you to meet my boys and I know that Cleon will be happy to see you again.’

Knowing he was fighting a losing battle, Amador gracefully accepted both Merason’s and Finnlach’s offer.

As he and Merason left, Finnlach pulled up a chair to watch Orrison’s regular breathing until he awakened.

Merason thanked Finnlach again and said, 'I'll send refreshments to you and one of the other healers, so you can get a message to us if you need to.'

On leaving the infirmary, Amador stopped to take in the view of the bay before him. The children at play in the water, the adjustment of the tide, which was now high, the rolling hills and cliffs that protected the bay on either side. He relished the sea breeze on his face and the fresh smell of the air. 'What a beautiful home you have here,' he said.

'Those children look like they are having fun,' he said pointing in the direction of the water. 'Your Taye will be amongst them no doubt?'

Merason replied, 'Yes, she's the one who bobs up every now and then for air. As I said before, I'm sure she was a baby seal in another life. Come and meet her Amador, she's wonderful, even if I do say so myself,' he continued enthusiastically, smiling broadly.

Amador joined his friend, matching his long purposeful strides to the foreshore.

On the way they passed the Smith, who assured him that the horses were Free once more and that they had left the bay earlier that morning.

They also stopped to chat to Rachel as she repaired and stacked the lobster creels. An important job as any, as the village's economy was largely dependent on their catch. Half of which they kept and the other half was traded for goods they needed, but couldn't either make or catch themselves.

Arriving at the foreshore, Merason called to Taye to join them.

Amador thought that she must be around eight or nine years old by now and watched the lovely young girl run out of the water, stopping only to jump the last wave, before joining them.

'Hello Papa,' she said.

'Hello Taye,' he replied, hunkering down onto one knee so that he could give his daughter a hug, regardless of the fact that she was dripping wet.

'Amador, I want you to meet Taye again. She is still the joy of my life,' he said cupping her chin and smiling. Do you remember my friend Taye?' he enquired.

'No Papa, I'm sorry', she replied.

Copying Merason, Amador also dropped to her height and said, 'Don't be sorry Taye, it's been a long time since I was here last and you were just a tot then. Now you have grown into a lovely young girl.'

'Oh Papa, your friend's just like you!' Taye exclaimed. 'I'm not young anymore. I'm big. I can swim all the way out there,' she said pointing towards a rock half way across the bay. 'I'll show you too.' And with that she ran off back towards the water.

Both men chuckled at her determination and obvious 'bigness'. Both watching her all the while as she bobbed up every now and again for air, as she swam mostly underwater, towards the rock.

'Oh Amador, she brings joy to my heart,' Merason said.

'I can see why, the little, 'big' seal!' he replied and they both laughed.

Amador spent a hugely enjoyable afternoon with Merason's family, reminiscing and catching up on all the news since they last met. Dinner was almost finished when news came that Orrison had reawakened. Excusing themselves, he and Merason left and returned to the infirmary in all haste. Amador pressed ahead with his friend following his lead.

Arriving at the infirmary again, Amador was relieved to find Orrison sitting up in bed sipping a glass of water. He was worried too though as the lad looked completely worn out. 'I came as soon as I heard you were awake Orrison, how do you feel?' he asked.

Flashing Amador what could on be described as a scathing look, Orrison said, 'Well met Amador. I'm wondering where I am and why you have brought me here. And, I would like to go home as soon as possible please.'

Making a show of looking for something, Orrison continued, 'I seem to have misplaced my obsidian and that doesn't bode well for my Clan.'

Amador could tell that Orrison was feeling way out of his depth. The lad was scared and probably rightly so. He silently admonished himself for being so easily persuaded to leave him. He knew that he really should have been there when Orrison woke up. It was bound to be very confusing for him on waking and finding himself in a strange place with strange people.

Amador's heart went out to this confused, fragile little lad, who sat accusing him for taking him from his home and all that he knew. 'First things first Orrison, well met Orrison, my apologies, and my apologies for not being here when you woke up.'

He didn't explain that he had no idea when that was likely to be, or the long, tiring journey that he had endured to bring the lad back to himself. Instinctively knowing that Orrison wasn't looking for excuses, only facts to help him make some sense of what had happened and what was happening to him. This was entirely natural though he thought.

He continued as Orrison fixed him with his piercingly blue eyes, 'On the matter of where you are, we are just over a week's horse ride from your home. It was very necessary to bring you here as you became very ill following the branding ceremony and your father said…'

Orrison interjected, 'I'm not very interested in what my father said Amador. Please tell me what Ayesha said.'

Taken aback by the vehemence in Orrison's voice at the mention of Viktor, Amador wondered what had happened to cause such a reaction. His clear memory was of a young lad going to great lengths to impress his father with the killing of the big cat and the obsidian he had recovered from the top of Mount Sepit Mhor.

Amador thought that he should try a different tact with Orrison, to try to reassure him that all was now well, or at least better than it had been. So, he moved to sit on his bed, which had the effect of bobbing both of them up and down for a few moments, until the water in the mattress resumed its equilibrium.

'Orrison, both your father and Ayesha wanted me to bring you here to try to help you. You have been very ill. A fire was raging through you and needed to be brought under control. Finnlach managed to do what no one else could and here we are amongst the Water Peoples, who are renowned for their healing abilities and who are also my friends. Your father said…'

Speaking over Amador again, Orrison said, 'I told you already Amador that I am no longer interested in what my father has to say or what he thinks or what he has done for that matter. I know some things about him now and I don't even want to think about him anymore, so try to avoid referring to him if you can. I would appreciate it greatly.'

Clearly Orrison is left with his full faculties Amador thought somewhat relieved, but he was becoming increasingly concerned by the way he was talking about his father.

He replied, 'As you wish Orrison for now, although we will talk on this matter further at a later time, when you are feeling more rested perhaps?'

Giving no indication whether he would or wouldn't talk on it further later, Orrison just stared back at Amador.

Knowing he had marked a card to return to this matter, Amador pressed on. 'Don't worry about your obsidian Orrison I have kept it very safe for you. I realise how important this is to both you and the Clan. It's in my room at Merason's house and I will bring it back to you tomorrow.'

He noted that Orrison's boyish features lit up at this news.

'Really, you have it Amador! I was so worried. I thought that I had really messed things up this time.'

Patting Orrison's arm, Amador was glad to see the youthful concern shine through. 'Don't worry Orrison, you've been through a lot more than you can ever know, but you're safe here now. Once you're feeling better, back to yourself again, of course I'll take you back home. Get some more rest meantime and I promise to bring your obsidian back to you tomorrow.'

Orrison was beginning to feel drowsy again. The conversation with Amador had left him feeling weak in more ways than one.

Perhaps he should have listened to hear what his father had said? No, he had heard Amador talking to the big man with the funny hair and beard. He knew he hadn't dreamt it because the man was there again standing in the corner of his room.

His father didn't want him to come home. He didn't want him in the first place, only needed him so that his own family was safe. Miele had warned him. He had known too! But he did love his father and still wanted to please him, even although he now knew that his father didn't care a jot for him.

What was so hard to bear was that he had truly believed that he could change his father's opinion of him. Show him how good he could be in all things and he would change his mind. He would be proud of his son after all, and everyone would know this and smile and nod to each other, wishing that they too could be part of this happiness and the respect that they shared.

Orrison almost sobbed his way into the pillow again, dark and warm thoughts vying for his consideration. Blissfully, sleep was not long in claiming him.

Watching over the lad for a few more moments, Amador was worried. He had briefly felt the fire mounting in Orrison, albeit nothing like before. Both times he had referred to his father. Turning away from the bed, Amador crossed the room to his friend thinking that the less said the better at the moment.

Merason could read the worry on Amador's face, but decided not to mention it. Instead he said, 'At least the boy's awake now Amador.' And then he couldn't help himself, 'Don't worry, the healing will come.'

After replacing the fire crystal on Orrison's forehead, Finnlach joined the others. 'I think the boy could use a little more help this night Amador,' he said keeping his own suspicions to himself.

Nodding in response, Amador said, 'Yes, thank you again Finnlach, you have helped Orrison so much and I really don't think there's any harm in giving him an extra dose of crystal healing. Just to be sure mind!'

Merason had asked two healers to keep watch over the boy overnight again. As far as he was concerned the boy was still on the critical list and needed to be watched to make sure he slept through the night. Instructions were left that should there be any change in his condition to wake Amador and so all three retired to their own beds. It had been a very long day.

Next morning, Amador woke early, collected Orrison's obsidian and headed for the infirmary. He had complied with Merason's request the previous day to secure the Liferod in a special box which was in his room and he couldn't resist opening the lid to make sure that it was still there and intact before leaving.

Marvelling once more at the artefact, he considered its origins and purpose once more, searching his brain for a trace of uncovered knowledge. Perhaps from something he had read before, but there was nothing.

Greeting Rachel as he made his way past the small harbour on his way to the infirmary, 'It's a fine morning Rachel, good luck with your catch today,' he continued his short journey.

Rachel called back her thanks and he marched on. At the top of the embankment, he entered the infirmary to find Orrison already awake. He was lying listlessly in his bed and Amador noted that the crystal was once more placed on the table by his bed. 'Good morning Orrison, how are you today? Did you sleep well?'

'Yes, thank you Amador. Did you bring it, my obsidian I mean?' he said hopefully.

'Course I did!' Amador replied, holding out the black shining stone to Orrison for him to take.

'Great, thanks,' Orrison said taking back the obsidian from Amador. 'I thought it was lost or that someone had stolen it when I first woke up yesterday. It was in the pouch in my skins. I don't suppose you still have those?' he enquired hopefully.

'I'm afraid not Orrison. They were thoroughly ruined on the journey. I did my best to keep you cool, but you just poured sweat and then you burned them a bit.'

Surprised by this news, he said, 'Burned them a bit. How could I do that if I was unconscious Amador?'

'I'm sure I don't know Orrison. Like I said yesterday, there was a fire raging through you. It was so hot at times, things just got burned. I'm not sure you realise just how bad things were for you Orrison,' he offered.

Considering this news, Orrison managed to reply through his shock, 'Obviously not Amador. I was hoping for my skins though. Ayesha made them for me and she'll be so mad with me. She really hates sewing you know,' he said absently as he held up his obsidian and examined it from all angles.

Amador watched him intently, until he looked up and for the first time since wakening, smiled at him. The smile transformed Orrison's face from sullen little lad to a happy handsome one in an instant he noticed.

'I know what I will fashion Amador. It will be so good. Perfect in fact,' Orrison said with both enthusiasm and conviction. 'Do you have a knife I can use?'

Amador didn't have a knife and promised to bring one later, but later wasn't soon enough for Orrison, so he found himself hurrying back down to Merason's house to get the knife that would keep the lad happy. Thinking all the while that he really did like Orrison when he was happy, and he returned to the infirmary as quickly as he could, with the smallest, sharpest knife he could find amongst Cleon's utensils. He did hope it wasn't one of her favourites.

Hoping that Orrison would find renewed motivation and purpose, Amador wasn't disappointed on his return.

He asked, 'What will you carve Orrison?' in the knowledge that this process was a kind of sacred ritual to the Clans. What Orrison made would eventually become the Clans emblem, and if it were a strong carving, then so too would the Clan be strong.

'I'm going to carve a tooth Amador. Not just any tooth though, a big cat tooth. It will make our Clan strong Amador, if I can shape it just right,' he replied.

Smiling at the concentration on Orrison's face as he chipped away at the black stone, Amador decided to leave him to his work. In fact, Orrison was so engrossed in his work; he thought that the lad didn't even notice him leave.

For the next few days Orrison's whole focus was on his carving of the obsidian. Each time that he would visit the infirmary, Orrison told him in great detail about every chip he had made, and what he still had to do. He was impressed at the lad's dedication, but he still wanted to try to coax him out of bed, so he offered to go for a walk with him outside.

However, the furthest that Orrison was prepared to go was into the adjoining room, where he would sit in the window seat to work.

Amador was pleased to note that Orrison did look up from his carving from time to time to watch the other children at play in the water.

Orrison was however, focussed on his man's work, not child play and Amador's heart reached out to him once again.

He did try to suggest that he join the other children, if only for a little while, but Orrison just said that he couldn't swim and that he was far too busy just now anyway.

Orrison really wanted to finish the carving before he went home. He would show Viktor. He had stopped himself thinking of his father as father. He could just about cope with Viktor, but he realised that he also still wanted to please him more than anything, to make him proud of his son.

Wait till Viktor sees my carving, he will be so proud, he just has to be, and he worked on.

Journal of the Living

Seems we are to march to our new home. The big man has said that we must and so we must. I remind myself once more that I'm a survivor. I did not end up on the mountain of the dead.

The big man didn't eat. I didn't see him eat, but when we left he waddled. He was definitely bigger than when he arrived. How can anyone be so big with so little food!

I will watch. After all, I'm a survivor.

Did I tell you? I found my friend stub. Right there in the muddy footprint the big man left. I'm so very happy to have my friend back.

The big man tried to stub the life out of stub. Boom boom! I really don't like the big man.

An extract from a survivor's journal of unknown origin but marked by Air.

CHAPTER THIRTEEN

SWIM

Time was dwindling as Amador settled back into the slow easy pace of life amongst the Water Peoples. However, eventually he couldn't bear Orrison's lack of progress anymore. 'Orrison, you haven't been outside now for more than a week! Do you plan to stay in this infirmary forever? You need to get some air. You are weak and will need to build up your strength again before I take you home to your family.'

That did it.

Strength, yes, he would build up his strength and he would have his carving finished. That ought to do it Orrison thought.

So, he walked with Amador, first along the cliffs to the harbour, where all manner of new sights met his young eyes. Then, down the grassy embankment to the foreshore, where he could watch the other children play and listen to their squeals of delight as each new wave brought an opportunity to ride it, to splash through it or jump over it. It seemed that there was no end to what you could do with a wave.

Orrison finally admitted to Amador that it did look like fun and eventually Cleon brought him a present of swimming shorts.

'I have seen you watching the children at play in the water Orrison,' she said, 'and thought you might like to join them, or to try it out, so I've brought these shorts for you to wear. I made them for you; I think I've judged your size about right. Anyway, they tie at the waist, so you shouldn't lose them in the waves.'

She left laughing at the look Orrison gave her when he said he wouldn't be needing shorts for swimming as they didn't wear them where he came from. Cleon told him that a lobster might reach out and pincer his private parts in that case.

Orrison didn't know exactly what a lobster was, but he didn't like the look of the pincer movement Cleon made with her hand. He had seen some strange creatures at the harbour with hard shells and big claws. No, he didn't like the thought of that at all and resolved again to stay safely on dry land.

He also thought that he would look silly in the shorts that Cleon had made for him to wear. They looked like undergarments. He didn't understand though why they all covered themselves up all of the time. It was a wholly confusing experience.

Orrison kept the shorts, but made no move to wear them. He was undone though when finally, Taye came over and with big earnest brown eyes said, 'Don't be scared Orrison, I'll help you, honest I will.'

'I can't swim,' he replied.

'That's alright; I can swim really good, all the way out to that rock and back. Do you want to see?' she invited.

He replied, 'Yeah I've seen you. You're good, but you go under the water an awful lot, how do you know where you're going?'

'It's easy peezy,' she replied, 'you just open your eyes.'

'What under the water?' he asked, not hiding his disbelief.

'You don't believe me,' Taye said. 'I'll prove it to you if you come in. Or maybe you're too scared?'

Orrison now faced a dilemma he knew. If he didn't go in this girl would know that he was a bit frightened, and if he did, well he didn't like the look of the big waves. He couldn't swim and he might just drown.

And he was going to look stupid in those stupid swimming shorts! But he just couldn't ignore the challenge from Taye, so he said, 'All right, I'll get changed and then you can prove it. I might even be a better swimmer than you!'

He huffed off to get changed and returned as quickly as he could, before fear got the better of him.

It was a bit too much though, he thought, when he came back and the adults laughed and clapped on his return. Taye came to hold his hand to go into the water for goodness sake!

The earth beneath his feet was soft and grainy and he noticed that his toes and feet made prints in it. The water was very cold and as he went deeper, up to his knees, he began to stand on small stones that made it difficult for him to keep his balance. So, he walked on tip toes to try to keep going, now welcoming Taye's hand, he flung his other arm out to try to keep his balance, as he inched his way towards the waves.

A wave caught him unawares. It seemed to come from nowhere, rose up and firmly splashed him all the way up to his tummy, stealing his breath away. 'Oohhhh!' he shouted, and beside him Taye squealed and laughed, so he laughed too, but still held on tight to her hand.

When he was in the water up to his waist, some of the other children joined them. They were all ducking and diving and splashing. He wasn't sure that he liked the splashing much and began to feel anxious.

Someone showed him how to float on top of the water. He told him that he had a lot of air in him, so he wouldn't go under. Holding his breath, he tried it, quickly went under the water and immediately panicked. He thought he would drown for sure, but no, he found his feet again and came out of the water coughing and spluttering.

The other children were laughing at him now. How dare they he thought. He felt foolish alright and wished he had never come into the water.

Then Taye was shouting at them to stop being horrid. 'We're supposed to help people, not make them feel bad,' she shouted. 'Come on Orrison, we'll go over there where there are no waves and I'll show you how to swim.'

Turning to the others she continued, 'And then you'll be better than all of them put together, just wait and see. Come on now,' she said taking his hand again, 'it's just over here.'

One of the bigger boys watched him closely as he followed Taye. He hadn't laughed at him, but he did look at him strangely, Orrison thought. He was the one Taye called

Finn he recalled, and he decided that he would have to watch out for him, for no particular reason.

Over the next few days he felt more confident in the water thanks to Taye's help. She was small sure enough, and she was a girl, but he couldn't help but like her.

Taye showed him that he could trust her, and she didn't laugh at him, only with him and they became fast friends. Inseparable really over a very short time in the way of children.

Feeling very happy, he thought that it was probably the first time in his whole young life where he could just play and be the child that he really was with other children who liked him, even although they didn't know that he was Viktor's son.

Growing stronger every day, Orrison enjoyed his time in the fresh air, the exercise in the sea and new tasty foods, all of which he knew meant that he was rushing towards recovery.

One morning as he sat on the grassy embankment engrossed in his carving, Taye and Finn came over to join him and discover what he was doing.

'What are you making Orrison?' Taye asked.

Deciding to relay his story, he told them of the hunt for the big cat and of his journey into Mount Sepit Mhor for the obsidian. Also, that he was now carving a tooth for his Clan's protection.

'Wow,' Taye exclaimed.

'Amazing!' Finn conceded.

He felt himself fill with pride at their obvious admiration.

Just at that Amador and Merason passed on their walk along the foreshore and Taye called out, 'Papa, Papa. Come and see Orrison's tooth. He killed a big cat and now he's copying the tooth in the stone, see?'

Walking over to where the three sat cementing their friendship, Amador and Merason wanted to see the progress he had made with his carving.

'I see you're nearly finished you're carving Orrison,' Amador commented, 'It's very impressive and very true to life.'

Orrison replied, 'Thank you Amador, I've worked hard to make it as real as possible, although it's black and a real big cat's tooth is yellow.'

'Yes, yes, but the likeness is still there.' Looking at the vibrant lad who sat before him with his carving, Amador decided that it was about time that he took him home to his family, so he said, 'You look much better Orrison, I will be able to take you back home to your Clan soon I think. Another couple of days and then we must leave this wonderful place. I'm sure that you will treasure the memories as much as I do though.'

Orrison felt like he had been hit in the face by a big cold wave. The words Amador spoke took his breath away and he realised that he was in no hurry to return to his responsibilities. He missed Ayesha for sure, but the rest of it left him feeling numb.

'Of course, Amador, whatever you think,' he replied covering the gut wrenching feeling in his stomach at the thought.

Merason saved the day by saying, 'As you're undoubtedly such a good hunter Orrison, why don't you try fishing with Taye?' Turning to his clearly excited daughter at his suggestion he continued, 'You can take the small creel Taye, but be careful.'

Taye squealed with delight, 'Oh Papa, can we?' and immediately turning to Orrison she said, 'Fishing is such good fun, you'll love it. It'll be great, a real treat. Oh, thank you Papa, thank you!'

Caught up as usual in Taye's enthusiasm, he thought that fishing must be good if this was her reaction and he wanted to go immediately.

'I'll come too,' said Finn butting into their happiness.

'Of course, you will Finn,' said Merason. 'You'll be in charge.'

Orrison thought that he didn't really want Finn to go at all. He was always hanging around Taye, taking her attention away. However, fishing sounded good and he had made up his mind that he was going whether Finn was or not. He only had a few days left here it would seem.

The three raced each other to the harbour and Orrison clearly would have won had he known exactly where they were racing to. In the end, Finn was the first to jump into the creel and take up the oars, he and Taye following him in. The boat rocked as he climbed in and he sat down quick on the nearest bench which happened to be at the prow of the little creel.

Finn rowed out of the harbour and into the bay towards the big rock that they all liked to swim to from the shore and they began to fish.

One hour passed by with no bite on the rod that he dangled into the water. Nothing was biting for Taye or Finn either. 'Is this what you wet landers call hunting? It's very boring,' he said.

'No, it's really good Orrison,' Taye admonished. 'Wait till you get a bite, I'll bet it's just as exciting as killing a big cat.'

He had been brooding for the last hour about having to leave this place and return home. He was beginning to feel mischievous. He said, 'I really don't think so Taye. The big cat killed our Huntsmaster, raked him with its big claws so that his stomach spilled out.'

As he said this he reached out with his hand mimicking the big cat and snarled.

Taye was clearly frightened.

Losing his inhibition of the boat, in an effort to really scare her for fun, Orrison stood up and lunged towards her, his face contorted into a grimace as he growled low in his throat.

Before he could take a step further towards Taye, Finn jumped up and said, 'Stop it Orrison, you're scaring her.'

Ignoring Finn, he tried to go around him, but Finn pushed him and shouted, 'I said stop it, you're scaring Taye.'

Caught off balance, Orrison fell backwards and the momentum of the push carried him right out of the boat and into the waiting water.

Immediately panicking, as although he could swim now, he still wasn't too confident and the weight of his clothes were dragging him down. The tide was coming in and the waves were smashing and eddying against the nearby rock. He flayed and gasped for air.

Noticing Taye's outstretched hand, he grasped for it, and then fear mixed with anger exploded through him from his head to his toes. Wait till he got hold of that Finn. He would be sorry.

Stretching to reach Taye, he caught hold of her wrist and it was then the fire came. It started in his stomach and lashed through his limbs uncontrollably. He could hear Taye scream as he burned her, but he just couldn't help it. Letting her hand go, he grasped onto the side of the boat, but the fire kept coming, pulsing through him and ignited the boat itself.

Finn half pushed half threw Taye clear of the boat and then followed her with a dive. Catching her into his arms he swam with her back to the shore, all the while holding her burned wrist and pouring all of his care for her into a healing mantra that he ran through his head on every kick, 'Please let her be alright, please let her be alright, please let her be alright, please let her be alright.'

On reaching the shore, both Merason and Cleon had wadded into the water to meet them. Taye was still crying, 'Papa, Mama, Papa,' she sobbed, 'Orrison burned me, it was very sore, Mama, look,' and she held out her arm, but there wasn't a mark on it.

'Taye, I know something bad happened out there, but I won't stand for lies,' Merason exclaimed in the heat of the moment. 'Please take yourself home and go to your room.'

Gulping back her tears as she hated getting into trouble of any sort, especially with her Papa, Taye was very confused. She had felt the pain and she knew that she wasn't lying so she turned to Finn and beseechingly said, 'Finn?'

Finn only shook his head in response. He had nothing to say at that moment. Nothing he could say. He had seen the burn on Taye's wrist with his own two eyes and now it had gone. Had he made that happen with his mantra? He felt sure that this was just not possible, but he had so wanted her to be alright. He wanted to protect her from any harm, but he had no idea just how much until this moment.

Splashing his way to the shore, Orrison was greeted by Amador who waited to see if he was alright. Coming out of the water completely he shook himself to get rid of the worst of the water and then ran right past Amador, up the grassy embankment, and on towards the cliffs. Trying to chase away the mixed emotions that still coursed through him.

Feeling both scared and upset now. He was glad that the anger had died down and with it the fire. Out there in the water, a boat, albeit a small boat, had disintegrated in his burning hands. And yet there was no mark on him. No sign of a burn anywhere on his person, he had checked. What was happening to him? It just didn't make any sense at all.

Truly concerned now, Amador realised that he had lulled himself into thinking that the lad was cured. Better even! That he could take Orrison back to Ayesha hale and well as he had promised. And now this! It really beggared belief.

Eventually he caught up with Orrison who was sitting on a large rock overlooking the bay, staring out over the water where a small creel had been wrecked. A few small parts of the boat still floated upon the water, providing the evidence, if any were needed, that there had indeed been a boat bobbing there not so long ago.

Sitting down beside Orrison, he asked gently, 'What happened out there Orrison?'

Looking at Amador directly in the eye, he replied, 'I don't know what happened. We were fishing one minute and then Finn pushed me into the water. I was scared and angry and fighting for breath, trying to get back into the boat. Then the fire came and here we are, you know the rest.'

Orrison was so precise and matter of fact in his response that Amador was taken aback slightly. He had thought that the lad was sure to be upset, unsure, and remorseful even, but he showed no sign of being any of these. It had happened; he didn't appear to know why and didn't appear to be too bothered in any event.

Silence descended between them for a while, with Orrison once more looking out over the water.

Breaking the silence eventually, Amador said, 'Orrison, I was wondering if you have been using the crystal in the way that Finnlach suggested?' It was the only possible explanation that he could think of for the fire's return.

Orrison replied scornfully, 'Of course I have Amador, but it's not doing me much good is it? I seem to have turned into some kind of freak!'

'You're no freak Orrison, but the fire in you is strange. I'm sure we will think of some way to bring it under control though. You know, I really thought that you would be going home soon, but now,' he left the words unspoken, hanging in the space between them.

'But, I want to go home soon Amador, right now in fact. Will you take me or do I have to find my own way home?' he challenged, knowing full well the response that he would get, even before it came.

'I can't just yet Orrison, I'm sorry,' Amador replied. 'You know that something has happened to you since the branding ceremony. Your father,' he corrected what he was saying quickly seeing the dark look descending onto Orrison's face at the mention of his father. 'Viktor has asked me to bring you home when you are cured. We're not quite there yet, although from where I'm sitting things look a lot brighter than they did.'

'I know why he doesn't want me home Amador,' Orrison replied heatedly. 'You said it yourself and I heard every word. It's because I'm different to the girls. He took another woman and he got me! That's why he can't look me in the eye. Do you know what it feels like when your own father's eyes slide over and away from you every time you just want him to see you?

Anyway, that's why he doesn't see me or anything I do! I've tried and tried all my life to please that man, always thinking that I was doing the wrong thing. Nothing I do pleases him. Nothing! And all along it's really him that's done the wrong thing.'

Amador noted that Orrison was becoming increasingly agitated, but it was all he could do to contain his own feelings. The lad had said he had heard him talking about his father. What had he heard, and when? Wracking his brains, Amador could find no answer.

Ranting on, Orrison continued, 'He hates me. Doesn't want me! Even Miele told me with his last breath. He knew! My father,' Orrison said scathingly, 'My father is a liar and a cheat. All he wants me for is to be his ticket to security, so he can stay as Clan Leader.'

The heat was building in intensity now in Orrison's eyes. Amador could feel it radiating from him. Pulling the lad towards him, Amador held him like a babe in arms, while release came in the way of tears for Orrison.

He's just a lad, Amador thought to himself, how can he be expected to deal with these huge changes going on inside him, as well as cope with speculation about his father's feelings towards him? He knew that Orrison was bound to be affected by either one of these things, but having to deal with both at the same time, and in strange surroundings, must be very hard to take.

He held on tight to Orrison, until all of his tears were spent.

Eventually Orrison pulled away and Amador said, 'I know this must be very hard for you to understand Orrison,

I confess that I have never seen anything quite like what is happening to you before, but I would still like to help you if I can.'

Orrison didn't respond as he was busy re building the shield around himself that would protect him from further hurt.

'Orrison, I don't know what you heard me say, or when you heard me say it,' Amador said, 'but I did make a promise to Viktor that I would try to help you. To find a cure for your condition, before I take you home.'

Muttering in response, Orrison said, 'It was in the infirmary. I woke up and heard you talking to Merson. It doesn't matter now,' he finished flatly.

Feeling like he had been punched in the stomach, Amador recalled the frank conversation he had had with Merson only a few weeks ago.

Now feeling the need to explain, he said, 'Orrison, what I said to Merson was only speculation on my part. I don't know for sure what has happened to you. What I do know though is that your father is bound to be concerned for both you and your sisters.'

'Whatever you say Amador, but if you ask me he is most concerned about himself. How could he do what he has done? There are other ways that he could have protected the girls. He could have let another care for them and openly taken another woman to have a son with. Instead, he chose deceit, and look what's happened as a result. A freak that sets things on fire! I wish that I had never been born Amador.'

'Be careful what you wish for Orrison. Everyone is born for a reason,' Amador replied quickly. 'We just don't know what that reason is until we reach the end of our journey here, so don't be so quick to wish away your purpose. We don't know why you are experiencing what you are yet. If you listened to me that day in the infirmary, you must know that we were also talking about the Liferod.'

Seeing the confusion and uncertainty in Orrison at the mention of the Liferod, he guessed that Orrison hadn't hung around to hear the whole of the conversation.

'I don't know anything about the Liferod Amador,' he replied, 'but I do know that you were right about Viktor. Miele told me to be strong when I find out who my real mother is as he lay dying. I didn't know what he meant then, but I think I do now.'

The defeat in Orrison's voice was palpable.

Amador thought that one so young should not be having to face up to the troubles of adults that he was clearly having to try to understand, so he tried to motivate him in the only way he could think of. 'Come Orrison. There are good people here who can help you. We can't do anything to change the past, but we can sure try to help you now. We need to think to the future Orrison. What's done is done! Let's try to find you a cure so that you can go home. I know that Ayesha would want that for one.'

The two climbed down from the cliff together and walked, each locked in their own thoughts, back towards the infirmary.

Breaking the easy silence only once, Amador said, 'Orrison, I don't know what Merason will have to say, but boats are precious to these people. The loss of one will be hard for them.'

Orrison didn't reply.

Right enough, as day broke, Orrison wakened to the realisation that he would not be swimming or fishing that day. Merason informed him personally that the boat was indeed important and that he would now be expected to work to repay the damage that he had caused.

He was given two main chores, the first of which was to attend to Rachel each morning to help with net and creel repairs.

This took up most of his morning as his fingers learned new skills. He moved the shuttle back and forth to mend the nets. After he had learned the technique, his hands used the small black shuttle to form the patterns that Rachel had shown him. His fingers were sore from running them over the tight mesh of the creels and he had picked up a couple of splinters from the wood for his troubles too.

At the end of the morning Merson arrived with Finnbarr to check on his progress. Taye was nowhere in sight, Orrison noted. He straightened up to his full height as Merason addressed him.

'Hello Orrison, how has your morning gone?'

'Alright, I guess,' he replied glancing towards Rachel seeking her agreement or otherwise.

Rachel didn't offer any insight to her thoughts. She was a quiet woman and was still fully focussed on her work. Not much recognition there then for his efforts he noted.

Merason didn't seem to be very concerned about the lack of response from Rachel though.

Finnbarr hung by Merson's side looking rather uncomfortable and Orrison noted that he seemed to be having some difficulty looking him in the eye.

'You can report back to Rachel tomorrow morning Orrison,' Merason said, 'but for now I want Finn to show you where you will be working for the afternoon. We have a freshwater well where we collect water for cooking and drinking for the village. It needs to be both collected and delivered. Finn has offered to help you by doing the deliveries, but you will need to draw the water yourself. Do you think you can manage that?' he asked.

'I guess so,' Orrison replied, wondering why Finn had offered to help him, as he clearly hadn't set the boat on fire.

Setting off to the freshwater well together, it became clear to Orrison fairly quickly just why Finn was there when he said, 'I shouldn't have pushed you Orrison, I'm sorry about that. But you were scaring Taye and I didn't like that. Anyway, she's not allowed to come out, so I might as well help you.'

'Is Taye alright?' Orrison asked. 'I really didn't mean to hurt her and her Papa seems to be more concerned about a boat than he is about her. I just don't get it?'

'You didn't hurt her,' Finn replied, 'but she can't come out anyway.'

Orrison stopped walking and stared at Finn, 'What do you mean I didn't hurt her? I remember burning her arm.'

Finn continued to walk along the foreshore and Orrison had to strain to hear the words he spoke.

'She's not burned.'

Thinking he must have heard funny, Orrison ran to catch up with Finn. He decided not to pursue it though. If Finn wanted to play at being the guilty responsible person then let him, he couldn't care less.

Finn always wanted the attention anyway, Orrison thought. And yes, he had started it by pushing him into the water. Although he would rather die than be seen to blame someone else for his own actions.

Deciding that he didn't think any more of Finn for his supposed help, he followed him in silence to the well.

Arriving at the water well, Finn explained the task ahead. He had to draw the water by dropping a bucket down deep into the well, let it fill and then use the rope to pull it back up again.

It wasn't easy. His fingers were already sore from the work on the creels that morning, but he wouldn't show this to Finn. There was a stack of containers of all shapes and sizes that needed to be filled and it took at least five buckets to fill the smallest of these. Groaning inwardly, Orrison buckled down to his task.

'Why can't you just take the water from the sea Finn, wouldn't it be a whole lot easier filling these containers in there?' he asked.

'It's not fresh water Orrison,' Finn replied. 'It's full of salt and we can't drink that! You sure don't think straight, even if you are a big cat killer. This is our only freshwater supply, so we have to do this each day.'

The jibe from Finn didn't miss its mark and Orrison wished he hadn't asked the question as Finn had the chance to make him feel foolish. He didn't say anything else and as Finn left with the first water carrier, he was glad to see the back of him. Thinking that really, he would have preferred to do Finn's part of the task.

Over the next few hours, Orrison dropped and hauled the bucket to fill the water carriers, that Finn then rolled away to deliver to the village. His hands felt sore and were blistering from the friction caused by the rope that was tethered to the bucket. It had slipped through his fingers on more than one occasion.

Beginning to feel the results of the day's work, he once again strained to pull the bucket back up out of the well, thinking all the while that there must be a better way to do this.

He recalled the pulley system used to winch Miele and others to the top of their pyre and he thought he could copy the technique to aid his own work here at the well. After all, he was going to have to do this chore for the rest of the week.

Scouting around, he found a long stick that would stretch across the mouth of the well. Trying to recall the knot that was used, Orrison had to try several variations before he was satisfied that it would work. But this all took time.

When Finn returned for the next carrier, there was nothing in it. But, Orrison reassured him that his new way of getting the water would speed things up.

Sure enough, it was easier for him to roll the stick up and down and Finn grudgingly admitted that the carrier was filled more quickly.

Finn rolled it away when it was ready.

Getting into his stride, Orrison filled three more carriers before Finn returned. Feeling rather proud of himself, he noted the look of surprise and admiration that crossed Finn's features. Then the acknowledgement dawning on him that he would have to move faster himself if he were to keep up with the new production line.

As Finn rolled the next water carrier away, Orrison smiled inwardly.

A few more carriers to fill and then I'll be done for the day, he thought. Settling back into his task. However, he immediately encountered a problem.

The rolling of the stick had shredded the rope in a weak spot and the bucket now dangled precariously, losing some of its precious cargo. Horrified, he watched helplessly, unable to reach the bucket in time to save it from plunging down the well into the darkness.

Orrison tried to grasp for the rope that snaked over the stick, but it was at the centre of the well and by the time he had realised what was happening, he was just too late. Fingers tantalisingly brushing against the frayed ends of the rope, like a promise missed.

Hearing the conclusion as the bucket splashed as it hit the water below, he was annoyed. I'll have to climb down the well to get it he thought, peering down into the dark depths below.

However, he spotted some footholds that descended and without a further thought, he levered himself over the small wall that he had until very recently, rolled the stick across.

Finding the first foothold, Orrison lowered himself and began the journey down the well, wondering if he could get down, retrieve the bucket and get back up to the top before Finn returned?

He thought wryly that he had left the evidence of his failure, with the remains of the rope still wrapped around the stick that now lay discarded at the side of the well.

So much for his great idea, he was going to feel foolish again, even although he knew that his idea had been a good one. He now wished that he had taken the time to check the rope before he had started.

Descending quickly and smoothly, he used his natural ability to manoeuvre himself in the darkness. This well is deeper than I thought, but the footholds and handholds are well placed and fairly secure, he found. The smooth structure of the walls reminded Orrison of the smooth walls of the infirmary and the houses in the village. He thought the only difference was that it wasn't painted white. A bit the painter missed, he chuckled to himself. He would have to report it to Merason!

Around the halfway point, Orrison was drawn to a chink of light in the darkness. It was weird he thought, it seemed to come from a way off, and then he was able to discern the opening of a tunnel on the opposite side of the well. If he hadn't been trying to see how far it was to the bottom at that moment, he would have missed it completely.

Sure enough, hand and footholds enabled him to move around the circumference of the well and gain access to what he could only describe as a tunnel, with a small amount of light coming from some way along it.

The tunnel wasn't as smooth as the wall of the well, but seemed fairly secure, as he ran his hands across the top of the tunnel to check. He certainly wouldn't want to get trapped down here.

He knew he could easily crawl on all fours along the tunnel, so he did. Curiosity as always getting the better of him. He wondered what he would find.

As he neared the end he began to hear the murmur of low voices and so he proceeded more carefully. Now entirely caught up in his investigation, all thought of his chores and the bucket forgotten in the moment.

Peering towards the light, Orrison found that he couldn't see anything too well, so adjusting his position, he looked out onto water. This was a bit confusing as he was now able to make out the voice of Merason. He just couldn't see him, and then quietly almost out of nowhere it seemed, a big man came into his view.

At first Orrison thought that the man walked right upon the water, but then he noticed that he skirted what could only be described as a pool. The big man looked up and gestured for him to come down.

Orrison felt his mouth go dry at being caught and was about to comply when another figure, very close, stood up and walked towards the big man who was now placing a towel on a slab of stone.

Relief washed over him. He hadn't been discovered after all. And then it dawned on him that he must be looking into the bathhouse, that all the men liked to visit, but where children weren't welcome.

He realised too that Merason must be sitting just below him.

As if on cue Merason started talking again, only louder this time so that his voice reached the man he called Finnlach, who now lay upon the slab while the big man rubbed and chopped at his back.

This was very curious Orrison thought, a small bubble of excitement growing at his discovery.

Merason's voice called out to Finnlach from somewhere just below him.

'You know Finnlach, I just don't understand Taye. She insists that she was burned by the boy, but I've checked her all over and there's not a mark on her. I'm at a loss as she's never been one for making up stories. I'm afraid that the boy has influenced her in all the wrong ways.'

Finnlach grunted in response as his back was being pummelled by the big man.

Fascinated now, Orrison decided that he wasn't going anywhere until he heard some more. They were speaking about him after all he justified.

He wasn't disappointed.

Merason continued, 'You know, I've been wondering about Finn's part in all of this. He's offered to help the boy. Seems he's feeling a bit responsible. Taye said that Finn pushed him over the side of the boat and that's why the boy panicked. It's just not like Finn to do something like that either, is it?'

Indicating to the big man to stop what he was doing, Finnlach said, 'Thanks Walker, a minute if you please. Finn told me that the boy was scaring Taye and that's why he pushed him. He said that he didn't mean for him to fall out, just to get him to stop talking about blood and guts. I reckon that he was trying to protect Taye by his actions Merason.'

'I think you might be right at that Finnlach,' Merason replied. 'This is going to sound crazy, but do you think he wanted to protect her so much that he healed her?'

Drawing in a deep breath, Finnlach hung his head. Running his fingers through his wet hair, he shrugged, 'That's a massive jump you're making to a very strange conclusion Merason. I know you don't want to think of Taye telling untruths for sure, but just because Finn has healing hands doesn't mean that he can cure something like a burn just like that. Or at least, I've never seen any indication that he could do something like that, or anything like it for that matter. What I do know is that he really does care about Taye. They will make a good couple one day.'

Merason agreed in the affirmative. A conversation that had obviously often been shared between the two, so familiar were they.

Before he could help himself, Orrison blurted out, 'No!' He immediately had a strange feeling inside when he thought of Taye and Finn together. Being a couple! It just wasn't right.

The big man they called Walker's eye's alighted on his hiding place. There was no mistaking where he looked now and Orrison retreated back up the tunnel as quickly as he could. Back towards the security of the darkness.

The man may not be able to speak, he had heard the stories from the other children, but there was obviously nothing wrong with his hearing.

Scrambling back up the tunnel, he approached the well and feet first, found the foothold. He traversed the inside of the well just in time to hear Finn call down.

'Are you down there Orrison?'

'Yes,' he replied, heart hammering in his chest. He tried to sound nonchalant as he continued, 'The rope snapped. Stupid really, won't be long,' and he climbed down the remaining footholds, retrieved the bucket and returned to the surface as quickly as he could.

'Are you alright Orrison?' Finn asked as he clamoured over the wall that defined the well.

'I guess,' he shrugged. 'The rope snapped and I had to climb down the well. It's deeper than I thought.'

Finn looked at the two remaining water carriers that needed to be filled, and there were still two to be delivered. 'Alright Orrison, you try to fix the rope and I'll deliver these two. I'll help you to fill the last two and we can still get the job done.

As he started to roll one of the water carriers, Finn said, 'I was about to go for help Orrison. I thought you had fallen down and hurt yourself or something. I called a couple of times before you answered.'

'Sorry Finn, I didn't mean to worry you. It's just some of the footholds are a bit tricky and I had to concentrate.' Seeing that his hurried explanation seemed to satisfy Finn, he felt relieved.

Finn really was a good help, but what he had heard changed everything between them. Not that we were great friends in the first place, he thought wryly.

What he had heard made him realise just how much he did like Taye though. For a girl she was good fun and easy to be around. She somehow managed to make him feel special and she never gave up on him, even when he couldn't let the air out of his lungs to swim underwater.

Completing his chores for the day he managed to thank Finn for his help. What was it about him anyway that so irked, Orrison wondered? He thought he knew though… Finn just seems to do everything right all of the time!

Putting Finn to the back of his mind, he walked back from the freshwater well towards the infirmary. The day's chores had not dented his spirits or his energy, being used to the like at home. Dusk was descending as he walked back along the foreshore towards the infirmary and the sand he walked upon tickled his toes as he left his mark in it, like sealed memories struggling to surface.

Wondering how things were going at home didn't help though and he realised that he was feeling very lonely. So, he found his obsidian and chipped away at his big cat tooth.

The next few days pretty much followed the same pattern. To the harbour with Rachel in the morning and to the well to collect the water in the afternoon. Having secured some good rope from Rachel, his technique of pulling the bucket up with the stick and rope taking all of the weight, meant that his chores were completed in half the time they would have taken. His invention was a good one.

Merason and Amador had dropped by on hearing of his invention and Merason was most impressed.

Somewhat cheekily, he asked Merason when Taye would be able to come out again.

Merason had left giving no commitment, but the very next day she was back, laughing and chatting as if nothing had happened. Feeling relieved at this, Orrison decided that he liked her even more. Some girls would whine and moan, but not Taye, she was almost like a boy.

Each night he would work on his talisman and it was nearing completion. Perhaps when I finish this I can go home? After all, I seem to be fine now he imagined.

He collected all of the pieces that he had chipped away from the obsidian. What a waste, he thought. There were a few larger pieces and he rolled them in his hand thinking about what he could make with them, then he had an idea.

Always passionate when he knew what he wanted to do, he began right away.

It's just not working the way that I want it to, he thought. Beginning to feel frustrated about his inability to work the small chips, he gathered them all together in his hand and squeezed.

It's just not working, why can't I do anything right anymore? I hate it here! I just want to go home.

Becoming more and more agitated, he felt the fire begin to build in his belly. No. not that again!

He was panicking now he knew, but couldn't help himself, so he took deep breaths, to try and calm himself. Go away, go away please, he thought. I want to go home and if this happens again, Amador will never take me home.

Looking around frantically, trying to assess the damage he might cause, he decided that it would be better if he went outside.

Unclenching his fist to leave the obsidian pieces, he realised he couldn't as they were melting and sticking to his fingers.

The obsidian was now pliable and using his other hand he rolled the pieces into a ball, detached three quarters of which he proceeded to fashion into a petal shape with his thumb.

Now totally consumed in working the obsidian, it wasn't until it began to reset in its new shape that he realised that the fire had left his belly.

He inserted the point of the knife into the obsidian making a small round hole in the top the flower petal that would allow a leather thong to pass through. It would make a lovely necklace for Taye, he thought. Already excited to know what her reaction would be when he gave it to her.

You know, this fire thing might be alright if I could just learn to control it, he mused.

The very next day he went in search of Taye, even before he reported to Rachel for his morning chores.

Feeling happier than he had in a long while, he thought that what had happened last night was almost as good as getting the big cat skin for his seat at the animal dance. Almost, but not quite, I don't think that anything can ever top that, he reminded himself.

It had been raining overnight and the smell of the wet grass filled his nostrils. Deciding that he really liked that smell, he ran through the grass, down the embankment, prize in hand, towards Taye's home.

The closer he got though, the slower he went. Realising that he had never been to her home before, he began to wonder if he should go there now?

Where he came from the skins of a tent didn't have the same feel as the walls of a house. Walls were like a barrier that screamed at him to stay away. The walls were anything but easy, or welcoming.

As he was about to turn and go away, Taye's mother Cleon came out of the house.

'Orrison, it's good to see you. You look well,' she said appraising him. 'How are you feeling now?' she asked as she moved towards a wooden butt at the side of the house to empty some waste for composting.

'Much better now, thank you Cleon.' It was about as much as he could manage with this woman who was almost a stranger to him.

'Good!' she said, eyes fixing on him so that it would be rude to just walk away.

Clearing his throat, he said, 'I wondered if Taye is up yet?'

Cleon laughed out loud, clearing the tension that he had felt starting to build up between them, with the merry sound. She said, 'Just about up Orrison, why don't you come in and share breakfast with us? Taye will join us soon enough when she smells the cooking!'

Stuffing his present for Taye into the pocket of his trousers, he smiled and accepted the invitation. Orrison walked through the doorway in the walls and stepped into a loving home; thinking to himself then that the walls weren't meant for keeping people out, but for keeping the good things safe inside.

He watched with big eyes as the family came together for breakfast, all the while trying to make him feel both included and welcome.

Taye eventually joined the hubbub of family life, squealing with delight when she spied him sitting there. There was no standing on ceremony though as he discovered when he was passed one of the twins to entertain.

In due course, Amador joined the group, and then Finnlach arrived who was closely followed by his son Finn.

Feeling slightly vexed at the latter, Orrison wondered if he would now be able to give Taye his gift. He was hanging off leaving, looking for an opportunity, but he knew that Rachel would expect him soon, so he resolved to leave without giving the talisman to Taye.

Rising to leave, he passed the baby boy back to Cleon and said, 'I guess I should be getting along to help Rachel, my thanks to you for the lovely breakfast. It's nice to have company to share breakfast with.'

There was a general buzz in the room with conversation flowing in and around the individuals present, but he was now acutely aware of another strange buzzing in his left ear. It was quite a strange sensation and was a bit distracting, so he stuck his small finger into his ear to try to stop it, but if anything, the result was the buzzing intensified.

Shaking his head slightly, he realised that the source of the buzzing was too far in to do anything about with his pinkie.

Noticing that Taye was watching him he quickly tried to appear nonchalant. Grinning at her he said as light-heartedly as he could, 'I made something for you, it's nothing much, but I thought you might like it?'

He fished the necklace out of his pocket and passed it to her. All conversation ceased and silence descended over the room. Even the buzzing in his ear had stopped.

There was a sense of importance in the air for no particular reason. He could almost taste it.

Taye reached out her small fingers and took the necklace from him.

Orrison watched her delight as she examined the necklace, which felt really nice. He realised that it made him feel very happy inside to see her happiness. He was glad that he had given it to her now and he smiled broadly, importantly even, around the room.

The reaction of the small group who sat around the breakfast table was interesting though. Not one of them smiled back at him.

Cleon looked genuinely pleased, but was quickly distracted by one of the twins who had managed to knock over a cup of milk before letting out a wail. His brother joined his chorus.

Merason somewhat grudgingly said, 'I assume that this is your way of saying sorry and if so then Taye may keep your gift to her, though it seems to far surpass what an eight-year-old girl should have.'

Merason took a drink from his teacup.

Finnlach's face was closed and Finn studied his own hands.

Probably most surprising of all was Amador. He had the darkest look on his face that Orrison had ever seen there.

Rising from the table, breakfast forgotten, Amador said, 'Very, very nice Orrison. It's a beautiful gift. Come now; let me walk you to the harbour.'

Everything went quiet again as they made to exit. Taye ran over to him and gave him a genuine hug, which was a little bit embarrassing, but felt really good.

Not wanting the moment to end, he said to Taye, 'Here let me put it on for you.'

The necklace fastened around Taye's throat with a practiced knot, sealing their fate.

Orrison liked the look of the obsidian's shiny blackness against her pale skin, it just looked and felt right somehow to see it there. Realising then that Amador was still waiting for him and feeling the awkward silence in the room again, he said his goodbyes and joined him.

No sooner than the door had closed behind them than Amador said, 'What do you think you are doing here with Taye Orrison? Why did you give a marriage necklace to an eight-year-old girl? One, I might add, who is not of your race! And where did you find the obsidian? I know that you only had one piece and yet suddenly you have managed to make a small girl an adult necklace!' The questions and statements tumbled from Amador in a very frustrated rush.

Orrison stopped walking. He had been trying to match the furious strides of Amador, but really this was just too much. And the accusations he was making, just who did he think he was? He wasn't his keeper or even his father. Amador had no right to question what he did or didn't do.

He replied coolly, 'Whatever do you mean Amador? It's a gift of friendship I give, not of marriage. I know that the Clan custom is to give the necklace, but I had some spare obsidian and just wanted to make something special with it.'

'What of your own big cat tooth Orrison, why was it no longer important to you to have that? I know that you had nearly finished it,' Amador said trying to make sense of what was going on in the boy's head.

'It is important Amador! Very important to me in fact. It's the Clan's future protection. You know that. I didn't make the necklace from it, I still have it.'

Orrison started walking again, setting a new pace for both.

'What do you mean Orrison? Please explain to me how you can still have it, yet I clearly saw a big lump of obsidian fashioned as a marriage necklace that you have very obviously just given to Taye of the Water. You are of the Fire race. This cannot possibly be Orrison, not now and not ever,' Amador ranted, almost shouting.

Orrison walked on a bit in silence then asked quietly, 'You were curious about mixing when it was my father were you not Amador?' When Amador didn't respond he continued, 'I still have my cat tooth. I melted the shavings to make the necklace.

I don't really know why I made the marriage necklace; it just seemed the right thing to do. I'm not intending to marry her though Amador. She is, as you say, of the Water and forbidden to me, and she is only eight years old for goodness sake! It was just a simple present from me to her. Maybe it's just like Merason said; it's my way of saying sorry.'

They had arrived at the harbour and he turned away from Amador and took up his now familiar position amongst the ropes and lobster creels.

Watching him for a while, Amador realised that he probably hadn't handled the conversation between them too well. Knowing that Orrison was right about the observation he had made about him being interested in the possible mixing of the races, and in particular what had happened to

Orrison didn't help matters. Now he was wondering just what had happened to this lad.

Orrison had said that he had melted the shavings from his own carving as if this was an everyday occurrence. Finding it hard to comprehend this, Amador, not for the first time, wished he wasn't so well read, as he knew the kind of heat required to create obsidian. It was made in the heart of the earth at extreme volcanic temperatures and yet here was Orrison calmly stating that he had melted pieces of the stone that he had gathered from the mouth of Mount Sepit Mhor.

Perhaps he had been given a 'gift' like his own ability to move the air? If that were the case then he would never be welcome back amongst his own people. No, his fate would be the same as his own. Torn from his roots. There weren't many who had the gift of fire that he knew and of those that did, their talent didn't come anywhere close to what Orrison had just achieved.

Amador decided to walk on further alone, dark thoughts racing around his head.

Little Taye was another concern. She had claimed that Orrison had burned her and yet there was nothing to see. Now Orrison had made her a marriage necklace of all things. She was eight and he only ten. They were both just children and from different races.

Merason had shared his own and Finnlach's hopes for their children's future with him before. Alliances were made at an early age, with friendships encouraged and supported, in the hope that they would blossom into something stronger in future years.

Feeling torn, Amador wondered if he should let Merason know about the marriage necklace custom of the Fire Clan? Earthlanders followed that custom too, if more extravagantly due to their wealth, or was it just as Orrison had said a nice gift?

It might compound Orrison's problems amongst the Water Peoples if he said anything about this Fire Clan custom to Merason, and Orrison still clearly needed help. Amador was at a loss as to what to do for the best, so he kept walking hoping for some inspiration.

Looking around, he realised he had walked from the harbour right around the bay which was horseshoe shaped, and was now almost at the most southern tip which was edged in rock and cliff.

Stopping to look out over the water, Amador was delighted by the splash of the dolphins as they swam quickly across the mouth of the bay, following a large boat which looked like it was headed towards the harbour.

He realised then that he had decided not to say anything at all for the moment, but resolved to keep a closer eye on the lad. And to try and keep him away from Taye as much as possible, until Orrison had the help he needed that would allow him to take him home again.

Having thoroughly enjoyed his walk around the bay, he turned to make the return journey, in a slightly lighter mood.

Journal of the Living

Fifty-two. That's how many stubs there have been, but none is so precise as the first. I reflect that small piece of wood likely saved me from the mound.

'Sort the wheat from the chaff' the big man told me, so that's what I do. I do it well. I keep a record of those survivors and the group they now belong to. They all have the mark so they are relatively easy to sort–fire, earth, air and water. The chaff to the mound! Along with one or two strong ones from each batch we come across. Yes, I'm good at my work, so good I have managed fifty-two stumps and recorded many names.

I have many friends now, fifty-two to be precise!

An extract from a survivor's journal of unknown origin but marked by Air.

Chapter Fourteen
Huntsmaster

Ayesha was in her element. She couldn't quite believe what had happened in so short a time. Her whole world had changed beyond recognition and she thought that she was possibly happier now than she had ever been in her whole life.

Deep inside, she knew that she shouldn't be quite as happy, as Orrison, the brother who was almost like a son, nestled in her thoughts always. He had been away for several months now and she was anxious about what was happening to him. He had left with Amador that fateful morning following his branding ceremony and was yet to return.

However, she felt that she could truly trust Amador, and this factor alone made Orrison's absence easier to bear. She was sure that Amador would have returned if anything fatal had befallen Orrison to let them know. So, there was still hope.

Somehow this didn't assuage the guilty feeling inside that she couldn't quite square with the happiness at developments in the Clan since they had left.

Right now, though, she knew that she had to crush the happiness and the guilt and concentrate. It could all be futile if she didn't get this bit right. It was down to her now and she was determined not to let herself down.

So, picking up the pace of her jog, she scanned the landscape before her, searching for the perfect spot.

Knowing that her advantage of free time was slipping away, she had to find the spot where she could see the hunters approaching, but also to know their formation so that she could plan how to mark them one by one, in order that she was the last man standing. Or in this highly unusual situation, woman standing.

If she could achieve this, the prize was Huntsmaster. Ayesha just couldn't have imagined this opportunity in her wildest dreams.

Scanning high and low, she tried to consider what they would look for and what advantage she could give herself.

Her arrows were tipped with markers rather than blades and hung in a tube at her side.

She counted them with her fingers while she ran. Nine markers and the other one knocked in the bow she carried. There were also two marker sacs that she could throw and hope to take out more than one of her hunters at a time.

She knew that she had to stop soon and choose her position. The terrain was becoming more possible though.

There were trees down the right, an open area and some rocks leading to higher ground.

Favouring height, she started to climb. This posed no difficulty as she was agile and she kept up the gruelling pace that she had set herself, ever conscious of the need to pick the right spot.

The hunters would follow her tracks easily. She had splashed through a couple of streams, but it was the best in the Clan who would hunt her down. The position of Huntsmaster wasn't won easily and she knew more than half of the group who hunted her feverently wanted her to fail and had openly opposed her right to even try.

Derrik had been great though and she smiled at the memory of his challenge to them. He had said that if what they said was true, that a woman wasn't up to the job, then it should cause them no difficulty to demonstrate this by hunting her down thereby proving once and for all time, that a woman couldn't possibly be Huntsmaster.

They had been swiftly out manoeuvred, but like it they did not! She knew that they wouldn't rest or give her any quarter, until they had her.

This left her cringing at the thought of failure, as she knew them all to be good men. They would commiserate with her and tell her that Huntsmaster was really no position for a woman.

In fact, she had already heard one mention her need of a good man to settle down with and have the children that the Clan needed for their future. Those were the small-minded ones with no vision in her opinion. One had even offered to tame her telling her that she wasn't a bad looking lass!

Firming her resolve, Ayesha planned to hit him in the ass with the marker.

Reaching a plateau, she turned to check the land below. Placing her bow and arrow in a nook in the rock, she flattened herself against the smooth rock and looked around.

Yes, she would see anyone coming over the open ground to the base of the rocks. She would also see anyone trying to climb up to her position. The treeline would provide cover for the group though.

She now had to hope that they would come more than one at a time, as she would be giving her position away immediately.

They would probably think that she was being stupid though and that she couldn't possibly hit with all of her shots. That it would only be a matter of time until one of them reached her and put their mark onto her.

Time was slipping away now and she checked the rocks around the plateaux. She knew this terrain and had checked out the markings on the rocks as she had climbed.

There had to be an entrance nearby, she just knew that there had to be, all she had to do was find it, follow it and hope it would take her out to the treeline below.

Ayesha reckoned that she had about half an hour to discover if her instincts were right. If not, she thought wryly, she didn't deserve to be Huntsmaster.

There, she knew it! It was a cave mouth with old picked bones adorning the entrance. Entering the cave, she was assailed by the strong scent of bear. It had marked its territory well and choking back a gag reflex, she covered her nose and mouth with her arm, but didn't hang about as she explored deeper into the cave.

Heart beating fast now, knife in hand, she hoped that her calculation was right that the big brown she had passed at the river would stay to fish long enough to let her use the passage through to the trees, not once, but twice this day.

Sure enough, the floor started to slope downwards. Following it to its conclusion, she came out into the light just short of the treeline.

Damn! She would just have to make it work as best she could. There was nothing else for it, no time to formulate another plan; she would have to try to take out as many as possible from the plateaux on the rock. She hoped the bear was hungry. It's going to be touch and go with this timing she thought.

Returning to her lofty position on the plateaux, she settled down to wait. Knowing that it wouldn't be for long, she concentrated with every fibre of her being, whilst taking long slow breaths to help remain calm and focussed.

Leading the group, Derrik knew that they were approaching the place where Ayesha would make her stand. She had led them on a merry dance though on the way, backtracking and crossing streams from which she emerged on one side, only to lose her tracks on small rocks and not find them again, until they emerged someway back downstream on the opposite side.

His admiration grew as he followed her lead like a hound.

Having been part of the group hunting Miele many years ago, this was clearly different.

These men were hungry. Hungry to prove that a mere girl couldn't take on this important role in the Clan. It had never been heard of before, and they would do just about anything to make sure it didn't happen now either.

If there had been a feeling of fun in the air when Miele had tried out for Huntsmaster, there was certainly no evidence of that camaraderie now. At least Viktor had stayed out of the hunting group.

It would have been too hard for her to be marked by her father, but he had let his displeasure about the whole process be known. He hadn't stopped it though.

Derrik knew that he needed a new Huntsmaster now more than ever. Day by day the Clan were slipping away from Viktor and he feverently hoped that Ayesha would be successful today and help her father in her role as Huntsmaster. She deserved the position in his opinion.

Where was Orrison? The stray thought about Orrison marred Derrik's thoughts and he really hoped that he would be home soon. He had no real affinity with the boy, but he knew down deep in his bones that the Clan needed him back and soon.

Two of the group broke out of the cover of the trees. Annoyed at allowing his concentration to lapse when he knew they were close, Derrik hissed at them to return to the safety of the trees, already knowing that they had given Ayesha the warning that she would be looking for.

Shaking his head, he knew it wasn't going to be an easy afternoon. They were just too keen.

Calling the men together he said scathingly, 'Alright, we've given our position away now, but we need to start thinking before we hand ourselves over to Ayesha on a plate. I know some of you are keen to get this over, but I caution you not to underestimate her. She was trained by Miele after all.'

The men shuffled their feet at Derrik's wise words. He continued, 'We need a plan so I'm going to have a look at the position she's chosen. Drummond, come with me, the rest of you, wait here.'

Retracing his steps, he stayed within the treeline, then hunkered down onto his belly and indicated to Drummond that he should do likewise.

Crawling through the bracken to the cover of a bush, he peered out. Assessing the terrain, he could see that Ayesha had given herself every advantage. She had chosen her spot well, but she was only one and they were ten.

The ground from the treeline to the rocks was just too big to allow for a sneak attack, he surmised, so he was going to need all the men he could get rushing forward together, otherwise she would just pick them off one by one.

Ayesha's skill with the bow wasn't lost on him. If he rushed her however, one or two may just reach the cover of the rocks. It was a gamble he decided that they would have to take.

Where would she be? How high amongst those rocks and which did she hide behind he wondered? He guessed that he would find out soon enough.

Discussing his initial thoughts with Drummond, they agreed it was their best strategy.

North of where they now lay in the bracken, Drummond pointed out that the rockface didn't seem to offer an alternative as its sheared face rose up with no apparent purchase. Derrik agreed.

In fact, he had dismissed the possibility of circling around on first sight. While Ayesha's position was good, she may well have boxed herself into a corner he thought.

The trouble with things trapped in corners though was that they tended to fight for their very lives. It wasn't the first time he would face the unpredictability of a cornered animal he thought wryly, but he did intend to be very careful with Ayesha. She was no wild animal he reminded himself.

Half chuckling to himself, he knew that she was never very predictable at the best of times. Shaking his head to return to hunt concentration, Derrik realised that she was going to rely on her supreme skill with the bow and was impressed at her guts.

Back with the group now, they drew lots to see who would be the first two to go. 'We need to know her exact position so we must give two, one coming from the North, the other from the South. Let's find out where she is and what side she favours,' he suggested.

None were keen to be the first to go, knowing that they would be out of the hunt thereafter, but the strategy was sound so Normand and Douglass accepted their luck in the draw of straws, having both drawn short straws from the bunch that he had offered to all of them.

Long minutes ticked by for Ayesha as she waited for the hunt proper to begin. She felt relaxed, but adrenaline still pumped through her veins from when she had first sight of the hunters as they broke the treeline some time back.

She counted her arrows again with her fingers. When would Derrik show his hand?

Soon, it must be soon, unless they were going to try to wait her out. Panicking slightly at that possibility, she counted her arrows again, deliberately slowed her breathing, and worked the muscles in her legs from the toes upwards to keep the blood circulating for later. She knew she would have to move quickly.

Soon, it will be soon, she reminded herself unnecessarily.

Derrik looked at his men and said, 'On my mark.' Both men were now in position. 'I want you to emerge from the treeline at precisely the same time. That's the only way we will know for sure which side she favours, the left or the right. We need to know this for our next assault. Do you both understand how important this is?'

Both nodded that they did.

'Alright, get into a position that you can emerge quickly from. Normand, take the North, Douglass, you go south. I will snap a twig loudly when it is time. Listen for it and then bolt out running in the direction of the rocks,' he concluded, clapping each man on the shoulder as they turned to take up their positions.

The crack from the branch Derrik had found for the job could be heard within the treeline, but also echoed across the clearing to Ayesha, startling her momentarily. At the same time, two familiar people darted from their cover.

Acting on instinct, she marked first one and then the other easily, long before either had the chance to make it anywhere near to the rocks.

It had begun!

Both men walked off towards the south, their part in the days hunt acknowledged and swiftly concluded. They were not permitted by Fire Clan custom to assist the hunt further in any way, shape or form. To try to do so would bring great shame.

Knowing this fact, Ayesha immediately dismissed them from her thoughts.

Eight to go! Her fingers moved to a new beat, counting the remaining arrows in her quiver.

The men regrouped around Derrik, quieter now that they had witnessed first-hand just how easily Ayesha had dispatched with their friends. Neither had come anywhere close to reaching the rocks and although both had bobbed and weaved, Ayesha's marker had firmly made its mark on both men, with no near miss to lift their spirits.

Derrik took one look at them and said, 'Did you really think that it would be easy to mark Ayesha?' He half laughed at the dark expressions he saw on their faces. 'Look,' he continued, 'we planned that little skirmish to give us some information that we can use. We now know where she is on the rocks and that she favours the left side as she took Normand out first.

We also know that no matter how good she is with a bow in finding her mark, she won't have enough time to take out seven of us all running to the rocks at the same time.'

Drummond interjected, 'Seven of us! Surely not Derrik, what if she gets us all? That would only leave you. Are you trying to make this easy for her or something?'

'Don't be stupid man,' Derrik replied. 'I think it will take all seven to make sure that one or two reach the rocks. She's very skilled with that bow of hers Drummond,' he reasoned.

'Look Derrik, I'm willing to give this idea of yours a go with five. That will leave three of us to wait her out if the five fail.'

The look on Drummond's face was set and Derrik knew that he would have to try with just five.

'Alright Drummond, five it is. Two to the left and three to the right.' Eying them all, he said, 'You will need to run like the wind men.'

The crack of a snapping twig reverberated across the clearing, startling Ayesha yet again. There were five this time, coming in a rush. Two were marked almost before she had time to register this thought.

Whipping another arrow from her quiver, she set it calmly to her bow. It found its mark. Two more to go!

They were coming fast, but she would at least get one. Thwack, the bow made its mark and she was up and running, leaving the fifth man to find the rocks.

Ayesha ran at full pelt into the mouth of the cave, not stopping for any detour on the way to hide or cover her tracks as she left no indent with her feet on these rocks. She was conscious that Isaak, the man she had left at her back, would find the cave mouth soon enough. By that time, she aimed to be long gone.

The stench as she ran into the cave hit her like a wall, and she quickly covered her face once more with her arm, and both shortened and shallowed the breath she took.

Appreciating the pincer movement of the men, she had no choice but to dart from the bear's cave mouth and make for the treeline.

As she rushed forward to make for the treeline a green marker narrowly missed her. Luck was with her!

Quiet now, quiet, she stole between the trunks, finding first one and then another to mark. Two left of the ten! She couldn't find Derrik though, so she decided to go back for Isaak, who she felt sure she could almost feel creeping at her back, unmarked. She could only hope that the bear stench had made him wary of venturing into the mouth of the cave.

Ayesha knew, however, that going back would mean exposing herself in the narrow gully between the trees and the rocks.

She darted first one way and then the other, stopped dead for a heartbeat, and a green tipped arrow whizzed by her nose, as she dropped and tumbled into the cave mouth while a second green tipped arrow whizzed over her head, again missing her by a hairsbreadth.

She had been proved right in her estimations that Derrik had gone to ground to mark this very spot, guessing correctly that she would have to return to take out the man at her back. It was luck for her that his skill with the arrow was not as precise as her own.

Once more into the bear's lair, her heartbeat sounded in her own ears. That was too close for comfort she thought and number nine, as she now thought of the Clan members who hunted her, was directly ahead.

Trusting her own judgement that she wouldn't find him in the cave, she moved swiftly ahead, arrow knocked in her bow. As she approached the exit she slowed, then emerged swiftly and hit her mark firmly in the chest.

Nine down, one to go!

Isaak glared at her having been caught completely off guard and unprepared for her attack. Ayesha knew that he would resent that, but she had to keep focussed and so she completely ignored him, in the sure knowledge that he would now go to find his fellow failed hunters.

One arrow left and two marker sacs! Just Derrik to go she thought, not taking any pride for her achievements so far. It wasn't over until all ten were marked.

This hunt was not over by a long chalk and she had no clue as to which way Derrik would come at her.

There were two options, through the cave, the way she had come, or onto the rocks to circle behind her.

Had he already crossed the clearing, she wondered? Her green eyes darted here and there seeking the familiar figure and that's when she heard the roar.

A huge, deep throated, bellowing bear roar. Loud enough to put fear into any man's heart. Ayesha could feel the hairs on her arms and neck rise in response.

She had already deduced that Derrik was coming the way she had through the cave, but so was the bear and it clearly wasn't happy. Worse still, none of them had any real weapons with them.

Ayesha knew that she had gambled everything to win the coveted position of Huntsmaster, but she had endangered a member of the Clan to do so. Without a second thought, she launched herself back into the mouth of the cave, with only two marker sacs at her side and one arrow with no tip.

As she ran, she loosened the first marker sac. Screaming at Derrik as she did so, 'Duck,' she threw the first sac and it sailed over the top of him and found the bear's chest.

The bear roared again, enraged now.

Terror was etched on Derrik's face, but Ayesha was like a wild woman as she jumped over his now crouched form and threw her second marker sac directly into the bear's muzzle.

'Run Derrik, RUN!' she screamed as she turned from the surprised bear and started to sprint out from the cave hot on Derrik's heels.

She had filled the sacs the previous evening with pig's blood, hoping against hope that she wouldn't have to use them. But now was thankful that she hadn't been too arrogant about her own abilities with the bow to bring them.

Both she and Derrik half ran, half scrambled from the bear's domain. They kept running to put maximum distance between them and the bear as possible.

Becoming self-consciously aware that Derrik no longer ran beside her, she slowed and turned.

Too late, the green marker hit her on the back of her right shoulder.

It was over.

All she could muster to say was ‘I have been marked,’ but inside her stomach clenched in despair.

They walked now, she and Derrik in silence towards the rest of the hunters who waited by the river to hear the outcome of the hunt.

Walking forward with head held high, she moved past the waiting group and as she did so she said again for all to hear, ‘I have been marked.’

Derrik said, ‘I want you to remain standing there for a bit Ayesha. Look to what the water tells you about this day.’

Her humiliation was now complete as she gazed into the fast running stream; she stood ready to face her fate, a woman’s place within the Clan. How could she ever have aspired to be Huntsmaster, she chided herself wallowing in her predicament?

It was not proper for a woman to be that, and she had proven that to everyone today. She wondered if the men would laugh at her. If they would leave her on the banks of this river for being so presumptuous.

She wished that the very ground would open and swallow her at that moment.

Meanwhile Derrik was giving an account of what had transpired to the rest of the men.

Ayesha felt the shame of being marked rise to colour her cheeks, but she contemplated the water and tried to let its gurgling messages calm her mind.

‘So, men, what’s it to be?’ Derrik asked. ‘Is she good enough to be your Huntsmaster? If so, wash the mark from her back, or if she is beaten fair and square, let us talk to no man or woman of what has happened here this day.’

As one, all nine men ran towards Ayesha and pushed her into the river, thereby washing the mark from her shoulder.

As she swam to shore a little downstream she could hear their cries, 'Ayesha for Huntsmaster, Ayesha for Huntsmaster, Ayesha for Huntsmaster!' And she was overwhelmed.

Returning to camp at the base of Mount Sepit Mhor, the men carried her on their shoulders, all the while chanting, 'Ayesha for Huntsmaster, Ayesha for Huntsmaster!'

The commotion caused all of the men, women and children of the Clan to make their way to the 'animal dance' where Viktor stood waiting, watching the approaching men honouring his daughter by carrying her on their shoulders.

He could make out her face now. It glowed with happiness.

He could use a stiff drink, he thought. The irony of the situation wasn't lost on him. Here was his precious first daughter about to recreate the Clan's history by becoming the first ever woman to be Huntsmaster and thereby one of his most trusted Chief Flames.

Just what was to become of them now when the word spread, and spread it would, to other Fire Clans, he was sure he didn't know. But he didn't have the heart to take that look of happiness and triumph from her face.

Life was indeed cruel!

The procession ended before him and she smiled up at him, her eyes shining with pride.

Derrik said, 'Viktor, I bring you the victor of the hunt. She took us all and bested a big brown bear in the process. We offer her to you as the best hunter in this Clan. Proven against ten strong, powerful hunters of men. Let her be our Huntsmaster.'

Derrik was clearly caught up in the heat of the moment and the men cheered, 'Ayesha for Huntsmaster!'

He had played exactly the right move when he had offered the men a way out by marking Ayesha. Now they were all behind the nomination because they were giving it to her. She had not taken it from them.

His own eyes shone in that his clever strategy had paid off.

Viktor smiled back at his eldest daughter, but the smile barely reached his eyes, and said, 'So, my little Ayesha, my little Flame is to become my new Huntsmaster and one of my Chief Flames? You know the responsibility this position brings Ayesha, are you sure that you can manage this?

As Chief Flame and Huntsmaster, you will be second only to Derrik. Do you acknowledge and accept the weight of that responsibility? Our whole Clan depends on it that you do.'

'Oh yes father, yes Viktor. I am more than ready to be Clan Huntsmaster and Chief Flame if you will have me?' Lowering her eyes, she hoped against hope that her father would agree.

Ayesha wasn't stupid though and knew that a lot hung in the balance for him, but it was his decision alone to appoint her or not as the case may be.

It had been a highly emotional and physically draining day and as the seconds dragged out, she held her breath, awaiting her fate like a small child.

Viktor shouted, 'Clan, hear me! Ayesha shall be my new Huntsmaster. Celebrate our good fortune this night.'

A great cheer went up from a thousand throats all around her, the noise was deafening. But as she took in the expression on her father's face as he pulled her into a warm embrace, she knew that he had mixed emotions and some reservations about his decision.

Right there and then she vowed to herself that she would make him proud and hopefully in time to know that he had surely made the right decision. Even although she was his daughter and not his son.

Viktor had managed to find himself several stiff drinks that evening and was now feeling a bit morose as he faded into the background to watch from afar, the merriment amongst the Clan that evening.

Ayesha had danced the night away in the arms of many young men and he grunted to himself, once more questioning in his own mind if he had made the best decision for her future. But it was her night tonight and by all the Gods she deserved happiness he thought, whatever the cost to the Clan.

His thoughts became darker as they turned to thoughts of his son. Orrison was out there somewhere, but where he didn't know. He would need him home soon though. He had been reminded of this fact many times of late.

Yes, Ayesha would need protection from more than he and his Chief Flames if she was to stay Huntsmaster and the Clan was to survive attack by rival Clans looking to increase their numbers.

Change was coming; he could smell it in the air tonight. In fact, he could almost taste it!

It was time to speak with Seraphina.

Journal of the Living

I have a secret. The kind that gets you sent to the mound. I am careful with my secret and the big man will never know. I really think he will never know. I don't know why I do this, I must be mad. Someone has to record the people who go to the mound. They had a life once. I decide they go, so it's up to me to know. Fifty-two stumps and the list for the mound is twice as long as any other.

I watch the big man bless those on that list with their second brand. They escape with rapture. Their husks piled up into a mound and then burned. Yes, I am good at my work. Nothing left except my list, and the big man gets bigger.

An extract from a survivor's journal of unknown origin but marked by Air.

Chapter Fifteen

Watcher

The Watcher watched to see if the latest interference it had made had had any effect on fellow Watchers. It seemed to have gone unnoticed again and this was good.

Always working on the edge didn't attract too much attention and the Watcher had gone closer to the heart of things this time and was satisfied with the next small result that had been achieved.

The boy had heard something, enough anyway, to do the right thing. The two children were now connected in a way that would mean they would be together again, when it was time.

The Watcher knew there was more freedom now. The Keeper was absent and had been for several weeks. A blink really in the time measured by the Watcher, but enough to create a space to influence events.

The Keeper had been many things to this Watcher. Friend, mentor, killer, and keeper. Most of all Keeper.

The other Watchers seemed to be oblivious to the new freedom, but not this Watcher. This Watcher had been busier in this small time, than in all the eons gone before.

In fact, it was past time to be more than a Watcher. Action was needed if there was to be a change and this Watcher was prepared to take that action, knowing that more of the group were nearing time to be taken by the Keeper to satisfy his needs.

The Watchers had halved in number since the beginning, to provide the support the Keeper needed to sustain his life-force. He had gorged on their souls.

This Watcher knew it had been one of the first to be taken and had spent many years waiting for selection by the Keeper. Until realising that the old adage of he who is last shall be first and he who is first shall be last.

That's when this Watcher's slow plan began to be formed.

It was close now, so close. Release and freedom dangled, tantalising the Watcher. Yes, care was needed, but so too was action.

Another step had been taken and it had to be enough this time. The Watcher had spoken a seal as the marriage necklace was placed around the girl's neck. The races had to be merged again to bring forth the one who could find the release, but the road ahead was fraught with both danger and difficulty.

The Watcher could feel that the Liferod containing their souls had been passed to the Guardian. The one they called Amador who had assumed the Keeper was his mentor also.

It mattered little.

The Keeper was fat on the souls he had already consumed in an effort to sustain his own life. He could last a while yet without more souls. Long enough to regain the Liferod and consume more of the Watcher's essence.

The Guardian had much to learn about the Keeper's ways if he was to succeed, thought the Watcher.

Journal of the Living

I am washed clean. My head is shorn and my beard is no more. I have been set apart. I do not know what I have done to deserve this honour. I keep quiet and I learn my new tasks. I have found myself working for the big man. He watches me still. I will not quiver or shrink from the tasks. I have warm clothes and food. It is nearly enough now.

I sort the people out as we travel about the land. It makes sense I guess. We have the brands and we should stick with our own kind. That's what the big man has said. It makes sense. Fire with fire, air with air, earth with earth and water with water. Most are willing enough.

Every now and again though I need to break them up. Fire does not go with earth no matter how hard they cry. I close my ears and direct many to the mound. Those are the ones who just can't see the sense. I don't waste time, we travel fast. I nearly have another stub.

An extract from a survivor's journal of unknown origin but marked by Air.

Chapter Sixteen

Visit

Orrison gaped at the boat that made its way towards the harbour. It was a small replica of the larger vessel that floated further out to sea, but it was like nothing he had ever seen before. The prow of the boat was high and carved into what could only be described as a furl, the wood depicting concentric circles that were painted alternately blue and white.

There was then a long body to the boat with six oars, manned by twelve burly men, who were clearly practiced to pull in unison. This gave the effect that the boat glided across the top of the water.

Towards the back of the craft a small tent had been erected and the fabric billowed in the breeze, its bright colours of greens, reds and oranges clashing with the blue and white stripped wood of the boat.

Rachel was watching Orrison's reaction to the new arrival and said, 'Different to our boats wouldn't you say Orrison?'

Realising that he had basically downed tools, Orrison recovered his composure and replied, 'Yes, it's a lot different. Where does it come from Rachel?'

'From the Earthlands, where else,' Rachel replied as if his question was daft.

Everyone, or at least she thought everyone, knew about the garish show of the Earthlanders. No one else that she knew either had the money or the inclination to have the pomp and ceremony that the Earthlanders did. The boy was obviously a bit backward or had led a very sheltered life.

She went back to work.

Noticing Rachel's assessment of him asking a stupid question, he said, 'I've never seen anyone from the Earthlands before. They sure do like to shout that there're coming, don't they?'

Laughing out loud, Rachel replied, 'Yes Orrison, they shout very loud.'

As the boat came closer, children from all around started to descend upon the harbour to watch what was starting to look like a procession on water.

It reminded him of his own Clan's ceremonies at the 'animal dance'. The children always came to watch the antics of the adults. It was a nice time.

He watched Taye and Finn run towards the harbour. The jealousy from seeing them together was lessened when he saw his necklace bouncing against Taye's neck as she ran.

He looked over to Rachel and she gave him a smile and a nod to indicate he was relieved of his duties for the rest of the morning.

Orrison was now used to her communication style, she never did use many words when she could say what she needed to with a gesture.

Grinning back, he said, 'Thanks Rachel,' before running over to join Taye and Finn.

'Hello Orrison,' said Taye. 'It's Bella de la Rella who's coming from the Earthlands,' she breathed, clearly excited. 'She comes every year. Wait till you see her Orrison, she's beautiful. All silk and jewels. She is the richest person in the whole wide world, I just know she is.'

Getting caught up in Taye's excitement, they pressed on to find a seat on the harbour wall from where they would be able to see everything.

'Come over here,' Finn said pulling on Taye's arm, indicating a space where there was definitely only room for the two of them.

Without missing a beat, Taye said, 'Oh Finn, the best spots are just over there. That's where they will berth and we will all get the best view,' pointing to a space where there was clearly room for all three of them.

Orrison thought, that's just like Taye, wanting to keep everyone happy, even if it meant that she had to give up a better position in order to do so.

Finn insisted, 'No Taye, they will berth where they always do and that's the best spot there,' he said pointing to the smaller space. 'Come on, you won't mind will you Orrison?' he challenged.

'No, of course not,' Orrison replied. But he did mind. He minded a lot as Finn and Taye claimed their seats on the harbour wall, dangling their legs over the side to wait for the show.

Orrison decided then that he didn't know what all the fuss was about, and that he didn't care to see what would be coming off that ugly boat anyway. He moved to the back of the crowd that was now gathering on the Quayside. It seemed like the whole village was coming together to watch and welcome their Earthlander guest.

Also deciding that he might as well make a start with his afternoon chores of gathering the water from the well, thinking that if he hurried with it, he may just finish early enough which would have the added bonus of taking Finn out of the equation for a little while in the afternoon, so he moved even further back.

Surprisingly this gave him a better view, so he hung off to see what would emerge from behind the billowing curtains of the tent on the boat.

He found himself gaping again as a big woman threw back one of the curtains with a stick that she then opened. The stick was circular, colourful and very frilly. He overheard someone call it her parasol.

The rest was just more colour.

She wore a long dress of green. The kind of green that was bright and bordered on being yellow. It was all tight up top and bushed out in layers that fell to the ground. She wore a hat on her head that sat to one side and was adorned with feathers of green and blue hues. The other side of her head was a mass of hair that appeared to be encrusted with gems, none of which matched the size of the bright, shining green stone clasped around the woman's throat.

The woman was being helped up the gangplank when Orrison decided that he had seen enough. So that was what a rich person looked like, all fancy and frilly.

He couldn't help be a bit impressed and intrigued, but in the end completing his task quickly was more important to him, so he left the harbour area and headed along the foreshore to the water well, passing Taye's house on the way.

Going over the events of the day in his head, he began to wonder about why he had given an eight-year-old girl a marriage necklace and why it was so important to him that he did? The strange buzzing that he had heard forgotten until that moment.

He was nearing the water well when he heard a scuffling noise coming from that direction. Instinctively he pressed his body against the trunk of a nearby tree and waited.

As it happened, he didn't have to wait for long as a head emerged from the mouth of the well, looked around, before finishing the climb out of the well.

It was the big man Walker that he had seen in the bathhouse. The one who couldn't speak that everyone knew left once every year, but no one knew where he went to.

Oh, this is too good, Orrison thought to himself. I can track him and see where he goes on his annual foray.

The man was obviously counting on the distraction at the harbour to make good his exit, but hadn't counted on Orrison arriving early to undertake his allotted chores for the afternoon.

Walker was crouching against the wall of the well. Watching and listening, but Orrison was good at this game and outwaited him, secure against the trunk of the tree against which he hid.

After a few minutes he heard Walker move off in a northerly direction. Orrison waited some more and then followed at a safe distance. Watching where he placed his feet, least he snapped a twig and bring attention. He easily tracked the big man.

Actually, he thought he could have tracked him by smell alone, so sweet did Walker smell. Come to think of it, Orrison thought, he looks just like one of those Earthlanders manning the oars of the boat that had arrived in the harbour only a short time ago.

It became clear to him fairly quickly just where Walker was headed. It wasn't away from the village as he had first thought. He was just using the cover of the trees to take him around the outskirts.

He had to break cover soon though Orrison thought.

He was right!

Walker sprinted with his head down directly towards the infirmary.

Now this was confusing, why would he be going there the only time he left the bathhouse in a whole year?

Observing the man from his vantage point in the treeline, he watched as Walker expertly prised open one of the windows at the back of the building and climbed in.

Now ordinarily he wouldn't be too interested in any man's movements, but he had a hunch that he was onto something here. Rather than break his own cover, Orrison decided it would be best to travel back the way he had come, as he didn't want to take the chance that Walker would see him from the window of the infirmary.

Deciding then that he would investigate further later. After all, he was also a guest at the infirmary and would hardly need an excuse to go there.

Intrigued and puzzled, he began his afternoon chores, all thoughts of Taye put to one side for the moment.

Arriving back at the harbour from his long walk, Amador noted that there was a new arrival. One of the Earthlanders. He had seen the garish boat cross the bay. It was what had attracted the dolphins who loved to frolic around any boat that moved through the water.

This was obviously an important guest as many of the villagers had gathered around the harbour to greet the boat. The smaller boat that had been used for transport into the harbour, was now making its way back out towards the larger vessel having deposited its contents.

Already some of the men were lifting and carrying large trunks towards the infirmary. Amador's heart sank.

This important guest would be staying right next to Orrison and he just didn't know what the lad would do next. He had to speak to Merason after all, he thought. Perhaps Orrison should move into the guestroom with him meantime? He knew that Merason and the village relied heavily on the 'treatments' that they offered the Earthlanders.

Nearing the centre of the harbour area, Amador nearly laughed aloud when he saw the woman who was busy handing out treats as she made her way along the quayside towards Merason, who waited patiently to greet her.

Why would she wear such a formal gown to arrive amongst the Water People? There was not a flaw in her makeup, face whitened with two well-placed beauty spots. Her hair was fastened in curls with jewels and baubles encrusting one side with a feathered fascinator on the other. Her silk gown fell to just short of her slippered feet.

The woman was ready for a ball and looked decidedly out of place in the harbour that daily saw fish, lobster and crabs adorn its quayside, he mused.

Wondering at the ingenuity of the woman, Amador decided that he would never understand them. Women that is! How she had managed to look like that after a long boat trip, he would never know.

Stifling his desire to laugh out loud, he moved to where Merason and Cleon waited. Noting that Taye and Finn were together following the overdressed woman.

Amador was relieved to see that Orrison wasn't with them, although the black obsidian necklace continued to grace Taye's throat.

Frowning slightly, he decided that he would have to intervene in the nonsense that Orrison had started. A marriage necklace was no laughing matter, even one adorning a young girl.

'Hello Amador,' Merason said greeting him with a wide smile, 'Glad you could join us to meet our guest. She comes every year from the Earthlands for a whole week. We really depend on her contribution,' he confided. 'Her name's Bella de la Rella. She's from one of the most powerful families.'

As Bella de la Rella had just joined them, Amador had no time to respond.

Up close, he could see that she was a beautiful woman. She was what some people would call voluptuous, he thought, noting her full powdered bosom that struggled to break free of the restrictive bodice that she wore.

He guessed that Bella de la Rella was acutely aware of this fact and the affect it would have on many men. This lady didn't leave much to chance in her appearance, if anything at all, Amador surmised. He also noted the marriage necklace around her throat. It couldn't be missed and spoke of her being a valuable possession to some man.

Although why he would let her venture off alone was a riddle that he decided not to explore.

Amador coughed to cover his thoughts as she beamed a wide smile in his direction.

After the welcome and re introductions of friends, he stepped forward to introduce himself. 'It's wonderful to meet you Bella. I'm not sure if you know, but my protégé has been living at the infirmary for a number of weeks now, but I'm sure he can move into my quarters for your comfort and privacy.'

Bella replied in a strong melodic voice, 'Of course not Amador, I wouldn't hear of it. He can stay as I will have the quarters to the back of the infirmary, is this not so Merason?' She enquired in a way that assumed that this would indeed be the case. She was always very specific about her desires and was confident that her expectations would be met.

Continuing, Bella said, 'There are sometimes other guests, but I can make do of course. I have just travelled for a number of weeks by boat to reach this shore Amador; I am not, despite what you see and may think of what you see, a woman without compromise.'

Amador considered this woman before him who had just managed to put him roundly in his place with a smile on her face. She had simpered for sure, but clearly knew what she wanted and expected to get it.

No, she was not all she was made up to be, he thought. There was a toughness about her that shone from her eyes, that the make-up helped to hide if one didn't look closely enough, he discovered.

But, she didn't know anything about Orrison, so he turned to Merason, decidedly ignoring her position, and said, 'What do you think Merason? Orrison has had his moments recently. I would hate for something to happen to your guest.'

'The boy seems to be alright now Amador,' Merason replied, making light of the situation. Clearly appeasing Bella de la Rella by siding with her.

Smiling again, she proclaimed, 'Well, that's sorted then, but you must tell me more about this protégé of yours Amador, is he here?'

'Not at the moment, no. He has had an illness with fire and air. One of the boats he used for fishing caught fire through him,' he replied realising he was now trying to shock this self-contained woman into changing her mind.

'Well, I'm sure he had a reason,' was all she said. The matter was clearly closed. Bella would not go back on what she had decreed no matter what he said he realised.

'Merason, it's so nice to stand and chat here, but I've had a long journey and I would like to retire now if you don't mind?'

'Of course, of course,' Merason bustled, drawing Amador a look that showed his displeasure. 'You must be tired Bella, we are not looking after you as we should this year.'

Amador just shook his head in exasperation. 'My fault entirely Bella. Please accept my sincere apologies. I had no thought other than your good welfare, I can assure you.'

At this point Taye pushed forward and bravely asked, 'Can I carry your bag for you Bella de la Rella?'

Bella regarded Taye and at once exclaimed about the exquisite obsidian necklace that was fastened around her neck. 'I just love your marriage necklace little one, and wherever did you get it?'

'From my friend Orrison only this morning, didn't I Papa?' Taye replied openly, but it's not for marriage, just a token of friendship.'

'Oh, I see. Customs are different here I guess,' Bella said touching her own necklace. 'Is he the same boy who is currently staying at the infirmary?' Bella asked.

When Taye nodded yes, Bella continued, 'I'm intrigued to meet this boy. It's one of the loveliest pieces I have ever seen. Perhaps I can ask him to make me one?'

Bella's laughter filled the clear air. Passing her bag to Taye, they started to make their way, together with the entourage, towards the infirmary.

Orrison finished his chores with little help from Finn that day. His good plans for meeting with Taye had now been put to one side.

Still intrigued with Walkers movements he decided that he would have to have a good check over his own space in the infirmary and then do a little investigation of his own.

The day was closing in as he passed the bathhouse on his way back to his room at the infirmary and he was thinking about finishing his big cat tooth later.

Entering the infirmary, he was first struck by the darkness caused by doors being closed which were usually open, allowing light to flow freely through the infirmary.

Deciding to move quietly, he let himself into the area he called home for the moment. A quick check reassured him that his belongings were indeed intact.

He could hear muffled voices coming through the wall which was both unfamiliar and disconcerting. There was also a different smell about the place. It wasn't horrid exactly, just a bit false. He knew that his sense of smell was good, but this new flowery fragrance interfered with the natural smells he was used to.

Putting this fact to one side, Orrison brought out his obsidian and examined his work. Knowing he was close to finishing, he spent the next hour doing just that and was pleased with the result.

There had been laughter, chatting and now familiar noises to him, who had lived in a tented village with many passionate people.

Not fazed by the later, he guessed that Walker had found some happiness.

What was really funny though, was that he could actually talk. He had heard the deep male tones and hearty laughter. The illusion that he had created, not talking, not venturing from the bathhouse, but for one week each year, and the elaborate arrangements with the tunnel, in addition to sneaking around, obviously meant that he had something important to hide.

Orrison thought it quite sad really. There must be a reason though he thought and tried to imagine what it might be?

Maybe the woman made him come to her? Come to think of it he did look a lot like the men who had been in the bright boat earlier that day and that had confirmed to him that Walker was an Earthlander.

Somehow, he thought this made Walker more interesting as he was an outsider too.

Picking up the remaining piece of obsidian that he had previously welded together, he started to shape it.

Not thinking much about what he was doing, he shaped a perfect teardrop. In fact, it wasn't until he had finished shaping it, that he realised what he had made.

Shrugging inwardly, Orrison realised that his obsidian now had its purpose. His talisman to protect the Clan, the necklace for Taye and now this teardrop. Placing it on the table beside the bed, he had no plans for it yet, although he did know that he would give it to someone. Even although he didn't know who or why, he knew that he would and that he wanted to also which was even stranger, he thought.

As he finished his work, someone arrived with a bite to eat for him. He had become familiar with this routine, often eating supper alone. It was fish. Again!

It never failed to amaze him how many times these people had fish for supper and the variety of ways that it was cooked and presented.

Tonight's supper was fish pie which he ate once again longing for some real meat to eat. It was no wonder he was still like a stick, he thought. He was eating plenty, but there was just no proper meat to fill out his bones.

Readying himself for bed, he realised that the familiar noises of people enjoying each other's company, made him wish for home again. It had been weeks now and he had become used to the silence.

Making up his mind to talk to Amador in the morning about fish pie and his talisman being finished, he drifted off to sleep.

Next morning, he awoke to a strong smell of flowers. It wasn't quite right that smell, unfamiliar and yet familiar too.

Remembering the smell from the night before, his eyes flew open as he realised that there was someone in the room with him.

There she was, the painted, jewelled lady from the Earthlands sitting watching him with a drink in her hand.

‘So, you’re the little fireball,’ she said in a deep husky voice, and then she burst out laughing at the incredulous look he was giving her.

Go away, Orrison thought to himself, not liking the fact that she had been watching him when he didn’t know about it and didn’t know her. But, he didn’t say anything, he just returned her look.

Little, she had called him. His pride was wounded on many levels.

Noting the sparkle in her eye, Orrison realised that she was here to have a bit of fun.

‘Hello Fireball, I’m Bella de la Rella,’ she continued.

Now he knew he had to respond. She had respected him by giving him her name, so he responded formally, ‘Well met Bella de la Rella, I am Orrison of the Fire Clan led by Viktor at Mount Sepit Mhor.’

‘Well that sounds very impressive Orrison. You must miss your home,’ she responded seriously.

Orrison considered her. She was more than twice his age, quite big, but she had attractive warm eyes that were full of fun and he liked that.

He was always quick to decide who he really liked and he immediately knew that he really liked this Bella de la Rella. ‘That’s quite a special name you have. It rolls over my tongue when I try to say it,’ he ventured.

Bella laughed out loud at this. A joyous sound that came up from her belly and out through her mouth. It was quite infectious he decided.

He couldn’t help but smile back at her in return.

‘Tell me all about it Orrison, I want to know everything,’ Bella said in a conspiratorial tone, ‘Can you really make things hot? Can you really make fire just by thinking about it?' she enthused.

Feeling somehow important in this woman's intense gaze he replied, 'I guess so, but it just kind of happens. I don't have much control over it.'

'Maybe you can try now, just for me?' she pleaded. 'Here, my drink can do with heating. I do prefer mulled wine. Pop your finger in it and think about heating it up and let's see what happens,' she prompted.

Orrison wasn't sure. He looked at her to check that she wasn't trying to make fun of him. Deciding that she still seemed sincere, he thought he would give it a go and put his finger into the red wine in her drinking glass.

Not sure what to do next, when Bella giggled again in an excited way, he closed his eyes and for a brief moment thought of fire coming from his finger.

'That's it!' she squealed jumping up and pulling her glass out from below his finger.

He couldn't quite believe it. He had hardly tried and surely wouldn't have tried if it hadn't been for her.

Bella exclaimed, 'Oh, this is so exciting! We could surely use someone of your talents in the Earthlands Orrison. If you ever come there you must look me up and stay for a while.'

Orrison had the uncomfortable feeling of being like a new toy, but was quite impressed with what he had done himself, so he returned her big smile and said, 'Thank you Bella, I would like that.'

'You're so formal Orrison. You don't need to be with me, I'm your friend,' she said.

Immediately after Bella had said friend, he had another bout of buzzing in his ear and instinctively knew that the obsidian tear he had crafted was meant for this woman, who was now his friend.

He said, 'Bella, I would like to give something to you. It's quite special and I made it myself. It's not as beautiful as the jewels you wear, but I hope that you will like it.' He collected the tear from his bedside table and passed it to her.

'I love it, I love it, I love it Orrison!' Bella exclaimed happily. I saw the little girl wearing the necklace you made yesterday and I knew I just had to have something made of the black stone. I'm so happy I could kiss you Orrison.'

Shifting uncomfortably at this suggestion, he squirmed. The thought of anyone kissing him was just not a good one at all, and especially this Bella woman. But, he didn't say anything.

'Oh, don't look so worried Orrison, I'm only fooling around. I don't really mean to kiss you,' she laughed.

'I think you have your man for that anyway,' he replied somewhat relieved. He felt himself colouring as Bella looked at him somewhat shocked.

'So, what do you know Orrison? Shall I share my secret with you?' Bella asked.

Shifting position on his bed, Orrison decided it would be nice to know her secret. He told Bella everything about finding the tunnel in the well, to watching Walker climb out of the same well and following him only to see him climb into the back rooms of the infirmary. He concluded by saying, 'I know that you were with someone last night Bella.'

'Well you certainly do know a lot already Orrison. I think in a few short weeks here you know more than the people that Jonathon has lived amongst for the last ten years,' she said wistfully.

He was confused and he thought that he must have got it wrong, so he said, 'I'm sorry Bella, I don't know a Jonathon. I was talking about Walker, the man who works at the bathhouse.'

'Jonathon is Walker Orrison. Now let me tell you about my husband. He is a very rich and powerful man in the Earthlands. He wanted to marry me, but I was in love with Jonathon. My father insisted that I forget about Jonathon and marry de la Rella. Between the two, my father and my husband, I had no choice. Jonathon was driven out, chased and nearly killed. You see, he wouldn't leave easily as he loved me too. My loving husband to be had toyed with him you see. Made him race on a horse to win me and he lost the race.

Tears were now sliding down Bella's beautiful face, leaving tracks in the make-up she wore.

'So Orrison, I leave my husband every year for a time and come here to spend a week with my love. Do you think I'm bad for doing this?' she asked, somewhat petulantly.

'No,' he replied shaking his head. It was like an adventure to think of her crossing the waters to see her love. And here she was now spending some of her precious time with him.

Wiping the tears from her face, she said, 'Oh, I must look frightful. Can I ask that you never tell my secret? My husband is a bad man. He would track Jonathon down and kill him just to make sure that he has me all to himself,' she said making a stabbing gesture in the air. 'He couldn't face a scandal either.'

This had the desired effect on Orrison, whose eyes were wide with wonder. He said, 'I won't ever tell, don't worry about that, not ever.'

'Good, because I would like you to come and visit me sometime, but you could never, ever tell my husband. There, that's settled then. You can come and stay with me anytime.'

With that pronouncement she gave a wide smile, and flounced out of the room in her petticoats, taking her warm wine and her perfumed smell with her.

She also took her new jewel.

In the way of all ten-year-old boys, he knew with conviction that he had made a good friend and that every single word that she had spoken was absolutely true. She really wanted him to visit her in the Earthlands and he made up his mind that he would do that one day.

Getting himself ready for the day ahead, Orrison was feeling positive as he made his way from the infirmary to the harbour, where he knew Rachel would already be hard at work repairing and setting the creels for use later in the morning. He wasn't wrong, she was already there.

'Morning Orrison,' Rachel acknowledged as he approached. 'Can you work on the nets this morning?' she asked, 'I'm getting on fine with the creels. Not so many to repair today and I have most stacked ready for collection.'

He knew the routine by now and went to sit on the crate he favoured for making the nets. With the small black shuttle, he made the knots in the way he had been taught by Rachel. It was quite an enjoyable task now that he knew what he was doing and he was able to appreciate the day beginning for the village, as his mind was free to think about other things.

This morning his thoughts were of Bella de la Rella. It was pretty amazing really what she had asked him to do and not only that, it had worked!

A few seconds only and he had warmed her wine.

It crossed his mind fleetingly that maybe she had tricked him, but he dismissed this thought immediately as he knew instinctively that he had indeed made a new friend.

Just to prove it to himself though, he concentrated on the rope in his fingers and thought of heat and fire.

Almost instantly the rope caught fire.

It was so small at first, but he couldn't quite stop thinking of heat and fire.

It was truly exhilarating, such an exciting feeling coursing through him. He felt consumed by his thoughts, and the heat built up. The fire started to spread, first slowly and then more quickly as it raced along the lines of the rope.

Turning around, Rachel's cry of despair pierced the morning air. Then she screamed at him, 'Fire, Orrison, fire! Get water now!'

As he heard Rachel scream, he closed off his thoughts of fire. But it was like he was watching something bad happening from a distance.

It was like it was unreal. His movements felt slow. Like he was in someone else's body that wouldn't quite work the way he wanted it to.

The fire grew bigger, greedily consuming the piles of nets that caught the fish for the village.

Rachel had sprung into action and was pushing the creels into the water of the harbour. The trouble with that was the tide was at low ebb and they had a long way to travel before they reached the water below.

Orrison realised that he could only just see her through the smoke now. Like an apparition or a dream half remembered.

A line of people had formed and were now passing buckets of water along the line to throw on the nets. Others were carrying sand from the foreshore to throw onto the flames.

Someone passed him a bucket and he threw it futilely onto the flames. It seemed like he was at the end of the line now. He hardly noticed the creels bump their way down into the water below, some being completely ruined in the process, the wood smashing against the harbour wall and other creels.

Rachel was crying. He could hear her.

The fire was out. Broken creels littered the harbour. What remained of the ropes was a black mess.

Everywhere he looked people stared angrily at him.

Rachel's crying was starting to irritate him now. Why was she crying anyway? She wasn't hurt. Some of the creels could be saved and it was easy enough to make new nets, he thought.

Turning to leave, he walked straight into Merason and Amador.

'What happened here Orrison?' Amador demanded.

Orrison didn't like his tone, so he replied sarcastically, 'There was a fire in the nets and Rachel scattered the creels.'

Merason said, 'No more Amador, we can take no more of this. The boy isn't even sorry. Look at him standing there showing no remorse or care for Rachel or anyone else for that matter.'

Turning to Orrison he continued, 'Don't you know that fishing is our livelihood boy?'

Orrison didn't reply.

Amador knew that things had gone too far. His normally placid friend was hugely upset, that much was clear. 'Orrison, go and collect your things from the infirmary. We must leave now,' Amador said as calmly as he could.

Orrison walked away, past Rachel without a word or a glance and made his way back to collect his belongings.

Inside he was feeling normal again. In fact, he was quite happy really. Now Amador would have to take him back home he thought. He should have done something like this before now. He was fed up doing their silly chores anyway. No one was ever grateful for his efforts.

He was glad he would be going home.

In some ways he wished he hadn't done it, but wishes were just wasted thoughts, so he quickly dismissed the desire.

His work here was done anyway. He had given the necklace to Taye and the tear to Bella. He was both aware and pleased about both.

Orrison didn't once stop to question why he knew that his work had been done.

Amador couldn't apologise enough.

Merason only shook his head somewhat defeated. It was a disaster of huge proportions for the village. Eventually he said, 'That boy's a liability Amador and he's just as likely to harm others as he is himself. Take him home. That's my best advice for you,' he concluded flatly.

Already some of the villagers were swimming in the harbour, trying to retrieve the ancient creels, which would pre-occupy many of them for weeks ahead.

Amador had tried to comfort Rachel, but there really were no words that were either appropriate or came anywhere close to making her feel better.

Leaving the scene of devastation, he sighed. Realising that he hadn't done that for a while made him reflect on what was to come.

Should he take the lad home and be done with him? Somehow that felt wrong and he couldn't work out why for the life of him.

Telling himself that there was nothing more he could do for Orrison; after all he was in a lot better condition than when they had left the Fire Clan encampment.

He knew that Orrison must have started the fire. He just didn't know how. Perhaps he was finding a gift, but if so, it would be like Merson said, a dangerous one. He was likely to get both himself and others into trouble for the rest of his life.

It had only been a few weeks and already there had been two disasters with fire.

Finding himself sighing again, Amador started to pack up his things, stopping at the box in which he had placed the Liferod.

He knew that he should really take the Liferod back to The First and pick up the pieces of his own life again. The First was bound to be angry with him for missing the testing too.

The Twelve had served him well over the years of his life and he had repaid them by leaving at a critical point without so much as a second thought.

There was something about the lad though. It was tantalising him and he just couldn't put his finger on it and grasp what it was he was so interested in. He certainly had an interest in the races and how they managed their lives and affairs. Albeit the races were all different, there was a vitality that he had witnessed in their everyday lives.

Amador knew that he was an observer, but sometimes it felt good to be part of it all. He had really and truly enjoyed these last few weeks here amongst the Water Peoples, but he had cost them dear by bringing Orrison.

Oh, he knew that his intentions had been good ones, but the reality was that he had been more interested in what was happening in the mixing of the races to really care about the impact that it might have on these gentle, caring people.

He sighed again.

Sitting on his bed, he opened the box that held the Liferod. It was an amazing thing really. He looked again at the carvings and instead of deciding to take it back to the Conclave, he suddenly knew what he must do.

Closing the lid of the box securely again, he packed the rest of his belongings and left the guestroom behind.

Purposeful strides took him up to the infirmary where Orrison was already waiting, some soot still marking his cheek. A reminder, if one were needed, of the morning's events.

Orrison had watched Amador striding towards him and just knew that he was in for another lecture, so he squared himself to face it.

Sitting down beside Orrison, Amador said, 'Time to go lad.'

'I suppose,' Orrison replied, staring at his feet.

'Do you have the fire crystal?' Amador asked.

'Yes, I thought that it would be alright to take it. Is it?'

'I'm sure that Finnlach meant for you to have it Orrison,' he replied.

'Can I go home now Amador?' Orrison asked in a small voice.

Sighing, Amador really looked at the young lad standing before him and asked, 'Can you tell me how you started the fire Orrison?'

Orrison explained about warming the wine and needing to see if he could do it again and that before he could do anything, as his body wouldn't respond right, there was a raging fire in the nets.

'I thought that it must be something like that,' Amador acknowledged. 'You know when I was about your age; I was whipping up the air which resulted in a couple of trees in my village being uprooted. That's when my mother knew that I had the gift of air and sent me away from her and my home to study with The Twelve.'

Orrison could have asked many things of Amador then, but he had a feeling he knew where this was going so he asked, 'How did you manage to move the air to uproot a tree Amador?'

Explaining this was child's play to Amador as he conjured a mini whirlwind in the air before them. Perfectly controlled, but obviously powerful.

He said, 'This is a very, very small version of the winds I created and it has taken me many years to master control of the air in this way.'

Orrison was impressed.

'You need to learn control Orrison,' Amador said simply.

'I can't go home yet, can I Amador?'

'No son, not yet,' he replied gently.

Orrison asked, 'Where must I go to learn the control that you speak of Amador?'

'The way I see it is that you have two choices Orrison. You can do as I did and study at the Conclave. It's pretty gruelling and you will be bound by and to The Twelve.

You won't ever be able to go home again or contact your family. They will be gone from your life forever and you will have to face up to that fact from the very beginning.

The other choice open to you is to come home with me and I will try to teach you what I know so that you can find your own control and perhaps go home one day to lead your Clan. It's your choice Orrison. Think hard lad,' he cautioned.

Orrison's mind reeled. He wanted to go home more than anything, but if he couldn't go now, he thought it best that he should take his chances with Amador and perhaps make it home one day soon. And if not soon, then perhaps one day.

He said, 'I'm coming home with you Amador. I want to go home sometime. Ayesha and the girls will need me I think.'

Sealing their agreement with a handshake, the two left the infirmary and instead of walking back towards the foreshore, the harbour or the village, they took the back road and melted into the trees.

Acknowledgements

I would like to thank Andrew, Donald, Moira, Hugh, Billy and Rachel for their early encouragement in my embryonic hopes to write my story down in a book. Special thanks to Hugh and Rachel for sticking with it through the first draft of this book. They have their names in as requested, but Hugh will need to wait for the third book to be published to see his in print.

Thanks also go to my sister Brenda for her teacher's eye and for bringing the measures into the decimal age. I'm not getting any younger it seems… Brenda is the only person who knows the end of the story other than me. I was happy to hear that she enjoyed it.

What can I say to my sister Jill and Brother in Law Adam for their commitment to reading the whole manuscript and their advice on chapter length in particular. Dinner had to wait on more than one occasion! They read the book aloud! Their comments on believability and jeopardy were treasured. My thanks are huge to both as they helped me to keep going on more than one occasion!

I must mention the book club members – Karen, Sharon, Alison and Shelley for bringing a laugh to the proceedings. We were interrupted by Covid, as so many things were, but your direct insights were spot on. And thanks also to all my other friends and colleagues who have encouraged me along the way.

My thanks go also to my niece Danielle for reading the finished draft. She helped me to believe that publishing the book was definitely something I should do and that it actually read like a 'real' book!

And to Liam for his help when technology confounded me… Also to Anne for her advice on layout.

Music has been a huge part of our family life and my playlist has been a topic of conversation over the years. Huge thanks go to my brother Andrew, my son Liam and my sister Brenda for sharing their thoughts on tracks. My brother Andrew is a music legend and encyclopaedia, so special thanks go to his him for his input. Thanks also go to my friend Peter for offering to help compile my playlist on Spotify and sharing some ideas on tunes.

I must though take the time to acknowledge the many songwriters and musicians for sharing their music with all of us over the years. Hopefully I will be able to include my playlist in a future edition.

And a special thanks to CANVA. I mean who knew that design is at your fingertips? Fabulous! My cover artwork reflects their contribution, as does the designs for fire, earth, air and water which is truly the heart of my story. My efforts at design have been surpassed and then some by British Book Publishing and I owe them my gratitude for a truly spectacular jacket.

Huge thanks also to my solicitor Charlotte, without whom I would not have been able to self-publish this book.

I hope you as readers enjoy the journey through The Stones of Destiny series. I would like to acknowledge those of you take the time to read this book. A heartfelt thank you from me.

About the Author

Vivien Smith lives on the East Coast of Scotland on the banks of the Silvery Tay, no prizes for guessing where the name Taye originates…

Vivien has enjoyed a successful career in the public sector and has now retired having dedicated 43 years to serving people and communities.

This book, alongside the two companion books in the series, have been a fun, enjoyable escape from her busy life over many years. She has finished writing her story since retiring. The pleasure has been in the journey for Vivien, but she thinks the feeling coming from the books being published will be immensely satisfying too.

Music has been a huge part of Vivien's life and choosing tracks to complement each chapter has been almost as fulfilling as inventing and telling her story.

Vivien values her family and friends and is immensely happy to see the man her son Liam has become. She loves being his mum most of all.

Printed in Great Britain
by Amazon

56598bc2-0508-465b-89c0-05ce001c49b0R01